Ash and Cinder

Mads Re Kyron

Copyright © 2019
Mads Re Kyron
ISBN: 978-1-7777666-0-3
Cover art by Dane Low
The text type was set in Cardo

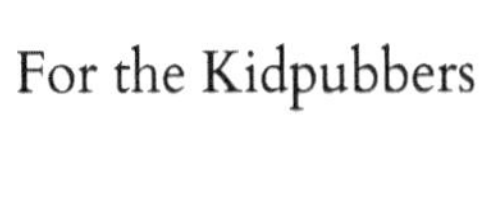

For the Kidpubbers

My world ended when I was twelve. Elle's ended when she was six. I can't remember how long ago that was. Six years? No. I glance at the nearest tray station where a reedy guard decked out in a ketchup uniform is lingering, hand resting on the hilt of his baton. He's not watching me but my skin prickles with nerves anyways. I fiddle with my spoon, mixing the top layer of dried-out oatmeal in with the goop underneath to make it look like I'm busy. Someone, somewhere, hums an achingly familiar melody.

I was supposed to be remembering something.

The lullaby. The year. The number seven. That's it, I've been in the Compound for seven years.

"Hey, Trick, pass the salt."

My head snaps up, and I correct my posture. There are no saltshakers in the Compound, but I slap Maverick's waiting hand anyways.

Experiments are packed into the cafeteria. Body odor clots the air, and the fluorescent lights have washed everything and everyone a lifeless, grey shade. The low drone of conversation fills the room. I rub my ear, grimacing. I guess no one was humming after all.

"Welcome back to the present." Maverick elbows the air next to my ribs, careful not to touch me. "Say hello to the new guy." He juts his sharp chin at a lump across the table from me.

I shove my glasses higher on my nose. "New kid?"

A pasty, pudgy guy ogles at me from the other side of the table. His hands rest folded over his bowl of porridge, and the metal clamped around each of his wrists is a sure sign that he's a newbie. Only two types of people in here wear shockers: instigators on probation, and first week newbies.

"Name's Trick," I say, reaching across the table with an open hand. The newbie takes it as well as he can with his hands tucked close to his body. If he stretches too far outside the circle of motion that the shockers allow, he'll get zapped. I've never worn them, but I've seen them in action. It doesn't look fun.

"Dieter," he replies, giving my hand a sweaty shake. I pull away and wipe my hand on my loose shirt. I'm used to Elle or the Whitecoats touching me, and none of them have particularly warm skin, let alone sweaty palms. Dieter gives me a sheepish grin. Baby fat makes his cheeks freakishly cherubic. How old is he, twelve? Bet that grin will be gone before the month-end.

"So, Trick, while you were up and away in wheresville, the rest of us were filling Dieter in on the Compound. He was wondering what your power was." Maverick, as usual, drags me back into the conversation before I have the chance to slip out of it. I shovel a spoonful of tasteless porridge into my mouth.

"Enhanced strength," I say around the porridge.

Dieter cracks a bigger grin like he doesn't believe me. I can't say I'm surprised. I'm not exactly the poster child for Bruno's Big and Buff. I'm shorter than most guys here, and all lean muscle where other strength Enhanceds have bulk. The glasses don't help either, thick and heavy as they are.

To my right, Maverick snorts. "Man, I would not judge this particular book by its cover."

Dieter gives him an uncertain look, and so do I.

"Even if its cover is a scrawny nerd."

Ah, there's the dig. I 'playfully' shove Maverick. His mouth drops in surprise as he pitches off the bench and meets nothing but empty air to slow his fall. He lands hard on the stained concrete, his elbow catching the brunt of the fall with a thud. He cackles while he picks himself up. He's an ass.

"For real, what do you do?" Dieter leans in, body relaxed. It's as if this is a normal conversation between friends. In which case, he would be the most well-adjusted newbie in this place. It took me months to accept what had happened and assimilate, and back then I was a hell of a lot more talkative.

"I told you."

"Prove it." He lifts his wrists, presenting the shockers. The bands holding him are thin and shiny new against his soft flesh. I eye the shockers and Dieter, gnawing the inside of my cheek. I could pop them in and out of place without too much effort. The Redcoats might not even notice a dent that small. Might. I'm about to tell him no when he scoffs and drops his hands. "You can't do it. I knew you were lying."

By the end of his sentence I reach across the table. Dieter jerks his arms back in surprise, and I roll my eyes. "Relax. I'm not gonna rip your hands off."

I lean forward again and grab a band. A simple pinch, a twist of the fingers, and voila, the shocker is split wide open. All he has to do is keep it in his lap. Dieter's eyes grow wide, his mouth is wider.

"I can move again!" he beams, stretching his free hand way above his head. Moron. Does he want to get in trouble?

"Put that down!" I bristle, lunging to pin his hand. He's too fast, arching his back, his bones popping as he revels in the new freedom. Good grief, he's going to attract the attention of every Redcoat in the cafeteria.

"You have no idea how long I've been stuck in those things," Dieter gushes. He looks happy, and I want to smack him. I lunge, trying to seize his waving arms, but someone beats me to it.

Dieter freezes as a pair of meaty hands clamp down on his shoulders. The Redcoat drags him out of his seat and spins him around. The Experiments sitting at surrounding tables have all stilled to a nervous stop. Listening. Watching out of the corners of their eyes.

"Experiment, it would seem that your shockers are a tad loose," the Redcoat snarls, his voice rumbling deep in his chest. Dieter goes from hyper-excited to downright terrified in less time than it takes Maverick to adopt a new friend—which is to say, not very long.

"I can explain, sir, I can explain." His face flushes the exact shade of the Redcoat's uniform.

He better not rat me out.

"Can you?" The Redcoat leers. "Well then, explain away, Experiment. I'm all ears."

A hush falls over the surrounding tables. Beside me, a short, dark-skinned guy shifts over subtly, moving out of the potential line of fire. I spare a glance at the Redcoat's nametag and almost feel bad for Dieter. This particular Redcoat has a reputation for being ruthless. I, personally, have never seen someone with quite the same level of permanent Monday morning blues. The dude seriously hates his job, and us.

Dieter swallows hard, squeezing his own fleshy arms. He cuts a look at me. I shake my head microscopically and duck to examine the scraped tabletop. I cannot afford to get in trouble. If I get caught up in something, the Whitecoats will take me off my pain meds. Or worse, take Elle off hers. My mouth goes dry as the image of my sister curled in a ball, choking on screams, flashes through my head.

Never again.

"It was Hendrix!" Dieter jabs a sausage finger at me. "He snapped the band, sir."

Idiot.

I bow my head, silently cursing out Dieter. I can feel the Redcoat's eyes boring holes in my skull.

"Experiment Sanchez." He draws out my name like it's a weapon. I lift my head a fraction to peer at him, feigning meekness.

"Yes, sir?" I keep my voice low and respectful.

"Did you break this lovely pair of shock restraints?"

"No, sir," I answer immediately. I'm not about to put myself and Elle on the line because some newbie can't keep his trap shut.

I cannot, and I will not. As a general rule, most Redcoats only get to know the powers of troublemakers, and I've never been one of those. It's a safe bet that this Redcoat doesn't know I could have easily broken that stupid metal bracelet.

By now, the cafeteria is silent. Maverick is on the floor still. He has one hand on the bench, and his eyes dart from the Redcoat to me. He's tense. I'm more tense.

The Redcoat huffs, pulling a new pair of shockers from the utility belt at his waist, and my heart rate kicks up a notch. I don't dare move.

Then the Redcoat turns back to Dieter. "Experiment Paxton put your hands above your head," he grumbles. I bite my lip. He has to know there's still a shocker on Dieter's other wrist.

"Wha—but he—I—" Dieter stammers.

"Paxton!" the Redcoat barks. Dieter's hands shoot into the air, the band clears his head and every fiber in his body snaps tight in a convulsion. He wails the moment the pulse ends, clutching his burned wrist. He looks to me, tears in his eyes, all but begging me not to let the Redcoat hurt him more. I turn away. Maybe next time Dieter won't be that reckless.

The Redcoat slaps new shockers on him and steers him towards the nearest exit. Every eye fixes on the pair as Dieter is frog-marched out of the cafeteria to receive his punishment for being unrestrained. The steel door bangs shut, and the usual clamor makes a slow return to the cafeteria.

The second the door shuts, Maverick jumps up and dusts off his baggy sweatpants. He pauses to wave and smile at someone across the room, then turns to me.

"Someone just made a brand-new enemy," he says, leaning his hip against the edge of the table. He crosses his arms and tilts his head as if assessing something. Maybe he's replaying the scene, who knows. There's always too much going on inside his head, or so he claims.

"Yeah," I scoff, "I'm really scared."

"You're gonna be sorry for that later," he warns, shifting his weight off the table. "They'll figure out Dieter hasn't got powers and then they'll be all over you."

There's Mav for you, always three steps ahead of everyone else. I bite back a groan as I realize my mistake.

Damn it!

He's right, this is going to come back to haunt me. I give him a dirty look, shooting the messenger and all that, and push my glasses back up my face again. His response is to stare right back.

"And you didn't bother to warn me?" I snap.

"You need to learn to think ahead, man. I'm not always gonna be around to stop you, especially not with the way I perform in the dome," he replies.

What a pile of crap. I've dueled him before, and I ended up with a face full of dirt. He doesn't show up with bruised or broken body parts half as often as the other Experiments in this room. There's not a chance in hell he's getting beat down enough to garner the attention of the Whitecoats.

"Not beat up much, no, but not doing what the 'coats want either," he says, clicking his tongue reproachfully. He catches his slip-up a moment before me and frowns to himself.

"I thought I told you to stay out of my head," I say irritably. The brush with that guard has set me on edge, and I'm in no mood for Mav to be poking around in my mind. My only comfort is that I won't end up in as much trouble as I feared. Maverick's a lot of things, but he's not careless and he's not stupid. He wouldn't let me dive headfirst into something that would get me killed, or Elle hurt. The consequences of snapping that chain, however unpleasant, will be survivable.

I stand, taking my empty food tray with me. All around us, other Experiments do the same. Breakfast is nearly over according to the electric clock bolted to the wall, high out of reach. It's the only clock in the Compound, making the cafeteria the only place where time exists as it should.

I start towards the tray drop-off station. When Mav follows me, so does the rest of the table.

He's popular in the Compound, charismatic, friendly, and a bit of a legend. That means he always has a posse of Experiments with him. The roster changes every now and then when someone dies or gets shut up in infirm. I don't learn their names like I used to, there's no point. I find it irritating at times, but he's the closest thing to a friend I have in this place, so I keep my impatience under wraps.

"I thought you liked these guys. I'm hurt, Trick." He presses a hand to his chest mockingly. I ditch the tray. A blond guy I vaguely recognize stashes his tray after mine but doesn't move to leave. He's with Maverick. I skim over the Kinetics and Enhanceds standing around the tray drop-off station, seven in total. I'm sure if I tried, I would remember at least some of their names. I've met them all before. I think.

"Stop listening in on my thoughts," I warn him again.

Mav's a bit of an oddity; not an Enhanced and not truly a Kinetic. He was meant to be telekinetic, but instead he ended up telepathic and annoying. We have an agreement worked out where he doesn't root around in my brain and I don't drop-kick him to Mars. Clearly, we need a refresher on that agreement.

"Hey." He holds his hands up in the universal sign for surrender. "You weren't exactly being quiet. I can only block out so much."

"Right," I mutter, shouldering open the steel door. The chilly, early-spring air gusts in, raising goosebumps on my tan forearms. Patches of half-melted snow dot the paved yard. To one side of the cafeteria are the cell blocks, six in total, each its own rectangular beige building. Standing along the wall on either side of the cafeteria doors are lines of Redcoats. Weak sunlight bounces off the roofs of the buildings, turning their obnoxious vermillion suits even brighter. I start towards the infirmary, or rather, the laboratory built into the far side of the infirmary. I'm scheduled for dueling today.

A trio of Redcoats break from the wall to surround us. Not all of us need escorts, in fact most of us probably don't. But there's always a chance that some idiot is sneaking out with us.

"You coming out to the court later?" he pesters me. He must have a free afternoon. Older Experiments get breaks in their schedules every week or so. The Whitecoats found that it improved our performance. I, however, do not have an empty slot anywhere today.

"Nah, I'm busy."

"Ah, okay." He falls silent. When I look back to see why, he has a squinty expression on. That's his mind-reading face.

"Dude!" I flick his ear, snapping him out of his trance. "Get out of my head, that's creepy."

A smirk crosses his face, "I'm incorrigible, you can't stop me."

Incorrigible. I shove my hands in my pockets. That's one word for it.

"I'll check on her today," he says, dropping his voice to a whisper.

I nod gratefully. "Thanks."

Maverick is the only other person I trust around Elle.

We reach the lab, and half of Maverick's group breaks off to join me at the door. Maverick raises a hand in farewell and goes to wherever he has to go.

We stand outside the locked outer door, shivering as the cold bites through the thin fabric of our matching uniforms.

Another two or three Experiments arrive, all escorted by two guards each. The rule is that you have to be escorted by guards unless you've proven yourself trustworthy enough to get where you're supposed to be without making a break for freedom. Though I'm not sure who would be stupid enough to try running. The fence surrounding the Compound is ten feet high and electrified, with barbed wire entwined through the links to discourage electrokinetics. Guards are stationed every eight feet around the perimeter, armed day and night with semi-automatic rifles.

Only one person has successfully escaped the Compound, and that was ages ago, before even I was brought here. Needless to say, security has been tightened since then.

I stretch, the bones in my back pop. Another crack echoes from the forest. I spare a glimpse beyond the fence, where a few yards of open grass give way to a wall of slender trees. The shade of the forest obscures everything beyond that wall. A wild animal probably made the noise, I'm not the only person who noticed it though. One of the Redcoats guarding our group eyes the forest for a moment before muttering into his lapel.

After fifteen minutes of standing and freezing outside the locked laboratory, the door creaks open and a Redcoat lumbers out. He is followed by a Whitecoat wielding a clipboard.

"Make a line!" the Redcoat snaps, and, like good Experiments, we do as we're instructed. I try not to look at the people on my left and right. I don't want to familiarize myself in any way with them, especially since I'm dueling one of them today.

The Whitecoat strolls down the line, asking each Experiment their name, and tapping on a clear, flat tablet. "Name?" she asks the tall guy on my left. He's the blond from earlier, a part of Maverick's group.

Damn, I'm familiarizing myself. I try to block out his response, but it's too late.

"Experiment Wardrop."

I dig my fingernails into my palm. I hope I'm not dueling him today. Knowing their names makes fighting them worse. Not that it's pleasant to begin with. It's harder to pretend that they aren't people when I have a name to put to the face. It's why I stopped learning anything about anyone except, reluctantly, Maverick.

"Name?"

"Experiment Sanchez–Fernandez." I say.

Her beady eyes skim the newstab for my name. She finds it. Her stylus draws a mark beside it, and she moves on. This time I manage to ignore the interaction between her and the experiment to my right. The Whitecoat makes it to the end of the line and signals that she's done with a flick of her hand. She retreats into the lab, leaving the guards to deal with us.

When she's gone, we're frisked for any weapons we may have, which I find pointless. We're pretty much living weapons ourselves.

The guards don't seem to share my point of view.

Commotion from the east turns all of our heads. I spot a cluster of bright red creeping towards the forest as we're hurried inside the heavy metal doors. There's a short hall that ends in a crossroad. Chastin, a dark-haired woman, and I, are all shunted down the left hall. Everyone else peels away to the right.

We trudge down a corridor that stinks of ethanol. The clinical scent fails to completely mask the coppery flavor of blood in the air. A Redcoat walks ahead of the group, and another looms behind us. Dark stains spot the grey tile from years and years of the aftermaths of duels crossing this floor. Some of that is probably mine. The Redcoat behind me sidesteps the stains, but nobody else bothers. Our footsteps echo off the dull walls, the only sound to break up the silence.

Lining the right side of the final stretch of the hallway is a row of windowless steel doors, each with a black patch for a doorknob and a giant metal pinwheel set in the middle. Three of the six doors are open. The rooms beyond them are hidden in the dark, not that they would have been much to look at in the light.

We each step obediently over the slight ledges and into the concrete cells, waiting silently for the Redcoats to shut the doors and spin the locks into place. At the click and scrape of the deadbolts, I'm plunged into momentary darkness. It takes the span of two deep breaths for the red emergency lights to flicker to life.

The cell is four paces by four paces, its ceiling is lost somewhere in the shadows. These cells, of all the places in this awful Compound, are my least favorite. Dark and tight and made entirely of smooth-faced concrete, every single one of them. There's not enough room to breathe. But discomfort isn't something I have the luxury of indulging in right now, I have a duel coming up and if I want to survive I have to prepare.

The Whitecoats like to pitch us against each other in a fighting dome and take notes while we beat each other bloody. I'm one of the best fighters they have, possibly the best, not that it's something I'm proud of. If I don't perform well in the dome, or if I break a rule, or if, for any reason, the Whitecoats think I've failed, they take it out on Elle. And so I can never, ever fail.

I flex my fingers because they feel like they're burning, and squeeze anxiety-ridden thoughts out of my head. I have to concentrate. I have to get ready. Fixing my gaze on the red-washed cinderblock wall, I take a deep breath. Hold it. And shrug out of my skin.

Not literally, fortunately for everyone, my enhancement does not include transforming into a bloody, squishy nightmare creature. I mean, I let the part of me that cares, that would hesitate to crack someone's skull open; the part that stops me from becoming a total monster, slough away. It always takes a few moments, but it's easier than it once was. It's easier than it should be. Sometimes I wonder how many times a person can lose himself before he stops being able to find the missing pieces.

A gust of air hits me from behind, disrupting my concentration. My vision snaps back so fast my eyes ache briefly, and I wince. The door has been opened. It's too soon. I'm not ready yet, I spent too much time worrying about Elle. The Redcoat beckons with a single finger, and I hesitate for a half-second. But I know better than to resist. I go willingly and try to scrape the last of me out of my brain as we walk.

We pass the other waiting cells where Chastin and the woman also wait. I'll have to duel him or the woman, or both. I hope it's not both, there aren't many ways this day could get worse, but spending hours in the dome is one of them. The distraction lasts too long, and suddenly I'm being shoved past the door that leads into the dome, still not entirely ready for the duel. The instant the door bangs shut behind me, I slip into a defensive stance, reflexes taking over while my mind plays catch-up.

I scan the dome, searching for my opponent. It's a rectangular concrete basin, with a half-spherical web of aluminum bars anchored over top of it to act as a barrier between the dome and the observation deck. Some of the bars are newer than others. Dueling Experiments frequently get smashed into, or through, the barrier. It's not pretty when they do. All that sharp, broken metal.

My eyes land on my opponent. The Whitecoats almost always put me in last, giving my challenger the opportunity to set up an ambush. This time doesn't seem to be any different, except the other Experiment appears to have given up that advantage and is standing alone, unguarded.

I start to check for the second Experiment who must be pressed against the entrance wall, waiting for me to take the bait, when my brain finally registers who my opponent is.

This has to be a mistake, there's no way.

Standing on the opposite end of the dome, huddled with his back to the wall, is Dieter. His shockers are gone, and his eyes are so wide that from this distance all I can see are two white circles. Nervous sweat plasters his white-blond hair to his head as he grips a rubber training knife in both hands, too blunt to slice skin but a usable weapon regardless.

Confused, I look up past the dome to the huddle of Whitecoats on the observation deck.

He's too fresh to have powers. They've never cranked out an Experiment in less than a month, let alone less than a week. And anyways, he doesn't have any scars.

"Trick," he squeaks and starts towards me. I put a hand up to stop him before he takes another step. His naïve cherub face flushes a deep magenta, but the Whitecoats keep their stony silence. I turn my stare to Dieter. He couldn't hurt a fly. The training knife wobbles in his shaky hands. And they want me to fight him? Why? This won't give them feedback on either of us. It will just be me beating up a helpless opponent.

As I'm puzzling, the answer comes to me.

This is my punishment for breaking Dieter's shackles. Our punishment. They figured it out faster than I thought they would.

I let my defensive stance slip and stride across the dome towards Dieter, my moment of hesitation over now that I understand what the Whitecoats want. The movement breaks Dieter out of his terrified trance. He scuttles forward, but not to fight. In the back of my mind, a part of me wishes he would pass out from fear, so I don't have to hit him, but it is a very small part.

About three steps away, Dieter reads my hard expression, and realizes I'm not coming over to have a nice chat. He judders to a halt, his eyes going impossibly wider. I draw back my arm, turning my entire torso with it out of habit.

"Trick, please—" he starts to beg. My fist collides with his jaw with enough force to send him flying a few feet. He lands, ragdoll limp, and I hope that's the end of it. I hope he's knocked out, or that he's at least smart enough to pretend.

Then Dieter groans with a force that reverberates off the concrete walls and pushes himself up on shaky arms. With an internal sigh, I walk over to him and raise my leg to kick him. The Whitecoats won't let the battle finish until one of us is unconscious, or too wounded to keep dueling.

This time when Dieter collapses, he stays down.

3 | Day Ten Thousand

Weeks pass before Dieter reappears in GenPop, I broke his jaw and some ribs. I'm glad he's not dead. I don't know how I'd feel about killing someone who didn't try to kill me first. Experiments have left the dome in worse condition after fighting me, but they weren't defenseless like he was.

Pushing aside thoughts of Dieter, I distract myself by counting out finger taps on the infirmary front desk counter. Five taps left, five taps right. My knuckles hurt, dark red and purple bruises stretch over the bone and darken the spaces in between. Patches of skin are scraped away in places, and it stings, but that's nothing new. The painkillers the Whitecoats have me on go a long way, but they don't make me invincible.

I wish the Whitecoat running the infirm desk would hurry up, I want to see Elle today. It's been weeks since I saw her, too. Another part of the Whitecoats' punishment. The worst part.

The inside of the infirm is chilly and reeks of ethanol, though not as badly as it used to. Whether the scent leaks over from the lab or not is a mystery, but the floors in here are all white squares with no bloodstains so my bet is on the former.

A Whitecoat shuffles in from the hall to my right, a bottle clutched in her veiny hands. She eyes me while she fills out my Savella prescription. The usual pill-pusher is a guy with hair so red it hurts my eyes, and teeth lined with metal brackets. He's used to all the Experiments that need drugs to function, but this one isn't. I fix my glasses to peer at the bottle and make sure it's the same one my pills come in every month. I remember too well what it was like the last time a Whitecoat decided I only needed sugar pills. The Whitecoat behind the counter finishes and hands me the filled prescription bottle, waving me off with a flick of her bony hand.

They act like it's a show of trust to let me keep my own medication, but I know they know I'm too sick to pawn off the pills and too protective of Elle to kill myself and leave her here alone.

There's already an escort Redcoat waiting to take me to my sister. I know where to go but I'm not allowed to move freely in the infirm like I do in the yard. We make good time down the hall, with me walking dangerously far ahead of the Redcoat, forcing him to quicken his pace to keep me in reach. Grey walls blur into white doors, the scuffed tile barely registers in my mind's eye. I've seen this stretch of hall so many times. I could point out every nick in the paint without so much as glancing in its direction. I can't imagine how bored Elle must get living in here.

At the door marked '70' in black sharpie I halt. The Redcoat stomps past me, yanks out a ring of keycards, and flips through them until he finds the right one. The keycard swipes across the handle, and the lock clicks. With a grumble that sounds like rolling thunder, the Redcoat shoves open the door and motions me in.

I ease past him into the room. The soft beep of a heart monitor and the scent of bleach greets me. The room is small, with grey walls and white linoleum floors and no windows. One wall is dedicated to an array of metallic, whirring machinery. Wires snake out of some of the machines and converge with a mess of translucent plastic IV tubes around the lone hospital cot, where a small, fragile body nestles.

Elle's curly hair sits in a huge puff surrounding her face. Her dark brown eyes are glassy and tinted yellow from all the drugs. We have the same eyes, only hers are framed with long lashes that curl a touch at the ends. She smiles when she sees me, and I smile back, glad that she has the clarity of mind to recognize me.

"*Buenos dias, ¿como te sientes?*" I sit on the edge of her cot. Spanish is our native tongue. Unfortunately for us both, the only other Spanish-speaker in the Compound that I know of is Maverick, who's septlingual or something ridiculous like that.

Americans dominated the Compound when we first arrived, kids from the east coast who got sold by their parents. It's strange, buried in the back of my mind is a memory of other island kids with us on the trip over, but somewhere along the way we were all separated, and I don't remember those kids re-appearing in the Compound.

But I also don't remember my mom's name half the time.

There aren't many of the east coast kids left, but the English stuck around, passed from one newbie group to the next, remaining the common language. Elle and I stick to Spanglish with each other out of habit alone.

Well, habit and homesickness.

"Sick. *Me estoy comiendo un cable.*" Elle sticks her tongue out. "Will you check my horns?"

"Yeah, kiddo, sit up."

She scoots up on her elbows and leans forward. I brush the hair away from her back, where a pair of scars cut valleys down either side of her spine. Sprouting from the scars, right above the loose back of her grey Compound tank top, are nubby keratin horns. I tweak them both.

"Yep, they look bigger today." I say. They might be, by a thin layer or two. They don't seem to stop growing, but it's a slow growth. Like toenails.

"Heard you won again," she says, settling back onto the thin pillow. She means the fight in the dome. She doesn't know what the fights are, or what winning means, except that when I win it gets her more medicine. And that's how I want it to stay.

"That's right. Who told you?"

She shrugs, the IV tubes sway. "*Un guardia.* Was it hard?"

I hesitate before answering, swinging my legs up onto the cot and propping my elbows on my knees. She spots the cracked skin along my right knuckles and reaches out to take my hand. Her hands are cold and dry, the skin feels papery, like if I rubbed it too hard it would flake away.

"*Sí,*" I say at last, "it was extra hard."

After that, the conversation turns. We talk about Maverick and how he came to see her yesterday. We talk about a boy she saw the other day in radiology. His eyes glowed. I'm not sure if that's part of his power, or if she likes him. Either way, I hope they can see each other again, Elle needs a friend. Towards the end of our allotted time together she starts to drift off. Her head droops so her chin rests on her chest, her breathing slows, and her skin begins to take on the drab green of the blanket over her lower body.

Elle's enhancement allows her skin to take on the appearances of her environment, or lately whatever she wills it to take on. Color, texture, shadowing, it's all there on her skin as if she were made of the things she touches. When she sleeps, her skin shifts on its own, sometimes taking on the shades of her dream, but more often adhering to the nearest point of contact and leeching the color. When the edges of her skin blend with the blankets, she looks even smaller than she is.

I rest on the edge of the cot, lingering for the rest of my free time. Looking at Elle now, it's hard to remember there was ever a time that we didn't live here. We used to live in the world of humans and that world was huge. There were supercities the size of Spain. I don't remember much about them since Puerto Rico wasn't near one, but I do remember that when one of the American ones crashed, it took us down hard. Money became next to worthless, and half the country was bankrupt before the end of the week. That's where a lot of us older Experiments came from. Our parents couldn't afford us. It could be the same story for the newbies too, I've never bothered to ask.

It doesn't matter anyways. We're here, Elle is sick, and I have to keep fighting until her medicine works for good.

A sharp rap on the door is my cue, times up. I tuck Elle's hair behind her ear and give her a quick peck on the forehead before I go. Day number ten thousand, we're both still alive. That's something, I guess.

4 | THE COMPOUND

The manacles clink shut around my wrists. I wait patiently as a Whitecoat secures me to the wall of my cell. The chains are shiny replacements for the ones I broke a while back. These shackles aren't bad, actually, no scratchy rust, no bloodstains. The Redcoat finishes locking me in and gives me a small, encouraging smile. Another 'coat stands in the door, arms crossed over his chest. Normally there's only one 'coat, but the smiley one is on probation, I think. Allegedly for helping two Experiments' get married. It was a big deal, Maverick told Elle all about it and of course Elle told me a couple dozen times.

The cell door clicks shut behind the Whitecoat, cutting off light from the hall. I stretch and listen to every bone in my back pop. Today was an exhausting one but at least I got to visit Elle. It makes me antsy when I'm not allowed to see her, it feels like I'm not doing enough. Or worse, that she's faded away for good and they're not telling me because if they do, they'd have to kill me, too.

I slide my back down the wall to sit on the cold floor. A faint light from the small, barred window set in the door illuminates most of the cell. There's not much in here, just a single dresser, bolted to the floor and wall. Its drawers hold three sets of the same grey tank tops, and sweatpants, plus two sweaters for cold days. Resting on top of the dresser is a blue prescription bottle, half-full of oval pills. Savella, pain pills, for the fibromyalgia the Whitecoats triggered when they experimented on me.

They only kind of work but without them, I'd be neck-deep in agony and muscle spasms before the night is up. As if to tease me, a pinprick needles my chest. It's a bad night, then. I lean my head against the wall and squinch my eyes shut. The chains keeping me pinned to the wall are too short, I can't reach the pill bottle from here, and I can't risk getting in trouble for breaking another set of restraints. Especially not after what happened with Dieter. I suck in a huge breath, ignoring the twinge it sets off, and hold it.

Since I'm going to be curled in an agonized ball in a few hours, I might as well get some shut-eye now. I let the breath out all at once and shift to a more comfortable position. It doesn't take too long for me to drift off into a dreamless swirl of unconsciousness.

I wake up to the awful sensation of a chainsaw ripping through my chest. I gasp and make the mistake of bolting upright. Glass shards stab into my back, all along my spine, and thick hot metal bands tighten around my chest. Something akin to a white-hot iron burrows deep in my torso, and the manacles that were mere annoyances early are a sudden, bruising pressure on my wrists.

Don't fight it, don't fight it, don't fight it.

The mantra repeats in my head. The tenser I get, the worse this will be. I force my shoulders to relax, even though it puts that much more weight on my aching wrists. Sweat beads on my temples and nausea swirls at the back of my throat: Withdrawal on top of returning symptoms.

Slowly, slowly, I ease myself up to relieve some of the pressure. Despite my best efforts, the glass burrows deeper into my skin. I tip my chin up slightly, hoping that will help, and that's when I finally notice that it's no longer pitch dark in the cell. The emergency lights are on, bathing the room in an eerie blood red. Puzzled, my eyes flit to the door like it can give me answers. As if on cue it bursts open and crashes into the adjacent stone wall, and all at once an ear-piercing, keening tone floods the cell.

"Why are you still in here?" An angry Maverick storms in. He stalks over to me and makes like he's about to jerk on my chains, but his hand stops halfway, and he pulls back sharply. He must have got a wave of the pain.

"I just woke up." I have to shout to be heard above the high-pitched shriek. I clamber to my feet, grinding my teeth hard against the wave of dizzying pain that shoots from my neck right down through the soles of my feet.

"You slept through fifteen minutes of this racket?" Maverick spins on his heels and strides across the room to snatch up the bottle of pain pills.

"Speaker in here must be out, 'cause that could wake the dead."

Last time those alarms went off, three years ago, a pyrokinetic had nova'd her cell block. Kinetics, very occasionally, go nuclear. Normally a 'coat catches it and puts an end to them before it can get this far, but this time is different. Something must have gone wrong. This time Mac is dragging me out of my cell instead of a Redcoat.

Out of nowhere, the ground shudders, knocking us all to our knees. Plaster dust rains from the ceiling.

"King, help him." Maverick motions to me around a volley of coughs. King, a short black guy, who I recognize but don't know anything about, steps through the door towards me.

"I got it." I wave him off.

"Listen, I gotta make sure nobody else was stupid enough to stick around in here. Grab what you can and meet us out by the court ASAP," Maverick instructs, setting the pill bottle and something else back on the dresser.

"Will do."

He leaves, King on his heels. Not wasting a second, I wrap the chain around my arm, pause as the chainsaw punches through me again, and give a good hard yank. The bolt comes free of the stone wall and in a matter of seconds, I am chainless. I stumble across the cell to the dresser. Two pills rest beside the bottle. That must be the second thing Maverick set down. I pop them in my mouth and dry swallow. Unfortunately, their effect is not immediate, but I don't have time to waste. I open the top drawer and fish out a sweater. I pull the sweater over my head, grab the pill bottle, and shove it in my pocket. After that, I grab an extra shirt, pants, and the last sweater. Whatever is happening, I want Elle with me, and it's bound to be cold outside.

Tucking the extra clothes down my sweater, I jog out into the hall. My leg joints scream in pain as I run down the corridors of Block Three. The alarm blares like a scalpel in my eardrums, and the emergency lights give everything an ominous glow. Another blast rocks the building, sending me crashing into the wall. A scream echoes from one corridor. I make the executive decision not to go see who caused it.

A shadow appears on the wall, and I snap up straight. My right foot slides back a couple inches for better balance. Sure enough, the shadow belongs to a Redcoat. But he barrels past me, shouting something into a walkie-talkie, wielding a shiny black stick. I don't even think he registers that I'm here.

What the hell is going on?

I continue down the hallway, keeping my eyes peeled for other Redcoats and Whitecoats. The blocks aren't particularly big, so it doesn't take long to reach the exit. The door is gaping. Flickering orange light and distant shouting filters in from outside. I sidle up beside the opening and peek out, checking the area for any Redcoats that might take offense to me being out of my cell. The chilly wind nips at my ears and sends shivers down my back.

The Compound is in chaos. Fires are blazing, flames lick three walls of the mess hall. Scorched patches and the fallen forms of Redcoats and Experiments dot the ground. And the fence is broken. Experiments bottleneck the crude hole, Redcoats buzzing around them like flies, darting in and clubbing down an experiment where they can, but it's not slowing the flow. There aren't enough Redcoats to stop them. Where are the rest of the

Redcoats? I sneak out of Block Three and skirt along the outside wall. The Infirmary is on the far end of the yard.

The deafening roar of a gun going off cracks the air, and a cluster of fist-sized balls fly over the heads of scurrying guards. One lands in front of the mess hall as another clinks to the ground near Block Four.

The next moment has me skidding to a dead halt. A blinding light flashes, and I throw up my arms to shield my face. That was *not* a Kinetic. When I lower them, my lungs seize in my chest. The Compound has gone up in a fireball. The heatwave hits me at the same time as a great boom shatters my eardrums. I'm bowled over by the sheer force of the explosion. When it's past, I am left floundering, deaf, with a sickening feeling taking hold of my stomach.

"Elle!" The scream rips from my throat. I can't hear it over the ringing in my ears, but I can feel it scrape on the way out. I shoot to my feet, ready to sprint the rest of the way to the infirmary. Maverick is there suddenly. He and King grab me by the arms, holding me back. They're dragging me away. Maverick is trying to say something, I can see his lips moving, but I can't hear it. I have to get to Elle. I have to.

"She's gone!" Maverick's voice breaks through the ringing. He's wrong. The Infirmary is the farthest building from what I can now see was ground zero. It's still standing. It's also on fire. With a heave, I throw both King and Maverick off. They go flying, ten feet in either direction, and before they have time to recover I take off.

I pelt past still-burning building shells and charred remains of things I don't want to think about. The heat from all of the newly spawned fires is suffocating. Black smoke dries my throat and makes my eyes water. The mess hall is gone, and Block Two, Three, and Four haven't fared much better. As I reach the path leading to the front entrance of the Infirmary, my heart sinks. A blaze has engulfed the entire front entrance. There is no way inside.

No no no!

"Elle!" I call, desperate.

"Hendrix!" The cry is weak.

I whip towards the sound, my eyes searching. I find nothing. Then, miraculously, Elle materializes to my left. I run to her, scoop her up in my arms. Her matchstick limbs wrap around my neck, and she holds on tight. She's alive. Now we can run. I cradle her carefully and turn on my toes to sprint back to the basketball court. I can see Maverick's blurry shape through the smoky haze. Halfway across the yard, one of the round things clinks to the ground and rolls between my legs. Elle cries out, and I have only a moment to drop and cover as much of her frail body as possible before the explosion.

"Help me with him."

"And the girl?"

"Did you not just see what he did?"

A few sentences slip through the renewed ringing in my ears, but most get lost under a thick blur of pain. I think my back has been melted off. Hands hook under my prone shoulders and pull me to my feet. I can't suppress a cry at the wave of pain. I also can't see.

"Come on, man, you gotta stay with me, okay? I can't carry you."

My arms are empty. Where's Elle? Where is she? I had her, where did she go? I don't have to speak for Maverick to know what I'm asking.

"Chastin has her, she's fine." Maverick pulls me forward. I stumble. I can't see a damn thing. The scent of burning flesh clogs my throat, and searing pain ripples across my back at every step. Regardless, I clutch Maverick's steadying arm and break into a run for the millionth time this night. Thick smoke clogs the air and screams pierce the sky, overshadowed only by the pop of gunfire. Suddenly a familiar weight settles on the bridge of my nose, and my vision clears. With all the smoke it doesn't help much, but at least the silhouettes ahead are easier to see.

"Almost forgot those." Maverick remarks. Now that my glasses are back, I can see that we've made it past the fence, and we're bolting for the hills. There isn't a lot of coverage here, mostly sparse trees and the dark of night. Somehow, I doubt that the Redcoats are coming after us.

"Thanks," I rasp. My throat is raw.

"Save it." He keeps his arm around my lower back, a support that is the only thing keeping me upright.

The Compound becomes a red-orange beacon behind us. We slow to a jog when we realize no one is giving chase, whoever blew the Compound open is holding up all their personnel. Still, we keep going and going and going until even the fittest of us is gasping for breath. And then we slow again, to as brisk a walk as we can manage. We have to put as much distance as possible between us and the Compound, or else this entire escapade will be null and void. The Whitecoats will make *us* null and void.

When at last we come to a full and final stop, the Compound is a mere flicker behind us. The air out here should be clear of smoke, but the faint, choking scent clings to our skin. We stand at the base of a shallow rise the crescent moon is beginning its descent to the western horizon, but the sky has yet to start lightening. I almost choke at the sight of someone lingering at the top of the ridge. Then Maverick waves at the lingerer and they return the gesture.

Maverick guides me to a boulder jutting from the side of the rocky foothill and makes me sit. The world tips on its axis. I grind my teeth and clench my fists, but that does little to ease the pain.

"Chastin." Maverick beckons to the guy holding Elle. When he treads forward with Elle still on his back, Maverick shakes his head.

"Leave her with Delilah for a moment. She doesn't need to see this."

'This' I assume means the awful state of my back. I don't have to look at it to know it's a mess. Chastin shrugs Elle off and leads her by the hand to a woman who smiles sweetly and bends down on one knee to talk with her. Maverick paces around the rock, examining the damage.

"Can you get your sweater off?" he asks. I'm surprised I still have a sweater. The whole way here drafts of wind at my shoulders sent chills down my arms. I tug on the sleeves and am met with instant pain. My fingers seize, a spasm rocks up my shoulder. I bite down hard on a groan. Mav whistles.

"Okay. Don't worry, it looks like the heat fused what's left of the sweater to your back."

"Don't worry?" I hiss. Yeah, I have sweaters melted onto my skin every day. No big deal! I push my glasses up my face, fighting to stay in control of my racing thoughts.

"Chastin is going to ice the burn, and I'm going to peel the sweater off, got it?" Chastin steps up to the boulder, the fingers of his right-hand dancing. Tiny snowflakes float to the ground from his hand. So Chastin is a cryokinetic. Nice to know. As he traces the edges of my burn, deep, numbing frozenness follows the path his fingers make.

"Brace yourself, Trick, this'll hurt," Mav warns, then he peels my sweater off, along with what I'm sure is most of my remaining skin.

Hurt is the understatement of the century.

They get the sweater off, and Chastin gives my burn a final numbing. Maverick rips up what's left of the sweater and uses the strips as a crude bandage. By the time he's done, I've contracted a bad case of shivers. The tank top I grabbed earlier goes on, and Mav hands me the extra sweater too. I protest, that sweater is for Elle. She'll be cold. Mav makes me put it on anyways, and since I can't think in a straight line, let alone argue my case, I go along with it. Then, and only then, does Maverick let Elle come near me.

The woman from earlier brings her over. Elle crawls into my lap, safe and sound. I wrap my arms around her and rest my chin on her frizzy hair. At thirteen, she weighs less than most ten-year-olds. Chastin rises from his resting place at the foot of the boulder to join the woman. They wander a few paces away to settle down for the night. Far in the distance, explosions pop. With the sky is hinting that morning is around the corner, I slump. The little horns on Elle's back dig into my torso, but I don't mind. In a matter of minutes, I tumble headlong into an exhausted sleep.

"*Hendrix*!" A terrified scream shatters the black oblivion of my dreamless sleep.

Elle.

My eyes fly open, and I spring to my feet. Only it doesn't quite work that way because the ground tilts on its side, and instead of jumping up, I'm crashing sideways.

"*Hendrix ¡ayúdame!*" Elle shrieks again. A fleshy crack echoes through the air. I struggle to my knees, frantically searching for Elle through dizzying triple vision.

"Elle?" I call. Her answer is a muffled scream. The world stops spinning enough for me to just make out two forms on the ridge above me. One is Elle, and the other is a giant man in military dress. He has a clunky black gun pressed to Elle's temple, his other hand clamps around her mouth.

"Don't shoot!" I shout. The man narrows his eyes, his finger tightens around the trigger, turning my blood to ice in my veins. Elle's doe eyes are wide and glassy with tears. A sharp whimper escapes from between the man's fingers. Her skin shifts in a patchwork myriad, the way it always does when she's scared. Some parts of her I can see, while others have vanished, chameleon-like, into the surrounding landscape.

"Elle, *¡tranquila!* You're going to be fine." Maverick appears on the scene, as calm and collected as ever. He's facing the man, his hands in his pocket. "He doesn't speak English," he says, more as an idle observation than anything. Without turning away from the man, Maverick addresses me.

"Trick, tell your sister that everything is going to be okay," he instructs. *Okay?* I see no way in which this situation turns out okay.

"Where's your telepathy?" I whisper. If ever there was a time for him to start digging in his grab bag of mind tricks, it would be now. While Elle is in mortal danger.

"I'm trying." His voice is still calm and even, but I spot his grimace before he covers it. His eyes are swamped under purple blotches. I fill my lungs with frigid air and lie to my sister.

"*Estas bien, Elle, está bien.* We're going to get you away from him." The words stick to my throat on their way out. Elle's gaze finds mine and holds it. She breathes like a panicked mouse, her chest heaving rapidly. Her fingers spasm at the man's arm, red lines raise on his skin. "It's okay," I say again. Nausea turns my insides to mush.

The man decides that he's had enough of standing around. He takes a step back, and Elle kicks out wildly. His grip on her constricts and he shouts something at us in another language. Russian, I recognize the guttural flow from years of listening to the Whitecoats. He waves the gun around, pausing every now and then to point it at each one of us. Out of the corner of my eye, I see a glimmer of movement. Someone is sneaking up on the man. Suddenly, Maverick's plan becomes clear to me.

"Elle, calm down," I instruct, and she does. Her feet stop kicking and she stares straight at me. The lack of resistance affords the man an easy way to drag her back. "*Escucha*, I need you to be brave okay. When I say duck, duck."

An ATV idles at the top of the hill. A woman with hair so pale it's almost white sits on the saddle, facing away from the scene below. She leans on the handlebars, fingers hovering over the gas. The man is nearly to her now. I wish Maverick would get on with whatever he has planned because we're running out of time. Elle's toes drag along the stony ground, her too-wide eyes trained on me, waiting for the signal. The man is at the top and Elle is fighting tears. I glance sideways at Maverick. My vision fades in and out of blurriness. He waits, his eyes dart between the man and the other person. Then he tips his chin in affirmation.

"Duck now," I command the moment he nods.

Elle twists in the man's grip and sinks her little white teeth into the flesh of his arm. The man shouts in surprise but doesn't drop her. At the same time, Chastin, who had slowly but surely been sneaking up to an angle where he could get a clear shot, lunges, his hands out, fingers splayed, and launches a volley of glittering white ice daggers at the man.

With impressive reflex the man whips his gun in an arc, swinging it up and firing. A spray of scarlet blood mists the air. Chastin falls. His mouth frozen open in shock. Behind me, someone screams his name. At the same time, an ice dagger meets its mark and burrows deep in the man's shoulder, and he drops Elle. The pile of stones she snags her footing on gives out. Pebbles skitter and she slips, cracks her head on the unforgiving earth, and goes still. I lurch, read to launch myself onto the soldier. Mav's fingers dig into my shoulder.

He motions to someone out of the corner of my eye. The man sees him too and levels his smoking gun at the person Maverick was signaling. Elle lays at the man's feet. Her skin has stopped shifting. Her purple-stained eyelids are closed, but faint puffs swirl out of her nose in the morning chill. She's still breathing. The man barks out either warnings or orders as he crouches and grabs Elle by one skinny arm. Her head lolls. She's out cold.

"Don't do anything rash," Maverick warns, though he's gone noticeably paler. He's leaving bruises where his white-knuckle grip pins me.

"We don't have time for another plan," I say in response. The man hefts Elle as if she's a sack of flour and tosses her onto his shoulder. She flops, ragdoll limp. Blood mats her curls where he nailed her with the gun. Angry, I rise inch by inch to my feet. The man squints at me, his gun still pointed at a person who stands at the edge of my field of vision. Melting ice and blood mix together and roll in fat drops down the front of his camouflage fatigues.

I take a step forward, silently daring him to do something about it. And he does. The barrel of the gun points at me, his finger squeezes the trigger. A force like a sledgehammer thumps into me, knocking the air from my lungs and sending me sailing down the hill. I tumble and roll over sharp rocks and merciless stone, pebbles skitter in every which direction. I slide to a stop at the foot of the ridge.

My first thought is to get to Elle. My second is actually two thoughts at the same time, one: I cannot breathe, and two: I'm bleeding. I stagger to my feet, gasping for air that won't hit my lungs. The world pitches so violently that I have to lean forward and rest my hands on my knees. Not dead, but it feels like I'm getting there.

The black clears and my breathing sort of returns, which leaves room for me to focus briefly on the fact that I'm bleeding. Not heavily, as far as I can tell, so I get back up and struggle up the hill as fast as I can.

Maverick stands at the top of the slope, facing away from me. When I'm halfway to the top, he pivots and comes down to meet me.

"Where is she?" The words tumble from my mouth before he even makes it to my side. He draws his brows together and shuffles to a stop.

"Let's have a look at you," he murmurs, more to himself than anyone else. He puts a hand on either of my shoulders and turns me from side to side, searching for new injuries. "No bullet, at least. The rocks did a number on you, though."

Surprised, I look down at myself. The blood oozes from a number of minor scrapes and cuts, but there is no bullet hole, no bullet. What hit me, then?

In the background, I see forms pacing. None of them are small enough to be Elle. Where is she? I start forward, determined to check on her, but Maverick steps in front of me, blocking my path.

"Take them." He pushes his open hand towards me. I look down at the two white pills sitting in it.

"Mav, let me see her."

He shakes his hand at me, insistent. I grab the pills and shove them in my mouth. He hands me the bottle and waits for me to tuck it in my pocket before speaking again.

"They took Elle," he says, watching me warily.

"What?"

"They took Elle. She's gone—not dead," he hurries that last part, "just not here."

The air leaves my lungs for the second time today, only this time it doesn't come back. Strange, awful pain settles over my chest. I turn to the nearest rock, which happens to be the one I sat on last night and drive my knee down hard on it. The rock shudders, cracks with a satisfying hollow snap. The extra energy vibrates up my leg and dissipates around my hips, setting off phantom pain from an old injury and rattling the pins there. I stagger, limping and trying not to. It's then that the sound of weeping reaches my ears.

"We'll get her back," Mav promises, "but first…" He trails off, staring at the place where Chastin fell.

I wait for him to trudge back up, then we both make our way over to the others. The woman is on her knees now, Chastin's head in her lap, she's sobbing uncontrollably.

A bloodred rose blooms over his chest. A trickle of blood drips out the corner of his mouth. His eyes, half-open, stare permanently ahead at some unseeable thing. The woman strokes his face, running her fingers through his blond hair. Her chest heaves unevenly as she chokes on her tears.

Chastin's death is a loss that everyone feels. An East Asian guy I don't know the name of is blinking hard, tears form tracks in the soot on his cheeks. King has his arms folded across his chest, his chin tucked as he stares at Chastin. In the light of day, I make out old scars on his face, carved across his forehead in imperfect raised lines. When he frowns, the lines buckle.

Leaning on the boulder, not far away, is Dieter. He watches the others. I note with a slight twinge of regret that his left eyelid is swollen and black. The bruise flowers up across his temple and disappears into his fair hairline.

When the woman's sobbing has reduced to sniffling, Maverick crouches to rest a hand on her shoulder. A whispered communication passes between them. The woman nods, and Maverick stands up and steps back.

The woman folds Chastin's arms neatly across his bloody chest. She sets his head on the ground with care. Then words, soft at first, and in Russian, spill out of her mouth. A prayer of sorts. It is short, and by the end of it the woman is choking up again. This time, the Asian guy helps her to her feet and guides her back. Her hair falls like a curtain around her face, hiding her from the rest of the world. We give her space.

Maverick takes her place. Bending a knee, he brushes his fingers over Chastin's eyelids, shutting them forever.

"Rest in peace, Chastin Wardrop," he says. He hesitates a moment beside the body. Sadness passes over his face, mixed with a darker, more hideous emotion. Then he clenches his jaw and backs away, motioning for the rest of us to do the same.

There is no place in the rock to dig a grave.

Instead, King slides the ball of his foot along the ground in a sweeping motion. There is a deep rumble, then the earth splits open with a hollow crack that swallows Chastin. Another swipe of King's foot and Chastin is buried under a mound of fist-sized rocks. We all stare in silence for a long time, first at the grave, and then at Maverick. He is our leader, and we wait for answers. He stands still. A parade of dark emotions traipses across his face. His silence, I imagine, is more for him to process all that's happened than for him to come to a decision. At last, he speaks, his eyes alight with fury.

"We're going after them," he says. Nobody protests. That solider killed one of our own and stole another.

"Wait," Dieter speaks up, earning himself hard stares from everyone. He wanes under the sudden attention but doesn't take the hint. "We should head in the opposite direction— get as far away from those psychos as possible."

"*Those psychos* took Elle, and we do not leave one of our own." Maverick's jaw is tight as he explains this. His tone is even, but anyone can see he's not having a great time keeping it that way. I'm having difficulty too, as my anger swells, parts of me are slipping through the cracks, and I struggle to keep them attached.

Dieter argues, "what's the point of going after one person if we're all going to end up dead?"

"We can't abandon her!" I snap. More and more of the controlled part of me slips away. Dieter's attention shifts to me. He crosses his arms over his barrel chest and vaguely looks as though he's reconsidering.

"Dude, I'm sorry about your girlfriend, but it's not worth it," he says after a moment. I'm on him before the last word is out of his mouth. My fingers find his throat, squeeze, lift him. His tiptoes scrabble for traction on the earth.

"She's my sister, and she's worth more than you ever will be," I snarl. Dieter's face goes red-purple, his mouth gapes as he gasps for air, and his eyes roll back in his head. Call me crazy, but I find it hard to care. I know I should put him down, but the part of me that would is sloughing away like it does before a duel.

"Trick." Maverick's hand is on my shoulder.

I glance sideways at him, at the rest of the group. They're all staring at me with varying degrees of 'what the hell' painted on their face. Oh. I drop Dieter. He stumbles, gags, hacks like his lung is coming up. His hands fly to his neck. A flicker of regret wriggles its way into the back of my head as I note bruises darkening there. I shouldn't have done that. I turn on my heels and run my fingers through my hair, trying to pull back into myself. My glasses rest crookedly on the end of my nose, so I push them back up.

Behind me, Dieter takes a steadying breath and mutters, "Bastard."

That's it. I whirl around, my fist already balled, and nail Dieter across the cheek. A bone cracks and he crumples fast. Maverick jumps between the two of us, hands out, ready to stop an all-out battle, but I'm already done. I shake out my hand and stalk off in what I hope is the direction the ATV took.

I'm getting Elle back, now.

The cold sun shines on everything. I squint against the brightness. Mid-spring in Russia is always like this: too bright and sharp with borderline cold. Every other step my left knee twinges. My joints do that every time the barometric pressure goes down, always beginning with my knee. Part of it is the fibromyalgia, I think, but the knee only started aching after I shattered my legs and the 'coats patched the shards with pins and rods. There's probably more titanium than bone below my hip. My breath no longer swirls in the air, which is a positive, but with each passing minute the pain pills are wearing off.

It's not time for my next dose yet but I pat the pockets of my sweater, searching for the bottle. It's not there. It must have fallen out when I walloped Dieter. The scraps tied around my chest and over my shoulders feel like shackles. The fabric is like sandpaper against my burned skin, even so I get the idea that the pain pills are blocking most of the pain from my burn. That means when the drugs wear off, I'll be in six kinds of hell. I guess that means I'll have to rescue Elle all that much quicker, which is fine by me. The sooner I get her back, the better.

"Trick! Wait up," a familiar voice calls. I ignore it. The terrain is rocky, and foliage is sparse, only a towering oak or pine here and there. In the distance, angled to my left, the trees are much thicker.

"Come on man, you know you can't outrun me."

I sigh and slow down. Maverick jogs up beside me, matching me stride for stride.

"What do you want?" I ask, trying not to sound too bitter. I'm calm enough now to realize that Dieter had a good point. I wouldn't be that surprised if the others followed his reasoning over mine, in fact, I'm not sure I want anyone with me for this. What if more of us die?

"Did you think I was gonna let you run off on your own?" he scoffs.

"I don't need help," I say, though we both know that's a lie.

"You don't know where they took her," he points out.

"And you do?"

"Give me five minutes."

Because this is Maverick— and only because this is Mav— I slow to a stop.

"Shouldn't you be with your group?" I ask, crossing my arms over my chest for warmth, only to drop them because the motion stretches the burn in a painful way.

"I am." He nods in the direction we came from. Not far back is the rest of the group. Dieter trails behind them, and I can't help but notice with a measure of both smugness and self-loathing that the entire left side of his face is bruised an ugly gooseberry purple to match his black eye. Lower, my gaze finds blue-ish, finger-shaped welts on the soft flesh of his neck.

Maverick holds a fist out towards me, something in it rattling. "You forgot these."

I grin half-heartedly and take the bottle of pills. They rattle pleasantly in my hand. "Thanks."

"What're friends for."

I pop the lid on the pills and shake one into my hand. I wish I could down one now and kill the pain at its roots, but unfortunately that's not how these stupid things work. Resigning myself to the aches, I dump the pill back inside, slipping the bottle into my sweater pocket. When I turn to get a better look at everyone here, I spy Dieter eyeing the top of the pill bottle. Unsettled, I shove it deeper into my pocket.

"So, directions," I say, turning back to Maverick. He holds up a finger for me to wait. His focus is on King, who's bent over against a birch tree. The other guy, whose name I still don't know, gives his back a solid couple of bumps before moving off to check a nearby stream.

"We'll have them in a moment," Mav assures me offhandedly. "King, how's it going over there?"

"I'm good," King wheezes, straightening up. He pounds his chest with the side of his fist, coughing hard once. "Heart's working."

Not more than a minute later a blur zips into our midst and trips to a halt. A spray of gravel kicks up under the blur's feet. I step back instinctively, but Maverick stays impassive.

"Trick, meet Skyelar."

The blur, now that it's not moving, transforms into a person. A sweaty guy with a narrow build and wind-spiked ginger hair stands before us. Dirty goggles obscure his eyes.

"And while we're doing the name thing, this is Piper." Maverick points to the Asian dude. "Delilah." The only girl in the group. "And I hope you at least remember Bakari and Dieter, since you saw them both yesterday." The names all sound vaguely familiar, which means I've probably met them all before, except for Skyelar.

"Sky, this is Trick." Maverick draws an invisible line connecting me and Sky, confirming my suspicion that we've never met before.

"Fastest kid in the Compound, at your service." Sky pries his goggles off, mock curtseying as he does. His accent is distinctly British. Freckles smatter his olive skin, and his narrow blue eyes are full of mirth. We shake. His hand is slender like the rest of him. I can picture him racing around the dome, clutching a rubber knife.

None other than Dieter himself pipes up. "I don't see how he can help." His voice is nasally. I definitely broke his nose, and possibly his cheekbone too. I should have broken his jaw again, then at least he would be suffering in silence. Maverick claps Sky on the back.

"Speedy here has been trailing our guys since they made their escape."

"Where?" I demand.

Sky holds his hands up.

"Woah, mate, ice it," he says, eyebrows disappearing under ginger hair. I clamp my mouth shut, desperate for answers. Sky points a slender finger in the direction he came from.

"There's a camp fifteen miles due east. I'm not going to lie, there are at least a hundred people there, all military, not too friendly looking. You know, like in movies when they show the after shots of a failed big fight before—"

"Sky," Maverick interrupts, "focus."

"Right, at any rate, you could make it there easy enough, just not before nightfall, and some of the terrain you do not want to be navigating in the dark." Sky drops his hand to his side, finished delivering his news.

"Any good campsites?" Maverick asks.

"I might've seen a few. That's a big might, mind you, it's not easy spying details when you're going that fast."

Maverick nods thoughtfully. "Okay. Here's what's happening. We've already hiked at least three miles, and we're all tired from last night and this morning. So, we'll go as far as we can today, set up a camp, scavenge some food if we can, and get as much shuteye as possible." He looks from face to face as he speaks, gauging how we all look and probably skimming our minds to see if anyone's on the verge of collapse, which King might be, or mutiny, which Dieter definitely is.

"Tomorrow morning we'll hike the rest of the way to the camp, grab Elle and whatever else we can, and get out as fast as possible." He clasps his hands together and rocks back on his heels, "Questions, comments, complaints, concerns?"

In response, Dieter starts to shake his head, only to stop sharp. Probably because his head hurts like hell. He settles for a scoffing noise instead.

"Dieter?" Maverick's thumps back onto flat feet, meeting Dieter with a level gaze.

"Is no one concerned about the fact that this is a suicide mission?" Dieter fumes. Piper lets out a low whistle.

"Cheerful bugger you are, mate," Sky quips. Dieter shoots them both glares that could curdle milk.

"My man, you don't have to come with us." Maverick, forever the peacekeeper, steps in before things can escalate. Dieter shifts his angry gaze to him. They stare each other down, an endeavor that Maverick inevitably wins. "You're free to go whenever you like, just don't come back."

Dieter holds his tongue.

"Uh huh." Maverick turns to address the rest of the group. "Anyone else?"

Nobody is particularly enthusiastic, but they don't voice any concerns either. Delilah's eyes are flinty with wild determination. I doubt a rescue mission is the only thing she has in mind for that military camp.

"Alright, now that's settled, let's go." Maverick claps his hands together. "If you're thirsty, grab some snow, if you're hungry, well so is everybody else."

I stoop to scoop up a handful of snow and pop it in my mouth before picking up a brisk jog. The snow numbs the roof of my mouth and tastes like dirt and pine needles. It's a source of water though. I try not to think about the grit in the snow, or the discomfort that's rising in heatwaves off my burn. Focus, by this time tomorrow, I'll have Elle back.

We keep a steady pace, heading east into the foothills of the mountains. We stick to the patches of wooded areas where we can. A majority of the terrain is grassland, but the many rivers and streams are lined with tall pine trees and bushes that droop over the riverbank. The water flows downstream, providing us with a well-covered path to travel. The hills get steeper, and while my muscles are conditioned for this, my bones ache. The throbbing in my knee has gotten exponentially worse as the storm draws nearer, but I grit my teeth and march on. I can only imagine that the slant will get steeper and steeper as we go along. After all, we're headed straight at the Urals.

Delilah has a permanent frown, and Piper keeps casting uneasy peeks at the sky. King lags, breathing heavier than the rest of us. The steady pace wears on him, and I keep waiting for the moment he drops. I feel bad for him. The Whitecoats might have given me constant pain, but at least I can breathe and run at the same time. Maverick should have taken him and the others somewhere safer. If something happens to them, it will be on me.

I catch myself staring up at the roiling cloud that eats up the sky between us and the dark northern horizon. Bolts of bright gold lightning snap free of the growling thunderhead as the wind picks up. A few minutes ago, Maverick sent Sky to check out what was going on below the storm. If he reports back that the storm is more than a bad rain shower, we can use the time before it hits to find shelter. That shouldn't be too hard. From what I've seen, caves dot the landscape like braille.

With any luck, we'll only clip the edge of the storm. But the creaking of my warped bones and the heavy scent of ozone hanging in the air tell me that my luck ran out a long time ago.

The blur of orange and tan comes tearing from the north, a dust tail kicking up in Sky's wake as he speeds towards us. By the looks of it, he's moving much faster than he was headed there. That's a bad sign.

He yelps something unintelligible as he plows into the group. He slams down on his heels, skidding to a stop barely short of body-slamming King, bouncing back on the balls of his feet. Words fly a mile per minute from his mouth while rainwater runs down his freckled face and plasters his ginger hair to his forehead. "We have to haul serious arse right now, or we won't have any arse left to haul later."

Maverick springs into action less than two words into Sky's warning.

"Go, run!" He shoves Delilah and Piper between their shoulder blades to get them moving faster before breaking into a run himself. The rest of us, finally processing what Sky said, follow suit. The wind swirls between the tree trunks, setting the hair on the back of my arms on end. The trees groan in anticipation, and a nearby stream that was bubbling before is roaring now. We don't have much time.

"How bad is it?" King calls, or rather, wheezes. He's already out of breath from the trek, if we don't find a cave before the storm hits, I'm not sure he'll survive it. Sky, now running only slightly faster than me, throws his hands in the air to pantomime an explosion.

I want to convince myself that he's exaggerating, but the guy is soaked from head to toe and winded like he had to wrestle his way out of the rain. I grit my teeth and lean into the run. The woods we entered not long ago whizz by on either side. My calves burn and my lungs ache. Deep down in my bones each step vibrates dully. I'm not a sprinter, and I'm less of a runner. The Whitecoats made us run for hours on treadmills, side-by-side until we all collapsed one at a time. The running labs were the worst. The duels were bad, but at least I knew I had a chance at winning them.

Rain pelts down, soft for now but not for long. The only sound audible above the howling wind is the crash and rumble of the flooding stream. It's closer than before, so either we're angled towards it and we're about to run out of land to walk on, or it's swelling dangerously fast and we have a flash flood to worry about on top of everything else. A night in a damp cave, sleeping in an inch of water, isn't appealing. But I'd rather have that than nothing.

For all the caves and hovels that we passed before, there's nothing but roots and ridges now. Maverick looks like he's considering turning back. I already know that if he does, I'm going on ahead. I refuse to give up the distance we've already traveled. I don't know how many miles are left in my tank, or how many pills I have left, and I can't afford to lose any more time or distance than this storm is already going to cost me.

A deafening pop splits the air to my left, just another noise in the cacophony of the approaching storm until Delilah throws her hand in front of me. She stops me seconds before a jack pine crashes to the ground in front of us and splits the group in half.

"Thanks," I shout over the wind. She ignores me and vaults over the fallen tree.

Sky might've under-exaggerated a tad. Lightning cracks and thunder shatters the air every other breath. Rain like razors beats down, gusts of wind rip up trees by their roots and fling them like twigs. Guess we know why there isn't all that much greenery around here.

There's no other option except to trudge on now; we can barely tell which direction we're going. We wouldn't know if we were walking in circles. The going is slow, every other second the wind knocks someone down and it's a struggle to drag them back onto their feet against the gales. Delilah is the only one not getting completely bullied by the storm. I'm not sure why she isn't having as much trouble as the rest of us, she might be aerokinetic. At any rate, anyone not getting flattened by the wind is still blinded by the pouring rain.

Maverick supports King, with one arm around his waist and the other shielding his own eyes from the rain. The flashes of light reveal snapshots of King clutching his chest, the veins in his neck are popping out. I should be more concerned about whether he's going to make the next five feet without collapsing entirely, but a louder part of me realizes that with the only geokinetic member of our group struggling to keep his own heart beating, we have no chance of creating our own shelter.

We're moving too slow. Time is of the essence and we're wasting it trying to beat back an uncontrollable force of nature. Frustration builds as the minutes tick past, and we press on at a snail's pace. Where are all the damned caves!

Ice it, Trick.

Maverick's voice projects in my mind. It's crystal clear and laced with irritation.

Out of my head! I snap. My mind is off-limits. The rules don't change because we're in the middle of a disaster. To my minor satisfaction, he doesn't reply. Though that doesn't mean he's not still poking around my thoughts. It's hard to sense him if his face isn't visible, and impossible now in the discordant storm. I stop grumbling to myself, mostly because Mav might be lurking, ready to chide me again, and he doesn't need that distraction to add to his self-imposed responsibility of keeping us all alive.

"Shelter, ho!" Piper bellows. His words are nearly lost to the wind, but that faint shout feeds relief into me. A bright flash of lightning reveals the shelter: a teensy cave mouth that juts from the ground like a beastly maw. It could not be more inviting. The entrance is pitch black. For all we know a wild animal has made its home in there, prepared to tear apart any poor creature that dares seek shelter inside. The idea is none too concerning at the moment, not when there's a beast already beating down on us with ice rain and falling trees. We straggle to the cave, feet slipping in the silty ground.

Skyelar is the first to reach the cave. His hand grips the stone lip. He scrapes his palm dragging himself inside. Piper stumbles in after him, and I after him. The relief is instantaneous. Most of us fall to our hands and knees. There's a lot of coughing and sputtering, a lot of heavy breathing, and underneath all the noise I can hear Maverick talking to King. "Where's your glycine, hey? Which pocket is it in?" Followed by wet squishing and the rattle of a pill bottle.

Water runs from our sodden clothes and forms puddles on the cave floor. Thankfully, the cave mouth opens to the east, it blocks the wind swooping in from the north. Only the occasional frigid gust manages to sneak its way in. The cave itself isn't fantastically warm, and since we're all chilled to the bone from the icy rain, the cold is that much more noticeable.

Anyone not on the brink of dying shuffles around. Sky rubs his arms and Piper and Delilah shoulder up against one another. I shiver and tuck my knees up to try and bundle any body heat I might have left into one place. My glasses slip down my nose, I swipe at the lenses half-heartedly. The glass is fogging up, the temperature in here must be just high enough. With a tired grimace, I take them off and scrub at them with the corner of my sweater. While I wipe all the grit off my glasses, I watch Mav's blurry form slump over King, exhausted.

I wonder if King's alive.

Maverick answers as if I spoke out loud: *he's okay.*

Good, I don't want anyone else to die, even if I don't know these people.

Piper is the first to move. He is the only one not shivering, which I find strange considering he has the slightest build of our group. He extricates himself from Delilah and runs his hands over the cave wall and scuffs the floor. Lichen scrapes off the rocks into a neat pile. He kicks a dried-up twig, and it skitters deeper into the cave. Sighing, he follows it to add to his pile.

He skims the cave in search of more firestarter, and something catches his attention. A puzzled expression crosses his face. I close my eyes and silently beg for there not to be some angry bear glaring at us from the cave mouth. He says nothing, and after a moment I hear his footsteps coming closer. Relieved, I breathe a heavy sigh. We're safe, for now.

Then Piper speaks up.

"Where's Dieter?"

Damn it!

5 | A Small Tree

My eyes fly open, and I scan the cave. It's dark in here, but it's also small enough that it doesn't take long to confirm that Dieter is not with us. Piper lets loose a stream of colorful swear words, including a handful I've never heard before. I can only agree with him. I catch Maverick's gaze. His arms are crossed over his chest, and he chews on his bottom lip. I know that look. His guilt look. He turns away and stares out at the wailing storm. Probably thinking of ways he could go out on his own to find Dieter. He can't, end of. He can't see through the rain or command the wind to stop any more than a regular human could.

I would leave Dieter. It's not worth risking more people to look for him. Besides, I'm not all that fond of the guy, I don't think anyone in this cave is. I grimace as it dawns on me that that statement could be just as easily said about me. In the end, Dieter and I are both outsiders to the group, and the only reason either of us are here is because of Maverick. All of these people—including me, trust Mav, and with good reason too. Because Maverick is far nicer than me. He's too altruistic to leave someone out in the storm of the century.

When he looks back to me, I already know what his decision is, and I know that I'm involved in whatever plan he's cooked up.

"You would do it for Elle," he says.

"That's different."

"How?" a woman's voice interrupts. We both glance over at Delilah. "How is it different?" Her accent is wan, but I can picture how at one time maybe the only language she spoke was

Russian. A vision of Chastin falling, red flowers blooming from his wounded chest, enters my mind. If anyone has the right to be royally ticked off at me, it's Delilah. I don't know what Chastin was to her, but he was clearly important to her and he's dead because of me.

"It's…" Elle is small, and fragile, and helpless, and I can't lose her. Dieter is none of those things. One glance at Delilah's narrowed eyes, and I bite my tongue. "Not. It's not different. Never mind."

Dieter is a person, albeit an obnoxious one, but still a person. Who am I to decide who to help and who to ignore? Besides, there are far too few Experiments in the world for us to leave each other's backs wide open.

"I hate to bear bad news, but may I remind you all that the bloke is out there." Sky jabs a finger at the monstrous storm outside. Thunder rumbles as if to accentuate his point, deafening us all momentarily. "And none of us can bloody stand straight in that mess."

Maverick grunts in the back of his throat, acknowledging Sky's point.

"Most of us," he corrects, turning to face Delilah, "I know you're tired, we all are, but I need your help finding Dieter."

Delilah waves off whatever Maverick is about to say next, already rising to her feet.

"Don't you think it would be hypocritical of me to refuse after badgering Trick about the same thing?"

"Thank you."

He claps his hands, as if we weren't all paying attention to begin with. "Alright, Trick, you're with me and Delilah. King, you're in charge while we're gone. This should be a quick recon, he can't have gone far." Maverick backs towards the cave mouth as he speaks. Delilah and I flank him. Lightning sparks and thunder quakes a half-second after. I'm not liking our odds against that rager. Delilah had better be damned amazing with her kinesis, otherwise we are as screwed as Dieter.

"In the unlikely event that we don't make it back before morning, you are to continue the original mission," he instructs, then makes a point of turning and fixing Sky with a firm look. "You will not come looking for us," he orders.

"Your wish is the very air I breathe." Sky mock bows.

"See you soon." Maverick bids them goodbye, then it's out into the storm for us. I brace for the buffeting wind and piercing rain. None of those things strike us.

A glance forward shows Delilah wearing a mask of concentration so intense that I'm half-afraid she might pass out. Her arms are stiff at her side, her palms facing out and her fingers so flexed they're hyperextending. A dome of wind whips about us counterclockwise, forcing the storm away. In places, the dome bulges inward, only to snap into place like a reluctant rubber band.

We inch forwards. The area outside of Delilah's protective bubble is painted pitch black by the unforgiving rain, meaning we can't scope for Dieter. In fact, unless Maverick snags a drift of Dieter's thoughts to follow, we won't see Dieter until we're right on top of him. At this rate, it could take the rest of the day and night to find him. I glance at Delilah. Despite the icy temperatures a sheen of sweat wets her forehead. Veins pop out on her forearms and neck. She can't keep giving this much energy for very much longer.

"Up ahead," Maverick shouts. "I'm picking something up."

"Is it Dieter?" I shout back. Delilah's wind dome is only partially successful in blocking out the racket of the storm.

"Can't tell for sure." He shakes his head. "Their thoughts are too frantic. I can't decipher it."

It's a bare straw, but it's the only lead we have and it's better than nothing. We alter our course according to some rough guesswork on Maverick's part and trudge on. The wind dome weakens, ripping like tissues paper every few minutes to let gusts maul us until Delilah patches the tear. We're playing a dangerous game against mother nature.

At the trunk of a massive fallen tree, Maverick halts. His eyes sweep down the trunk and off into the pitch. He traces a squiggly line over the rain-slick surface with his fingertips, then stops and drums the trunk lightly.

"I've found him," he says, but his expression wavers. His lips tug down at the corners as if he's not entirely sure. Delilah and I share a glance, then turn to face the fallen tree. It is a monstrosity, huge compared to the saplings and skinny poplars that dominate the area. After a brief pause I voice the concern on both of our minds.

"Under the tree?"

"You bet."

"So, he's dead. Crushed."

Maverick scrunches his face. "Dead people can't think." He taps his right temple.

Oh, that's comforting. Dieter's not dead, he's only mostly dead, pinned under this giant of a tree, skewered by a branch or two and panicking so hard that Maverick can't even make sense of his thoughts. By the time we get to him, he's either going to be the rest of the way dead, or there's not going to be anything we can do except make his death more comfortable. There isn't a version of this where Dieter survives.

"This is where you come in." He taps the tree, being careful not to jostle it in any way. "But first we gotta find where Dieter has got himself pinned." He swings his arm around and points with two fingers down the trunk.

"That way first."

Once again, we set off following Maverick. I fall back to the very edge of Delilah's protective bubble. The wind nips at my heels like a bratty puppy. My eyes are glued to the side of the trunk closest to the ground. Upon closer inspection, I can make out an eensy weensy space between the heavy tree and the unforgiving ground. The tree is resting on something somewhere down the line. I cringe internally, I'm familiar with begin crushed under something impossibly heavy. And knowing you could never lift it in a hundred years. Knowing no one is coming to save you. Knowing you're going to die there, pinned. I wouldn't wish it on my worst enemy.

We carry on as fast as we dare, watching the ground beneath the tree for a body, or a sign we're getting close. I expect blood, but it's the glimmer of something lighter that catches my eye first. Tangled with the stub of a long-gone twig, fluttering slightly, is a clump of fine blonde hair. It's way too long to belong to Dieter. Before I have a chance to look closer at the clump, Maverick shouts.

"Found—" He cuts off as Delilah's bubble pops, plunging us both into the maelstrom. She jerks her arm to force the dome back up. Maverick wipes the rain out of his face but doesn't comment. He gestures down at the base of the trunk, and I crouch to get a better view of what he's showing us. I find myself inches away from a pale, feminine face.

Not Dieter, not by a long shot. I pull back in surprise. Her wide green eyes flit over me, straining to see. Branches on either side of her look like they took the brunt of the weight when the tree fell. Since then, they have sagged, and now the trunk rests almost entirely on her chest.

"It's not Dieter," I say for Delilah's benefit. The woman under the tree opens her mouth but no sound escapes. The tree must be crushing her lungs.

"What are we supposed to do?" I ask.

"We have to get her out of there," Mav answers. "Can you lift it?"

"Yes," I say, but uncertainty bleeds through. I'm sure I can lift the tree. I'm less sure I can keep it off the ground with this storm ripping around us.

"Do it fast," Delilah says, "I'm tapped out, we have to go back."

Mav bites his knuckle. "Okay, we'll get her out and then go back," he says.

"What about Dieter?" I ask. He's the whole reason we're out here.

"She's all I sense."

So, Dieter really is either dead or flung away out of Maverick's reach. Either way, we're not getting to him before the storm gets to us.

"Get ready to pull her out." I rock forward on my heels and jam my hands as far under the trunk as I can get them.

Maverick crouches by the woman's head. She stares up at us, a mixture of terror and disbelief plain on her sharp features. I heave, the tree rocks, and a sharp cry bursts from her.

Damn. She's lying too angled for me to roll the tree, it'll crush her legs. I'll have to lift straight up. I switch grips, brace, and haul up. This tree is nothing, I tell myself. My arms strain and I lift from my legs, like they taught me in the Compound. Two-point-nine tons, I can lift two-point-nine tons, this tree is inconsequential. The wood groans as it is lifted from its resting place. The bark bites into my bare skin, and I lean back a tad to distribute the weight more evenly.

Maverick moves in quickly. He hooks his hands under her armpits and drags her out from under the tree. During the process something snags on one of the branches, causing the tree to lurch. I jolt rapidly to keep the trunk from collapsing back onto the woman, crushing her for good. I over-correct, and the trunk ends up crushed into my face. Bark scrapes like sandpaper, the tree wobbles.

It reminds me of that day back at the Compound, with the huge concrete weights.

The heaving and the trembling limbs.

The knowing that I was pushing myself too far, and the worse knowledge of what they would do to Elle if I didn't keep pushing.

Then the collapsing, the falling, and the pain, and my legs—*my legs*—and the fear.

The absolute, overwhelming, fear.

My breath hitches in my chest and won't release. Not soon enough, Maverick gets the woman clear. I can't set the trunk down fast enough, but before it reaches the ground, Delilah's bubble snaps like a rubber band.

Rain blinds me. An overpowering gale gusts the trunk clean out of my grasp and threatens to fling my body into the air as well. The tree flies up as if possessed, and the wind pushes it over top of me.

It's falling. On me. It's going to crush me. *It's going to kill me.*

I'm already shaky from the burst of panic that came moments earlier. My muscles lock of their own accord at this new danger, and I can't force myself to jump out of the way.

Sharp pain cracks across my face, but it's not from the tree. I think somebody slapped me. My vision snaps back into crisp focus, blessed air hits my lungs and loosens my panic-cramped limbs. Delilah's bubble has made a reappearance. Maverick is in front of me, his hands on either side of my shoulders. His eyes search mine for a sign that I'm back from wherever my mind went. Residual strands of the panic he must have heard screaming from my brain peek from the corners of his eyes.

"You good?" he asks. I peer over his shoulder at the tree. It's now several feet away, lying flat on the ground.

"Yeah. Yeah, I'm fine." I reach up and wipe the lenses of my glasses. He claps my shoulders.

"Let's head back." He turns to address the other two. "We'll have to look for Dieter tomorrow." He says, thinly masking his resignation. He pauses a moment, considering the woman. I take the time to get a better look at her as well. She's on her feet, gripping a heavy pack in one hand while the other is wrapped tight around her ribs, her lean, muscled shoulders curve forward. She's clearly hurt. Her face is haggard, her nose is thin and sharp, her chin is pointed, and her eyes are hard like jagged shards of glass. Her hair is muddied and bracken from the dirty ground, but it's possible to make out strands of blonde, so pale it's almost white.

The woman driving the ATV had the same coloring. Suspicion washes over me. I step around Maverick and grab the woman by the collar of her stiff jacket, her eyes widen. She's sporting the unmistakable camouflage of army fatigues. Cool metal presses into my palm and I look down at the dog tags around her neck.

She's Army.

She helped steal Elle.

I grab her until her bones creak under my grip. She chokes, her mouth twists in a picture of surprise and pain.

"No—please." She gasps, "I-I have a—" I narrow my eyes and lift her, so her toes barely scrape the dirt. Her hands claw at mine.

"A little girl," she rasps. "Marsya."

"How ironic," I sneer and drop her. Her knees buckle, she crumples at my feet. "I had a little girl too, do you know what happened to her?"

"*Da*," she wheezes at the same time Maverick intervenes.

"By the stars, Trick, *calm down*." His hand clamps over my shoulder and he yanks me away from the woman. I bat him away, incensed.

"Tell me," I demand. The woman winces, her arm is wrapped protectively around her. To her credit, she doesn't shrink away. "What do you know? Where is she?"

"Trick, stop." Maverick jerks me back once again, this time he drags me farther away.

"She took Elle," I snarl, struggling to free myself. It should be easy, but my arms aren't cooperating quite like they should.

Another of Maverick's handy-dandy telepath tricks. One he never uses because it's exhausting and headache-inducing. Mind control.

"Ice it," he commands again, his words have taken on an ethereal tone. Sapped of the ability to move, my mind takes that moment to catch up, and suddenly I'm aware that, without realizing it, I've slipped into dueling mode. "She wants to help us get Elle back. She snuck away to come find us and take us to the camp because she thinks what the military is doing is wrong."

I look to the woman for confirmation. She dips her chin and stares at the ground, refusing to meet my gaze. Her long fingers twist around the chain of her dog tags, her chest rising and falling with rapid wheezes.

"My name is Anushka Tatyanin," she says, her accent is thick, and her English is broken. "I am a Sergeant in the thirty-sixth regiment of *Krovavaya Brigáda*." Her breathing evens. "We were on a mission to find escaped Experiments. I thought we were looking for animals but when we found your group, the lieutenant commanded us to—to," she hesitates, grasping for the right word.

"Capture us?" Maverick supplies. She nods.

Her fingers clench around her chain. "I am sorry. I want to return her to you, we should not have captured the little one."

By the time she's done apologizing, I've shrugged back into my own mental skin. A majority of me is unwilling to return to normal, but I quash the anger and stuff it where it can't be found. Maverick, sensing that I have control of myself, releases me. Free, I run a hand over my face, shoving my glasses out of the way, and heave a sigh. A knife of guilt for forcing him to pull that out when he's already in rough shape twists in my chest.

"Can you walk?" he asks Anushka. She raises her head to look at him.

"*Da.*"

"We found shelter not far from here, if you agree to help us get Elle back, then you can come back with us," he offers. He would probably let her hide from the storm with us anyways. Then again, the ultimatum he gave Dieter comes to mind.

"I want to help you, but." She holds up a hand to stop us. "You must also promise safety for my child, Marsya. What I am doing is treason, the Bloody Brigade will kill me if I am caught, and they will try to hurt her. Please, she is only four."

A sympathetic pang goes through my gut. I hadn't noticed earlier, but Anushka is young. She can't be that much older than me.

"We'll keep her safe," I promise before Maverick can answer. He shoots me a dubious look but holds his tongue. Anushka's relief is palpable.

"Thank you," she breathes. "I will help you get your *malyshku* back."

Delilah is a lot worse for wear. She all but collapses the moment we're in the cave. Her soaked limbs flop like limp ropes on the ground around her.

Sky leans on the cave wall near a meager fire, shoulder blades pressed against the curve as if they belong there. His goggles are shoved up on his forehead, emphasizing the crease between his brows, and his hand spins in an unending loop, fingers snapping impatiently. The moment he lays eyes on us the snapping halts and his forehead loses its stress crease. A wry smirk twists his lips when he sees Anushka.

"Funny, I thought Dieter was a dude."

"Stuff it," I grumble. I grab Anushka's arm and all but drag her to the back of the cave. Her feet scrape on the stone, but it doesn't make a difference. She's weak and light, and while she's here surrounded by kids who pack more power in their thumbs than she could dream of, the only defense she has is the gun in her holster. I push her in front of me. The force knocks her into the rock wall. I'm too rough and it's not entirely on purpose, but she doesn't need to know that. She turns, her face blank as it's been since Maverick decided to give her a chance. It's not until I reach for the gun at her side that she finally reacts. She sidesteps, face clouding over as her hand hovers protectively over the grip.

Maverick stops me.

"I got it, Trick," he says, "get some rest, you need it." He slides between me and Anushka easily, nudging me away.

The spot I'd curled up in earlier is open, I claim it again, easing my aching body to the floor. Piper has ended up at Delilah's side and is coaxing her closer to the fire. Half the group has stripped off their sweaters and shirts and spread them out to dry. I tug my soaking wet sweater and shirt over my head. They come off as one article, and it takes a bit of prying to separate the two so I can wring them out.

When I'm done, I contemplate the makeshift bandage around my shoulders and chest. The sodden fabric clings to my skin and rivers of pink-and-brown tinged water run down my sides when I move. It's not the healthiest idea to take it off, but it might be even worse to leave it on while it's soaking wet. Shivering, I pick at the knots with cold-dulled fingers until the strips come free. I have to peel the strips off, taking fresh scabs with them.

Stars, it's cold. I crush my hands into fists but that does next to nothing to stop my violent shivering. My teeth chatter. It feels like ice water drips through my veins and rests in blankets over my shoulders. I'm coldest where the grenade cooked off most of my skin. Maybe taking the bandages off wasn't such a good idea after all. Too late now. I crumple the strips up, squeezing rainwater and blood from them. The insides of the strips are stained with ugly red blotches.

The base of my neck twinges, an ache that settles in my stiff shoulders. I dig in my pocket for the pain pills. My hands meet with fabric and nothing else.

Frantically, I search the pocket again. I pinch the inside of both pockets and turn them inside out. Thin muck sloughs out and nothing more. The bottle of pain pills is gone.

I bite my tongue, holding in a bitter curse. The bottle must have fallen out while we were out in the storm. It could be anywhere by now, I'm never getting those pills back.

Unusual tightness pinches the skin across the back of my ribs. Without medication to numb it, the burn is going to hurt like hell. Without medication, all of me is going to hurt like hell. As if on cue, the pins and needles that have been plaguing me since before the storm begin to escalate into searing pain.

I glance up at the others. They're all bedding down on the cold rock floor of the cave, making the most of the thunderstorm by catching up on the sleep they lost last night. Nobody noticed my outburst, not even Maverick. Good, I don't want to be the one to cause another delay when we have no time to waste. I'll keep my trap shut. I can worry about getting more pain pills when Elle is safe. I pull my damp sweater on to hide the injury and gain as much heat as I can. For now, that's the best I can do.

I sigh and settle gingerly on my side, trying to find a position that doesn't press knots into my muscles. Normally I sleep sitting up and leaning on my back, but that's not possible with the burn. The cold seeps through the sweater, I shiver like a madman. I hope Elle is warmer than this, I hope that she at least has a bed. I close my eyes, clinging to these hopes.

Minutes into trying to rest, a creeping feeling sets my arm hair on end and makes my skin crawl. I shift, my eyes are drawn to the back of the cave, where Anushka is tucked into a corner that looks like it should be too small to fit her. Her crystal green eyes bore into mine, then flicker down to my shoulder. I follow her gaze, the neck of the sweater has drooped to expose the top of the shoulder she's staring at, where the swollen edges of the burn peek over. I narrow my eyes and tug on the sweater neck.

Anushka holds her tongue and as long as it stays that way there's nothing to worry about. Nothing at all.

It takes longer for me to let my eyes close a second time, but when they do, the plunge into sleep is instant.

I can't be asleep for more than a couple hours when the pain finally sinks its fangs to me. I wake to its claws in my breastbone, and the red-hot iron jammed up in my stomach, welding my organs together. The fire has dimmed to mere embers, and the storm outside has lightened to a shower.

I gasp as a paroxysm strikes like exploding cherry bombs up each individual vertebra. The spasm locks up my lungs. It doesn't last long but being robbed of the ability to breathe scares me. What if I suffocate to death in this instant and never see Elle again? The moment the spasm ends, I crush my palm against my mouth, partly to keep from waking anyone by shouting, and partly to keep from vomiting. Nausea twists my guts hard, and a headache throbs at the base of my skull.

Ow, that's a lot.

Another spasm clenches my abdomen, forcing me to curl up like a shrimp. But curling forward like that pulls my aching muscles too tight. I suck a harsh breath in through my nose, desperately trying to stay quiet. And, oddly enough, my back itches like hell. Bile rises in the back of my throat, and I rock to my knees, hand clamped even tighter. The new position helps my stomach settle.

"You cannot sleep?" A voice freezes me in place.

My watery eyes sweep up to find none other than Anushka staring at me. Her hair is down, hanging in tangled clumps over her shoulders. Mud darkens the platinum blonde and is smeared into the scrapes on her cheeks and hands. She looks as young and exhausted as the rest of us, if not for the fatigues she could be mistaken for an Experiment. She has a beaten look in her eyes that I'm used to seeing in others at the Compound.

I lower my hand and wipe the sweat from my forehead. Anushka's form blurs in time with the pulse in my head.

"Why are you awake?" I ask. Sweat forms beads on my forehead and slicks my palms. A bone-deep ache awakens in my hips, and my fingers are going numb. The pains haven't been this bad in years. I can barely think straight.

"Nightmares," she says.

"What do you have nightmares about, people stronger than your gun?" I spit back. The effort costs me, but at least she shuts up. Briefly.

"Your back will get infected," she says, folding her knees up to her chest. I shoot her a glare, but I'm not sure which of the swimming Anushka's to look at.

"It's deep, and it's not clean."

"Shut up."

"You won't be able to rescue your sister if you get blood poisoning and die."

"I'll be fine," I insist as if saying it more forcefully will make it true.

She gives me a curious look, her fingers twist the chain holding her tags. The scratched metal clinks together softly, reflecting dim orange light from the dying embers. She twists. The chain gets tighter around her neck.

"I am a coward," she says. "But I did not want to be a coward who kidnapped children."

"Then why did you?" I ease back, resting my weight on my heels. The conversation at least helps keep my mind distracted from the headache and nausea.

"For my daughter, she's only four, she needs a lot of stuff, and it costs a lot of money. The army keeps us housed and fed." Twist. Her hand is practically pinned to her neck now. A final twist, and it snaps. One of the tiny beads broke under the pressure. She tugs the tags loose from her neck, frees the broken section from the latch, and fastens the chain around her neck. Her hands shake.

"You look too young to have a kid," I say, flexing a cramped hand. Her gaze flickers over me, her fingers begin to twist the chain again.

"I am," she says. "I turned twenty the day we took your sister."

That stings, though I'm sure it's not meant to. "Then what's the deal, why do you have a kid?"

Anushka's face warps, her expression turning bitter where before it was empty. She grips the bead chain until her knuckles go white with the pressure "Do not talk to me about my daughter."

I almost apologize. I'll never be good or empathetic or diplomatic like Mav, but tonight I've been… mean.

"My name is Anushka Tatyanin." Anushka's shoulders rise to her ears and there's a tremor in her voice that I didn't expect. Her hand stays tangled in the chain. It twists. "I am a Sergeant in the thirty-sixth regiment of the Bloody Brigade."

I furrow my brow, a faraway look has washed over her features. From across the cave her irises look glazed.

"I'm twenty." Twist. "I have a daughter." Twist. She looks at me.

"Okay."

"I love her." No twist. A shudder creeps its way up her back. The light comes back to her eyes as she returns from wherever her mind took her. She opens her mouth as if to say something. Then she snaps it shut and drops the hand that was clenching her tags. Clearly this conversation is over. She melts into the shadows of the cave, her arms clasp tightly around her legs so she's curled up in a cramped little ball. I half expect her to start rocking back and forth after the episode she had, but she doesn't.

I turn my gaze to the mouth of the cave and stare at the rain falling in curtains outside. It's dark, and the temperature has dropped considerably. Thankfully, the nausea has alleviated, and the spasms have calmed to a dull throbbing. I take a few more deep breaths, then inch across the cave to the dying fire. There are unburned sticks mixed in with the embers, and with some nudging I get them all in one big pile over the glowing coals. I've never built a fire before, so I snatch a thinner stick from the stack and poke at the coals until a teensy flame erupts from the rippling orange embers. The fire catches, and the cave gains a bit more heat and light.

I sit for a while in the circle of light, prodding the tiny fire with my twig every now and then to keep the flames going. The ache in my bones pools in my legs and lower back. Moving hurts. Not moving hurts. Too much to sleep. Anushka shuffles in her teeny tiny corner, she moves like a puppet, all jerky and wooden. I turn back to the fire and roll my shoulders to ease the malaise, instead, the motion scrunches the burn, sending fiery prickles down my back. Anushka's warning coils in my mind.

Infection.

Gingerly, I turn my head to get a good look at the burn. Even as gentle as I'm trying to be, the movement hurts.

The first layer of my skin is gone. A crevice of scabby, fleshy mess sprawls down one shoulder and across my back. It ends at the base of my neck and encompasses both shoulder blades. Lesser burns decorate the backs of my arms where flames licked briefly. Angry red skin encircles the burn. The unburned, red skin is swollen and shiny from the tightness. When I poke it, pain sparks, and I yank my hand away. I bite my lip. I've spent enough time in the infirmary to know what an infection looks like. Anushka was right.

Sighing inwardly, I reach for the makeshift bandage strips to fasten them in place. The bandages are dried, but the spots of blood are crusty. I rub them away with my thumbs as well I can. Fibromyalgia rears its ugly head as I add more and more pressure to my back. What would normally feel like a slight discomfort is amplified to something akin to a vice crushing my chest. I grit my teeth and keep on re-tying the strips. These are all I have to keep dirt out of the wound.

I can only hope that the poor bandages and my immune system are enough to keep blood poisoning at bay for a little while.

"Need some company?" Maverick startles me when he comes to sit beside me in front of the fire. I fold my arms over my chest, shoving all thoughts of the looming infection out of my head. If he realizes what's going on, he'll stop me. Strap me to a tree and stick a twenty-four-hour guard on me until it passes. Sure, he'd send someone to rescue Elle, he'd go himself. But the idea of doing nothing while she's out there, alone and in danger, makes terror bubble under my skin like acid.

"What are you doing awake?" I ask, tilting my head to glance at him sideways. His hair sticks up at random and bags have formed under his eyes. His shoulders sag as if he's carting around a boulder.

"It's loud in here." He shrugs, staring at the fire. "The walls must reflect thoughts or something."

We sit in silence, letting that sentence hang in the air while the flames crackle. Mav shifts now and then and rubs a spot behind his ear the way he always does when his head aches from all the voices. Once again a knife of guilt for earlier twists in my chest. His finger traces a loose circle over the bone. I scratch at an itch on my elbow and squint at the fire, try to will the smoke to stop irritating my eyes.

"Does that mean they have physical form?" I ask, scrunching my nose.

"Hm?" he snaps out of his train of thought.

"If the thoughts are bouncing off the walls they have to be physical, like waves."

He lets out a short laugh. "Smart observation, for a dumbass."

He ducks to dodge a smack, narrowly avoiding searing his face in the fire. He hovers there for a moment, centimeters away from the flames. The skin on his cheek turns pink from the heat, and still he doesn't move, just works his jaw, pretending not to grin. When he sits up, the smile fades for real, and he's back to being Serious Mav, with too many responsibilities and not enough sleep.

"How are you feeling?" he asks as he folds his arms over his knees.

"Oh, we're back to the Mars agreement now, are we?"

That makes him roll his eyes, the effect is ruined by a huge yawn. "I don't have the energy to filter everything right now." He runs the back of his hand across his eyes. "I told you, it's loud in here."

Over in the corner, Anushka makes a noise that sounds suspiciously like a sob. We both glance over, expecting her to be awake but her eyes are closed. She's curled in a ball, her fingers clutching the dog tags like a lifeline and her leg twitches sporadically. She must be having another nightmare. She gasps again, quieter this time but no less sob-like and no less fearful.

"What's she dreaming about?" I ask without looking away. The line of her jaw is taut with the grinding of her teeth, and beads of sweat are forming on her forehead. Maybe she is dreaming about people who are stronger than her gun. Do I care? Should I?

When Maverick doesn't answer, I turn back to him to see that he's focusing hard on the fire. His face is a patchwork of bloodlessly pale and flushed red and his entire body is tense.

"Hey, you good?"

He opens his mouth to respond, then shuts it and squeezes his eyes closed instead. His breaths come shallow and shuddery. From the back of the cave Anushka groans, and Maverick winces in response. Whatever is playing out in her nightmare must be pretty damn bad. It takes a lot to make Mav flinch, he's seen more than the rest of us. He's been in all our heads. Another moment passes before he moves, scraping his fingers through his hair and prying his eyes open.

"It's too much right now," he whispers, "it's too loud in here."

I reach out to pull him closer. He breaks out of his trance, leaning into the hug until his cheekbone rests on my shoulder.

He lifts his hand and presses it to my forehead, "Think about something," he instructs in a trembling voice. His telepathy works ten times as well when he's touching the head of the person he's listening to. He used to only be able to hear that way. On a normal day I'd shove him off, but this time I tip my chin, ducking a little so it's easier for him to reach. On a normal day, there wouldn't be tears shining in his eyes.

The first memory that comes to mind is of the last conversation I had with Elle before the Compound was ripped open. As it replays, I linger on the better moments like her story about his visit the day before, and the way she went on and on about the boy she'd met earlier that day.

"*He has glowing eyes, they look like two little stars.*" I remember her saying. I'm still not sure what that means.

"His name's Carver," Maverick says when that part plays out.

"Who?"

"The kid with the glowing eyes, his name's Carver. He was brought in last year. They made him photokinetic."

"Oh." I wonder if Carver made it out of the Compound alive.

Maverick takes his hand off my head. I shouldn't be as relieved as I am about this, but it's getting harder and harder to mask the pain snarling in the back of my mind. I don't want to admit it, but his weight against my shoulder is starting to hurt. His breathing is getting deeper, his head is getting heavier, it won't be long before he drops off, and I can move him.

The firelight grows dimmer and dimmer. The pattering of the raindrops keeps pace with the beat of the pulse in Mav's wrist. I wait until I'm sure he's asleep, then reach over to nudge him. Before I even lay a finger on him, he shifts, lifting his head a little.

"You didn't take your meds?" he asks abruptly, turning to stare at me. Blazing telepath, I curse silently.

"I lost them." I pick at a loose thread on my pant leg. There's no point in hiding it now, besides, as long as I'm alert and functional he has no reason to try stopping me. Withdrawal and fibro pains won't take me out, not as fast as an infection anyways.

"Why didn't you tell me?"

"What would you have done, magicked them back into my pocket?"

His lips part, then snap back shut. His entire body deflates with an exhale, curling forward like a broken tree branch. Shadows are carved into secret lines under the edge of his collarbone and in the corners of his mouth, only visible in the flickering of the firelight. We sit in silence again, Maverick staring at the fire and me staring out at the cold drizzle.

Has it always been like this for him? Everything weighing down even when it's not his job to carry it. I know he's always been the one to take on newbies and watch out for his crew, but the game has changed now. Is he ready? Are any of us ready for it?

"You need to go to sleep." I pull him down, this time angling him so that he ends up laying across my lap instead of on my arm. He obliges, heaving his second gigantic yawn of the night.

"Is it my fault Dieter's gone?" His voice is thick with exhaustion but there's an unignorable urgency to his question.

Of course it isn't his fault, the very idea is ridiculous. Dieter got lost on his own, with help from whatever vengeful sky spirit conjured up that hellstorm. But it wouldn't take a master of telepathy to tell that Maverick doesn't see it that way.

"No." I shake my head, wincing when a sharp pain sparks at the base of my neck.

"I was supposed to look after him." He pauses, searching for something else to say. When he can't find the right words, he sighs. "He was a kid."

With that, he's out, finally too exhausted to stay conscious. His words hang in the air, taunting me. I guess I had forgotten that part, about Dieter being a kid. He's, what, three years younger than me? Four? One of us should have been watching him. I should have watched him, if for no other reason than to make sure he didn't make a run for a different mountain on his own. He could have made it out of the storm alive, if he was smart enough to take cover.

I hope we cross paths with Dieter again, if for no other reason than to ease Maverick's conscience.

9 | QUICKSAND

"Wakey wakey, eggs and bakey," Skyelar sings in my ear. Unfortunately, he jumps out of the way before I can take a swing at him. It can't be morning already. I closed my eyes barely five minutes ago. I groan, a sound that is akin to a dying whale.

Everything hurts. Everything.

Sitting up feels like too much effort, but I manage. Mornings are always the worst. I sway in place for a moment, keeping my eyes scrunched closed. Damn, is it hot in here. 'Warm' is not a temperature I'd expect from a cave in Russia, especially not in the middle of spring. Maybe we got lucky, for once in our collective lives. I pry my eyes open, crusty sleep crumbles on my lashes. I blink a couple times and fix my glasses while my vision eases into focus. The fire is a black pile of char on the chipped cave floor, and weak light floods in from outside. Maverick is gone.

I get stiffly to my feet. Every joint protests. Between the lack of pills, a burned back, and sleeping on a cold hard slab, I must confess that this is not my finest morning. I grimace as the dry heaving from last night makes a re-appearance. I smother my mouth with my hand and cover a lurch with a cough.

"Alright there, mate?" Sky cocks his head at me, bright ginger bangs fall across his forehead.

I clear my throat before answering. "Stomach cramp."

He chucks something silvery at me, and I jolt to catch it. The resulting pain is paralyzing. I crush my free hand into a fist, fingernails break skin, but I can't register the stinging over the sharp spasms. It feels a lot like someone is taking a nail gun to my back, right where the burn is. Sky gives me a weird look. I give a little wave, pretending to be fine, and force myself to focus on the thing he tossed me.

It's a protein bar. I can't read the Cyrillic letters on the silver packaging, but like most things the Compound used, I recognize the shape and packaging. The wrapper crinkles like Christmas paper as I rip it off. Saliva floods my mouth as I take a huge bite, not even nausea could keep me from eating this morning. Nothing has tasted so good in the history of food.

It isn't until I'm halfway through cramming the morsel of food into my mouth that I bother to ask where it came from. None of us packed food.

"Miss Tatyanin gave us some of her stolen rations," Sky answers.

"*Miss* Tatyanin?" I raise an eyebrow and wipe the last crumbs of the bar off my chin. Sky shrugs and plucks his shirt from the cave floor.

A weird sensation, exactly like the one from last night, washes over me. I look around, and—surprise, surprise—find Anushka staring at me. Correction, staring at my back.

"Can I help you?" I raise my voice enough to attract her attention and draw it away from my burn, which I'm sure isn't covered completely by the measly bandages. She purses her lips, and when she meets my gaze I can practically see the wheels turning in her mind.

"Thanks for the food." I wave the empty wrapper at her. She nods curtly but holds her tongue as she exits the cave. As soon as she's out of sight, and I'm sure that Sky isn't looking, I twist to examine my back. My sore muscles protest but being able to stand has helped the back pain from earlier—by pooling it all in my legs, but that's a more familiar, bearable problem. I can only spy slivers of red skin and flesh through the cloth strips, but there are wet spots where the wound has wept openly. Gingerly, I prod the border. Greenish-yellow slime oozes out, soaking the edge of the nearest strip.

"Nasty burn." King startles me. I jerk my hand away. His voice is deep and rumbly. I think this might be the first time I've ever heard him speak.

"It's not bad," I lie, wiping my hand on my pant leg.

"No?" His eyes, a shade lighter than his skin, sweep over me. He looks anything except convinced.

"I've had worse."

King snorts but leaves me be. First Anushka, now King. The numbers are stacking against me. I don't know how many of the others have caught on too, but I'm not going to let them stop me. I stoop to pick up my shirt and sweater, holding my back straight. I follow King out as I slip the tank top over my head.

A cool breeze floats through the trees. I relish in the relief from the sweltering heat and inhale a lungful of rain-fresh air. The piney branches of trees glitter with trapped water droplets, and the ground is slick and damp. Everyone has gathered outside the cave mouth. Everyone except Maverick, that is, and since I didn't see him inside, he must be wandering elsewhere.

"You should put that sweater on," Delilah advises. I stare at her like she's grown two heads.

A sweater? In this weather?

Then, I see her shiver. In fact, everyone except me has rashes of goosebumps that they are trying to rub away. Our breath swirls, opaque, in the air.

"Uh, here." I toss the sweater to Delilah.

She gives me a confused look but pulls the fabric over her head. The sweater fits well, she has a couple inches on me, so the bottom hugs the tops of her hips instead of the bottoms, but she flashes me a grateful smile. Then her gaze flickers to the damp bandages and her smile fades. Damn, I should have kept the sweater to hide this infection.

"Aren't you cold?" Sky asks.

"Not really." On the contrary, I'm burning up. King snorts again.

"You are sure you're all right?" he asks, he makes no pretense of sliding his gaze over the back of my neck.

"Fine."

"How fine?"

"Aw, leave the kid alone, King," Piper pipes up in a surprisingly strong Texan drawl, "you're just mad everyone else can walk without dropping dead."

King sneers at him. Thankfully, Maverick returns to interfere before things can progress to a flat-out fist fight.

"We're burning precious daylight, save your squabbles for when people's lives aren't on the line and let's move. Sky, Anushka, you lead." He makes shooing gestures as he steps between King and Piper. Sky splits from the group, followed by Anushka and the rest of us. I fall into step beside Maverick. He rolls his eyes up to the cloudless sky, mulling silently.

"Good walk?"

"I wanted to be alone," he murmurs. "I checked for signs of Dieter. I should send Sky to track him down, but who knows where he ended up after that storm."

"Mm," I grunt in agreement.

After that, I lapse into silence. Walking is hell, especially now that my system has begun cleansing itself completely of the Savella. I concentrate on putting one foot in front of the other and disguising my pain from Maverick's sensitive telepathy. Between my efforts and the distraction of keeping everyone else on the move he hasn't caught on, yet. I think. I just have to keep up until we rescue Elle.

We navigate the ever-steepening terrain for a long hour. Thick cloud cover hides the rising sun from view. Even so, it becomes ten times hotter as the morning gives way to afternoon. I'm sweating bullets despite the brisk wind. I run a tired hand through my damp hair and the strands stick right back down on my forehead, I must have a fever, though I'm denying it.

Everyone else is shivering while I can't begin to fathom being cold enough to shiver right now.

Out of the blue my vision blurs, and an invisible hand shoves me back.

"Trick?"

My vision clears enough that I can make out Maverick's ballooned head. He looks like someone stretched the skin of his face over a swollen watermelon. The ground under my feet swirls in a vortex of half-melted snow and wet brown mud. I jump out of the way, only to discover that my feet are stuck. I'm sinking, fast.

Quicksand? In the mountains?

The landscape blurs again, worse this time. I dig the heels of my hands into my eyes, trying to wipe away the dizziness and the nausea that's coming with it. The quicksand gulps my calves. This is bad. I need to concentrate. But I can't. I'm too dizzy, too nauseous, too hot, and— damn, I think my heart is skipping beats. It's not supposed to be going that fast, is it?

"Trick, what the hell, man?"

I open my eyes and the swirling of the ground sends my brain reeling. I don't think this is quicksand. I think I'm hallucinating. I open my mouth to tell Maverick, instead I vomit.

Maverick grips my upper arm. I suck in a breath, and then it all blinks out, like someone, somewhere, has flipped off a very important switch.

"He's burning up."

"Get some snow."

"Did you know?" A pause, a grunt. "Why didn't you tell someone?" Mav's angry. I don't know why.

"He did not want me to." Female, accent too heavy to be Delilah.

A groan. Me, or someone else?

"Trick, you *idiot*."

A biting cold dowses my back, my muscles lock up in shock. I can't move except to gasp in pain. A chilled hand pats my arm.

"Hang in there."

The switch flips again.

It feels like an eternity before the dark melts away, leaving my mind stripped of defenses and white-washed with burning bleach. At least now I'm awake. I'm lying flat on my back, the cold spreads its fingers over me. I peel my eyes open, which is an effort all in itself. What feels like a year's worth of glue-y sleep sticks my eyelids to each other. My heart drops to my toes when I only endless empty black, then a pinprick of light comes into focus, and another, and another. And flickering orange brightens my peripheral. I'm not trapped in limbo, it's night.

I let out a sigh. A faint crackling comes from the fire, and heavy breathing and snoring fills the air. For an instant I think it was all a bad nightmare, and I'm still in the cave. Then I realize the speckles of light above are stars.

With creaky bones and aching muscles all working against me, I sit up. Man, I feel like a corpse. But I'm glad that's all I feel like, it could be worse, considering the last time I remember being conscious.

"You're awake."

The statement comes from my left. I'm too stiff to jump at the disturbance, but I do turn to see who it is. All I can make out is a fuzzy blob against a background of taller fuzzy blobs. Where are my glasses? I squint at the ground beside me, trying to find them.

"On your left… other left."

My fingers finally meet the cool plastic frames, and I slip my glasses on. They're coated in smudges but at least they aren't smashed or lost. Maverick sits a few feet away, leaning on a tree, and in the dim light afforded by the campfire he looks ready to keel over. I've never seen him this ragged in all the time I've known him. I don't have time to speak before pain hits me like a fireball to the chest. Wheezing, I double over, but that hurts too.

I swallow a cry, wishing desperately for something to bite. I can't bite my hand for fear of breaking it, I can't scream for fear of waking everyone else. I'm trapped.

Maverick appears at my side. "Here, Tylenol," he says, holding a handful of pills to my lips. He's careful not to touch me as he feeds me three pills, then slips away back to his place by the tree.

For fifteen agonizing minutes I wait. I assume it's fifteen minutes anyway, since it feels like hours, but when the painkillers finally kick in I'm so relieved I could pass out. I nearly do. Instead, I heave a shaky sigh and look over at Maverick.

"I'm sorry," he says after a long break. His lips are chewed bloody. For a sickening moment I think that something horrible has happened, and we can't rescue Elle, until his gaze flickers to my burned back and he winces.

"It was nothing," I try to assure him.

"Clearly it was something!" he snaps, "I should have known something was wrong."

"It's my own fault for not telling you to start with. I didn't want to slow anyone down," I reply, pulling my knees up so I can rest my elbows on them. He relaxes in increments until he's leaning on the tree trunk again. It's a poplar, the smooth, white bark reflects the firelight. Similar towering trunks loom all around. There are certainly more trees here than the area around the Compound.

Maverick plucks a twig from the forest floor and twirls it between the pads of his thumb and forefinger. He's still on edge about the whole thing.

"You couldn't have known," I say.

"But I should have, damn it!" The twig breaks, he curses again, under his breath. "Damn it. It's my job to keep everyone safe, it's my responsibility." He tosses the twig away and glares at the ground.

"You can't keep everyone safe all the time. We're dangerous kids in a dangerous place. Thing's are bound to happen." I'm trying to talk some sense into him, but he doesn't seem to get it. "Look man, mope all you want, but don't pretend you're responsible for a mistake *I* made."

At that, the hard line of his brow softens, and a new crease appears over his nose. He glances up at me, nibbling on his lip.

"You're my friend," he says in a hushed tone. "Hell, you're my best friend. If I can't manage to watch your back at a time like this…" He trails off and lets out a heavy sigh.

"You can't keep an eye on everyone. You're not Eye Enhanced." I argue. I don't even think Eye Enhanceds are a thing.

He huffs, and I'm about to protest more when the slightest of wry grins lights on his torn lips. "Eye Enhanced. Can you imagine? Me with big buggy telescope eyes." He cups his hands around his eyes. An uncertain laugh works its way out of him, I try to picture it, and laugh a little too. Then he laughs some more, and I laugh some more, and soon we're both smothering childish giggles to keep from waking anyone else.

Punch-drunk from exhaustion, every time we make eye contact the hysterics start all over again. Gasping for breath, swiping at our eyes. It's ages before we calm down. When I can speak without bursting out laughing, I uncover my mouth and take a breath.

"Seriously, Mav, everyone makes mistakes, don't be so hard on yourself."

He ponders that for a moment, staring at the ground, then gives a slow nod. We both glance up at the sky. The clouds have finally cleared off, and thousands of glittering stars wink above us, twinkling like… I'm not really sure how to describe it. They're kind of like my *abuela's* dangly glass earrings, only a hundred times more captivating. The night wind rustles the budding leaves at the tops of the poplar trees. Out in the darkness beyond the campfire, an owl hoots.

"How long have I been out?" I ask. Maverick hesitates, his pause gives life to a ball of anticipation in my stomach. I look away from the stars and turn to him.

"Two and a half…maybe three days, if it's as late as I think it is," he mutters reluctantly.

"What?!"

Three *days?*

He holds out his hands.

"We moved, King used a slab of rock to carry you." He points to a craggy outcropping jutting out of the land east of us. "The military camp is right over that cliff. We were going to sneak in tomorrow."

Somehow, that only makes me feel marginally better.

"Three days," I scoff under my breath. We could have been here and gone in three days.

"Dude, you almost died. I'm surprised you're awake now."

I suck in a slow breath, silently forcing the frustration to disperse. He's right, of course, on both counts. People don't normally wake up when they collapse in the middle of nowhere. Which raises a whole other question.

"How…?" I leave the question open. He knows what I mean, perks of having a telepathic friend.

"Sergeant Tatyanin had the medicine." He taps his lower right shoulder, when I check the same spot on my shoulder, I find three teensy puncture wounds from a needle. "Tylenol too, in her pack."

"That's convenient." I rub the marks.

"I thought so, too. Seems blood poisoning is common in the Bloody Brigade. Soldiers get shot, and if the bullet doesn't kill them first, the poisoning does, so they started stocking everyone up with treatments."

"Huh." I throw a cursory glance down my shoulder to see clean bandages taped over the burn. The burn itself no longer hurts. "You know a lot about the Bloody Brigade?"

"I've been talking with the Sergeant."

"Talking?" I raise an eyebrow at him. He turns his hand lazily in a circle in a noncommittal 'so-so' gesture.

"Talking, skimming her thoughts, same difference."

I cough to cover a snort. He smirks, but that fades rapidly.

"Listen, there's something I need to tell you about, after we rescue Elle. There's a lot going on that you should know before anything else happens," he says, his expression dead serious.

"You got all that from talking to the Sergeant?" I ask skeptically.

"The Whitecoats think, too. There's a lot going on."

I narrowly avoid rolling my eyes. *A lot* is always going on.

"I'm serious." His voice drops to a whisper. "Heavy shit has been happening and we're right in the middle of it."

Someone near the fire shifts in their sleep, halting Maverick's tirade. He purses his lips and sighs through his nose. He seems to juggle something in his mind briefly before settling lower on the tree. He stills with just his shoulders and his head supported by the trunk.

"I'll tell you all about it tomorrow, we should both get some sleep now, before the sun rises." He yawns, crosses his arms over his chest, and closes his eyes. I would argue, but the very mention of sleep has me yawning too. I lay back down on the grassy chunk of earth and turn over on my side. My eyelids slide closed of their own accord. So much for being wide, wide awake.

10 | Rescue Mission

The following morning, I wake up to dew on the side of my face and grey light peeking over the tops of the trees. Drilling joint pain greets me, but no nausea comes with it. With the infection taken care of and the worst of the withdrawal over, I'm left with the shakes and the kind of pain that makes me feel more like a used pin cushion than a person. At least I'm not hallucinating anymore. I lay flat for a moment, trying to gauge where everyone is while I breathe through a shoulder cramp. How do I have muscle cramps? I haven't done anything yet.

Maverick snores, slumped against the same tree he was on last night. Over by the fire everybody else is sprawled out asleep, except King, who crouches next to the flames with a charred stick. When I slowly sit up, he glances over. The scars on his forehead are nearly invisible in the dim light. They don't look like typical surgery scars from the Compound.

"Thanks," is the first word out of my mouth. "Mav said you carried me on a rock."

King grunts and turns back to the fire.

"You are heavy for someone so small," he comments, dropping the stick into the fire. His accent is familiar, but I couldn't name it with certainty. Most newer Experiments at the Compound were African or East Asian, accents like King's were common.

"Sorry."

Piper rolls in his sleep, his arm falls dangerously close to the fire. I stare at his hand for a moment, trying to gauge the distance between the embers and his palm. I'm kind of curious if he'd even notice if he caught fire. Is he flammable?

While I'm considering this, Anushka stands up out of the blue and walks away. Her fatigues are muddied, and her hair is loose and tangled. I open my mouth to call to her, but King beats me to it.

"Don't bother, she is only wandering," he says, "she doesn't go far, and her radio is broken. We checked."

It's not exactly comforting but if they trust her that far I guess I have to, too. I watch her disappear under the crags of a nearby cliff before turning back to King.

"What are those from?" I ask, motioning to my own forehead. "If you don't mind me asking."

Not everyone likes to talk about their marks, but King smiles for the first time since I met him. He runs a thumb over his forehead, brushing the raised scars. "These are the scars I was given to mark my passage from boyhood to adulthood."

"They look like they hurt," Piper mutters sleepily. I hadn't realized he was awake.

King nods. "Yes, the ones who cry when they receive their marks bring disgrace on their family. I was a weak warrior, but I did not make a sound when I was given my marks, and now they keep my home close to me."

"That's real nice, King." Piper yawns and rolls closer to the fire. "Didn't you get sold to the Whitecoats though?"

"Didn't you?" King snaps back.

"Yeah," Piper mumbles. He scoops a flame from the fire and swirls it between his nimble fingers. He seems reluctant to get up, like if he stays half-asleep beside the fire he can pretend that he's not stranded in the middle of nowhere. "Delilah got sold, right? Not Sky though, he still likes his parents."

"And you?" King turns the conversation to me, obviously trying to get Piper to shut up. Piper lifts his head to see who

King's talking to. His eyebrows rise when he sees me, awake for the first time in days.

"Hey," he says. I wave in response. "Your parents like you and the kid?"

"Nah." A pang hits me at the mention of Elle. She's close, just over that ledge. I could scream, being this close and not knowing if she's okay. But I also can't take on whatever is behind that ledge on my own. I can't even hold my hands steady. It's pathetic.

"Figures. Mav's parents like him?"

"Ask him yourself," I deflect.

Piper rolls his eyes and lets his head flop on his arm. Maverick might as well be a brick wall when it comes to his past life, and obviously Piper has experience with this. Anyone who didn't know him when he first came to the Compound doesn't know anything about his life before, not even where his home was.

The sun rises higher, and the others begin to wake. Everyone seems mildly surprised to see me moving about. I get up to pace, to stretch out the muscles in my legs that insist on bunching up even while motionless.

"Good morning."

I jump, heart leaping to my throat. I turn too fast for my joints and my breath jams in my throat at the shooting pain. Sky throws his hands up in mock surrender, eyebrows shooting towards his hairline.

"You good?" He puts his arm out as if to steady me. I brush him off, pretending that I didn't almost take a knee because I flinched too hard. "We're getting your sister today. I was just scouting the camp." He shoves his goggles up his face, leaving sweaty red rings around his eyes. Hearing those words charges adrenaline into my veins. Elle will be safe soon.

"How is—" I'm interrupted by my own stomach growling.

"Can't eat while you're unconscious, huh?" Sky grins. He pats his pockets for something. A cramp I mistook for early morning fibro pains twists my gut, demanding food. Ironically, the cramp makes me too nauseous to stomach eating. And even if the thought of food didn't make me want to puke, there's nothing to eat.

"What have you guys been eating?" I ask. There must be some food since nobody looks starved. At the flick of Sky's wrist, a food bar appears in his hand. He throws it at me, forcing me to catch it.

"Food bars, small animals, and Piper has decided to become a flambé chef when we get back to civilization."

"A what?" Piper shouts, he still sounds half asleep. Sky laughs in response. He pulls his goggles off and aims them like a rubber band at Piper but stops when he spots Maverick across the campsite.

"Gotta go," he says, and darts off to talk to Mav. That leaves me, alone, with a food bar and a queasy stomach. I grimace at the silver packaging. I should save it for Elle. There's no telling whether she's had enough food these past few days. Or if she's been given water or kept warm. Three days is too long. They should have left me like we left Dieter.

I close my eyes as my thoughts start to spiral and take a couple deep breaths. I need a clear head this morning. I can't afford to slip out of my skin. That version of me is sharp, it's battle-ready, and maybe that's what I need to get past the soldiers that stand on the other side of that ridge. But I'm afraid of what I might do to Elle if I meet her like that.

"Eating will help." I open my eyes to see Delilah crouched over the smoking remnants of the doused fire. She flips her wrist to kick the wind up and rustle the crumbly remains of last autumn's leaves. Her hair is knotted at the nape of her neck, and she looks more haggard than the others, like she hasn't been getting the same amount of food or sleep. Her light eyes are dull, weighted down with dark, puffy circles. "If your head's fuzzy, eating will help clear it."

She doesn't move with the same energy as the others either, although keeping up with Sky's level of energy seems pretty much impossible. Even so, her entire being is taut with determination.

"You look tired," I say, which, admittedly, is not a sentence I thought through. I push my glasses back up my nose. The food bar wrapper crinkles in my hand.

"Haven't been sleeping well, it's just… ah." She drags the back of her hand across her face.

"I'm sorry," I apologize.

"Are you sorry because he died, or are you sorry because it was your sister he was trying to save?" Her tone takes me by surprise. When I don't answer, she shakes her head.

"It's not you I'm angry at," she says, standing. She flicks her wrist, sending a low gust towards the ridge. "It's them—him."

Not long after, Maverick calls a group meeting. We gather in a circle. Maverick waits until everyone has settled down to speak. He's squinting a little, probably skimming everyone's mind to check up on them.

"Okay, today we're rescuing Elle," he starts. I can practically feel the ripple of tension that goes through the group. "Anushka and I will go with Trick into the camp. Everyone else, you know where to go. If there's trouble, take 'em down. We're stronger than they are."

He ends the gathering with instructions to come back in five minutes so we can move out. I volunteer to fetch Anushka, since she still hasn't emerged from under her overhang.

I pick my way over small boulders towards the looming ridge. Moss makes the stone slippery. I reach the limestone wall and scan the dry area under the overhang. The rock is grey and riddled with imperfections. Lichen clings to the crags, lacing the stone with ribbons of bright color. Anushka isn't there.

Blazing stars. I pivot sharp on my toes to run back to the camp. Anushka could ruin this mission with a single word, and that can't happen. As I turn, I spot a shadowy cave mouth at the intersection of the end of the overhang and where the ridge juts out. The cave is almost invisible. Considering her penchant for tight spaces, I decide to check it. In spite of the way claustrophobia pinches my throat tight.

The cave looks undisturbed. There's no sign of Anushka anywhere. I creep inside. The ceiling is low, so I have to duck and try not to think about the tons of rock above my head. A few paces in, I stumble onto Anushka, curled in a ball, her back to the outside wall. She doesn't move when I squeeze around and crouch in front of her. Her gaze holds that spaced-out look that makes me think she's not even aware I'm here. Tiny silver balls litter the stony cave floor at her feet, among them lies the dog tags, threaded with what remains of the bead chain. It's far too short to be fastened around her neck now.

"Sergeant?" I say. She sucks in a sharp breath, her gaze stays focused eerily on an unseen object.

"My name is Anushka Tatyanin," she says with urgency that is borderline violent.

"Anushka," I correct myself. "We need to go."

"I'm a Sergeant in the thirty-sixth regiment of the *Krovavaya Brigáda*," she continues in that same urgent tone.

"Yeah, I know." I ease forward to check her pupils. I'm wary of getting closer, but I also have the niggling suspicion that she's whacked out on drugs. Somehow.

"I have a daughter."

"And you love her, I know, you already told me." Her pulse hammers in the hollow of her neck. It's elevated, and her breathing is sharp and shallow. She's afraid.

I go to stand, but her hands shoot out and latch on to my arms. Her nails dig in, her grip white-knuckle-tight.

"Ow!" I pull away, but she yanks me closer, so close that our noses are almost touching.

She stares hard into my eyes. "My. Name. Is. Anushka Tatyanin," she says slowly.

"You're a Sergeant, and you love your daughter," I finish, lifting her up. Her harsh grip squeezes even tighter, breaking the skin of my arm. I don't think she's blinked once in the past minute. Forget afraid, she's lost her marbles.

"My name," she begins again after she's completely satisfied that I won't interrupt her. "Is Anushka Tatyanin."

And then she waits, staring at me like she expects me to do something. Crazy, she's crazy. Totally, utterly, insane. Why am I in here with her?

She keeps right on staring at me, until it dawns on me that maybe I'm supposed to repeat after her. If it gets her to stop clinging to my arm, I'll bite.

"Your name is Anushka."

"Ye—no." She scowls.

I try again. "My name is Hendrix."

The scowl washes away, and her nails stop digging into my skin. "Remember that," she says. And, just like that, Crazy Anushka is gone. She stands, dusts her fatigues off, and strolls out the cave as if nothing is wrong. I wait for a beat, absorbing what happened. Then move to follow her. On second thought, I bend and snatch up the dog tags. She might want them later.

I tuck the tags in my pocket and head out the entrance. I can only hope Anushka can hold it together long enough to get us to Elle. This whole rescue mission rests on the shoulders of a nutjob.

11 | Wind Witch

Anushka has her hair tied back in a close approximation to a bun. Her army coat is tight around my shoulders, hiding the burn and doing a flimsy job of disguising me as one of them. The grey sweatpants are a dead giveaway in my opinion, but it's not like I have anything else. We look suitably haggard and distraught, enough to get us past the front gate and into the Infirm Tent, where Anushka swears Elle will be.

Yeah, that's our plan, waltz right in. What could go wrong?

Everyone else has crept off to their positions and Maverick perches on the tip of a boulder, eyes squinted, waiting for the right moment.

We're so close. If it were up to me, I'd be bursting over that ridge and tearing the assholes down there apart getting to Elle.

"If it were up to you, you'd be dead," Mav says, his voice vague like he's far away in his head.

"Good thing you're here, then," I say, only slightly sarcastic.

"Good thing," he repeats in that same distant tone. I bite the inside of my cheek and try to focus my nervous energy on the plan.

In through the gate.

Straight to the Infirm Tent.

If anyone starts trouble, Maverick will redirect them. We get Elle, we get out. And then… then we… something.

"Then we're free," Mav says.

Free. I don't know if I can hold that concept in my head. But I glance at Mav, and he's staring back at me with the clarity back in his eyes, and I think; if there's one person I'd trust to get us through to the other side, it's him. A small smile crosses his face.

Hopping off the boulder, he dusts my shoulder. "Everyone's ready, it's time."

Men and women in olive drab quick march between rows upon rows of tan tents. The ridge slopes downwards, and the camp is set in the flat middle of the bowl, taking up every square inch available. The tents are set up in rows encircling one that has been blocked off by loops of razor wire.

We near the outskirts of the camp. An army soldier who appears to be standing guard stares at us. Her hawkish eyes roam lazily over Anushka, then stall on me, then snap to Mav, who reaches out a hand to shake. She narrows her eyes at him, and he touches her shoulder briefly instead and says something in Russian that makes her glaze over. She lets us pass with a half-hearted salute.

The camp is busy with noise. The air buzzes with voices and steady footfalls, and clinking and scraping, and the crackling of multiple fires scattered haphazardly outside of this tent and that one. Grizzled, dirty faces mark every corner. Any person not marching or standing guard is slouched over, hands in their pockets or elbows on knees, and they all have the exact same world-weary expression carved into the dirt-caked lines of their mouths and eyes. Nobody looks up long enough to register us.

We're almost to the tent Anushka pointed out. Almost, but someone stops us. A gruff, mustached, grey-haired man steps into our path. He stands with rigid posture, glaring at us as if we are worms. My skin crawls as he peers at me from pale, steely eyes, and barks something in Russian.

Anushka replies in clipped, stiff words. The man narrows his eyes. Then, a glimmer. A hint of Maverick as he passes in front of the soldier and murmurs a command in his ear. Confusion crosses the soldier's face, replaced at once by passiveness. He nods and steps to the side, speaking something.

"*Da, Leytenánt.*" Anushka lowers her chin to hide the flicker of panic on her face. She nudges me past him and we're on our way, trudging down the path of clumpy, over-turned clay. We take a sharp corner to detour away from a particularly large cluster of scruffy soldiers, and I glimpse of movement behind us, that must be Maverick.

We cut the line, eliciting loud protests and vicious gestures that I'm sure don't mean anything nice from the injured soldiers waiting for their turn. Anushka pays them no mind, as she snaps her fingers to grab the attention of the guard in charge of letting people in.

He's a heavyset man with a jiggly face and a sour expression. He lumbers over and frowns like we are personally responsible for the line of soldiers he has to preside over. Anushka trades sharp words in Russian with the guard. Their exchange ends with Anushka spinning me roughly and yanking down the collar of the coat to show the guard the burn. They swap a few more words. I can't tell what they're saying, but by the end of it, the sour-faced guard relents at last and nods us past. Anushka jerks me around and we duck through the plastic tent flap, into the hospital.

We're in. Time for step two.

I'm keeping watch. Mav says inside my head. One look at the horrific scene before us and I'm glad he chose to stay out there. The tent hospital is not big, but there are at least a hundred people in here. Soldiers lie on narrow cots or sit on the stained tarp floor. There is a split down the center of the tent that nurses in dirty scrubs traverse, going from person to person, offering what help they can. A tired, sallow nurse approaches us. She flashes a penlight in either of my eyes, pinches my wrist with two fingers and a thumb, then mutters something in Russian and moves on to the next patient.

I can't help but stare as we maneuver our way down the middle. The people here are bloodied and bruised. They hold wet strips of clothes to their cuts and burns and gashes. A man moans into the gauze he cradles to the left side of his face. When a nurse makes him peel it away to let her see the injury, I can only make out bits of messy gore. Further in, I spot grizzled soldiers gagging and pinching their noses shut. It must stink something awful in here. For once, I'm grateful to the Compound. Years of breathing the cloying scent of formaldehyde and bleach have whittled my sense of smell away to nothing.

There are more blood-chilling sights here than I care to take in. Bullet wounds, shrapnel wounds, festered wounds. Missing flesh, missing limbs, if you look close enough, missing minds. Some souls have fled, but their bodies haven't been moved away yet.

We find Elle resting on the last cot of the row on the left side. She lies on her back, her fragile chest rises and falls shallowly under a paper-thin blanket. Her eyes are closed, and her eyelids are painted three shades darker than the rest of her skin. She's not asleep. When she sleeps her skin shifts lazily, and now it is perfectly still and normal. I wonder why she'd faking sleep, until I see who resides by her bed.

The man who kidnapped her sits firmly on an overturned bucket. He doesn't notice me, but you can bet I notice him. He has a thick black beard and coarse, thinning hair. His face is pockmarked and etched with deep grooves and crows-feet. A bandage peeks out from under the collar of his tight black shirt. My blood boils at the sight of him so near my sister. Who knows what he's been doing to her since he stole her.

It happens so seamlessly that I almost don't catch it. I notice my own mind shedding itself of humanity a second before it's gone completely, and I let it happen. The closer we come to Elle and the man, the more red floods my vision.

Mav, get Elle out of here, I think. I've got one thing to do before we get out of here.

My fist breaks the man's jaw before he realizes I'm there, the blow topples him from his perch, and he lets out a roar that goes unnoticed in the pandemonium of the tent hospital. Elle gasps behind me, and I sidestep to block her from the man's view. He jumps to his feet, but I'm more than ready for him. I pummel his gut hard and let him collapse backwards. He throws his head back, broken jaw and all, and for the first time gets a good look at my face.

Recognition flickers in his beady black eyes, he looks to the cot where Elle is supposed to be. She's not there. Anushka is carrying her away as fast as she can without raising suspicion. The nurses are all too occupied to pay her mind, there's too much else going on. He reaches behind himself, to where there appears to be another door, and I move to grab him, expecting him to try escaping out the back entrance.

Instead, he whips out a hefty, black handgun, points it at me, and fires.

Gunshots are deafening. I've never been so close to one before and it sets off a ringing in my ears that I can't hear anything over. It only takes a single shot to throw the already tumultuous tent hospital into utter chaos. I lunge forward and crack my elbow into the man's skull, striking him and his gun down. His shot missed its mark, and for that I am thankful.

I spin on my toes, my eyes skim what is ahead of me. A majority of the soldiers are scrambling for their own weapons, their instincts driving them to put an end to the threat before it puts an end to them. Others are screaming at the top of their lungs, clutching their ears. In the midst of this, is Anushka.

The man's bullet found its mark after all.

I'm just in time to see her collapse, Elle still in her arms. She falls forward, dead before she hits the ground. The back of her head has a hole the size of a dime in it. Blood pools onto the tarp, thick and dark and red. Her mouth and eyes are wide, wide open, but there's nothing in them anymore. Elle wriggles free of the corpse, fear marking her every motion. Soldiers and nurses are beginning to close in.

I dart forward and snatch her from the floor. She shrieks and struggles until she sees that it's me. Bodies are everywhere. Another shot goes off, accompanied by a shocked shout. Nurses rush to move the soldiers who can't move themselves out of danger. The aisles are overcrowded, so I duck to the side and hurdle over the cots. Every landing is hell on my knees, but we get to the exit that much faster. There are so many people pushing and shoving to get past the guard, that it's all too easy to slip past him and spill out into the camp.

A blaring klaxon assaults the air, Elle clamps her hands over her ears to block out the shrill screech. Soldiers come from all directions to control the panicked crowd before it can transform into a mob. My fingertips go numb. All I can do is hold Elle closer and plow through the tight-packed crowd.

Out of the blue, an elbow nails me as I go by. I stumble, which is the wrong thing to do in a crowd like this. Feet hook on my unsteadied ankles, hands shove me away from the bodies I crash against, and in a matter of seconds I'm down. Sharp rocks dig into my knees, striking in exactly the wrong spot, and my right leg all the way up my calf jolts with the kind of agony that makes me want to saw it off.

Elle jumps free of my grip. Her bony fingers wrap around my arm and she tugs insistently, trying to drag me to my feet. I force myself up. As soon as the rock is no longer jabbing the nerve, a buzz floods my leg. I take Elle's hand and limp for the edge of the camp. I can't bear to put weight on my right leg, and the hot, cramped crowd is pressing in from every side, giving my mind ample reason to race like a maniac. A hand grabs me. I twist and snap the arm it's attached to. Every body that gets in front of us, I bat away, clearing a path.

We reach the edge of the crowd and burst out, me limping, and Elle barely staying upright on her stick legs.

"Trick!" she cries.

"*No te preocupes*," I tell her.

Where the hell is Maverick? Where is anybody, for that matter? We had a plan, damn it.

As if on cue, Sky appears, mud sprayed all the way up his legs.

"Take her." I nudge Elle towards him. "Get her somewhere safe."

Elle's head swivels between me and Sky, her grip on my hand stays as tight as she can manage.

Sensing her hesitation, Sky takes her by the arm.

"It's alright, love, I won't hurt you," he says. She casts one last glance at me, then gives a single nod. He scoops her up and rests her on his hip, then holds a hand out to help me. I brush it off.

"I'll be right behind you, just go!"

Someone else bursts from the crowd and strikes me square between the shoulders before darting off. I grit my teeth, cutting off the shout building in the back of my throat. Sky is still standing there, uncertain whether he should leave me here. "Go!"

Finally, he takes off. Over the commotion of the crowd, a sound like the mountains cracking open rings out, followed by an eruption of flames along the north edge of the camp. Every soul in the camp freezes in wide-eyed awe at the explosion. In the brief calm, Maverick appears at my side, smeared in blood.

Come on, Trick, hustle!

Maverick's voice comes across loud and clear in my head. For once, I'm glad for his telepathy. My ears hold the remnants of the gunshot echoing inside them, making it difficult to hear much else. I brace myself for the running to come, and in doing so catch sight of the man who's nose I broke leading a posse of soldiers towards us.

One lifts her weapon. I grab Mav, yanking him out of the line of fire in the nick of time. He crashes into me and I keep moving, sliding back into the crowd, one arm around him to keep him upright. My thoughts whir and click machine-like into place.

What are they? Distance fighters.

As long as we stay in the crowd they can't fire at us, but the crowd is thinning fast.

"I've got left if you take right," Mav says.

We split, moving quickly. I lose sight of Mav in an instant. All my attention pins on the man and his soldiers. As I push through the remnants of the crowd, I cut the leftmost three soldiers out of the equation. Mav will take care of them. That leaves two soldiers and the man with the broken nose for me.

I snag a fleeing man on his way past and throw him at the man. Their bodies collide and sprawl. And now I'm out of the crowd, out of cover. Shock at the human projectile buys me a second. Just long enough to smack the gun out of the nearest woman's outstretched hand. Her partner jumps to action, raising his rifle. It's the same kind the Redcoats use. Black, sleek, automatic. A hungry thing I've seen spit a dozen bullet holes into an Experiment in seconds.

His fingers tighten on the trigger. I already know I won't have time to put the woman between me and the gun. I'll have to settle for diving and hoping he only puts holes in nonessential body parts.

At the last moment, a razor slice of wind plows over the soldiers. They stagger. I grab the woman and fling her at her partner with a resounding crunch of breaking bones, thanking Delilah, wherever she is. The impact knocks my two soldiers into Mav's last standing one.

"Let's go."

I've barely read the words off his lips when a force like a train slams into me from the right. I hit the ground hard and roll, avoiding a harsh kick by the skin of my teeth. A maddened cry cuts through the noise. I glimpse the sky above, where a giant swirling cloud has appeared from nowhere. It was sunny before we entered the camp.

There's no time to ponder the strange weather before a hefty weight comes down on my chest, pinning me in place. Meaty fingers grab a fistful of my hair, and the face of the man who kidnapped Elle sneers down at me a moment before his free fist knocks me across the face.

Stars explode behind my eyes and rust floods my mouth. I barely blink away my dazedness when he strikes again. My nose crunches under his knuckles and blood sprays out. I choke on the blood that streaks down my throat. He draws back his arm to pummel me again, but this time I'm prepared. I get my left foot planted firmly in the clay and heave up with my hip to throw him from me. He lands on his back with a wet thud and I scramble to my feet, wiping the blood from my face as I do. The man should be up and on me in a matter of seconds, but he isn't.

He's stuck on the ground, straining as if something is holding him down, but nothing is there. I didn't throw him hard enough to even knock his breath out, so I don't know what's going on, but I'm grateful for it. I back away, keeping my eyes trained on him, in case he's faking his struggle.

As I turn to make a run for it, Delilah storms past me, arms extended, palms out. Her lip curls into a snarl and her eyes glint like bits of broken glass. She reaches the man and clenches her hands. The edge of a gale-force wind nicks me as it rushes to heft the man into the air. He flails helplessly as Delilah raises him higher and higher.

"*You*," she spits, the wind tosses the man like a ragdoll. He's twenty feet up and she flicks her fingers open, the wind scatters, dropping the man to the ground.

He hits the ground with a loud smack and the whoosh of his breath leaving his lungs. Delilah throws both arms up, lacing her fingers together. The amalgamation of clouds above the camp reacts as if she's controlling it. She thrusts her arms down, aiming her palms at the man. The amalgamation whirls on a dime and comes thundering down, twisting, writhing, into something akin to a tornado. It roars towards the man with the broken nose.

The man's eyes widen, his mouth parts to release a scream, and then the tornado hammers into him.

I throw my hands up to shield myself from the blast, the gusts bat me through the air. A tent buckles and tears under me, it makes for a terrible landing pad. The plastic folds over me. A suffocating embrace. My legs are over my head, propped on something hard, shoulders screaming. Blinking away stars, I flounder out of the puddle of tent. Maverick finds me and hauls me free. My left arm hangs limp, out of its socket, but that's all. I'm intact. I think.

"Delilah is right behind us, let's get out of here," he says around gasps for breath. Fighting off the stun from being flung through the air, all I can manage is a nod. Wind howls behind us. I heave enough air in to clear the static threatening all five of my senses and break into a run without a second look back.

12 | MAVERICK

My feet pound the grassy ground, my arms pumping. Blood cakes around my nose, but no longer pours out my nostrils. My right leg protests with every step, but I don't dare stop because if I do, I might not start again.

The gate we came through is lost in a haze of dust and black smoke. We forego it and throw ourselves up the side of the ridge. I can hear Delilah causing an uproar in the camp. Sweat dampens my forehead and stings in the burn.

Almost there, come on!

Maverick is at my side, urging me on, his grip on my arm making sure I don't slip all the way back down to the bottom. Almost there. I repeat to myself, wiping the sweat from my forehead before it can drip into my eyes.

I see it before I hear it.

The glint of polished metal in the sun. The barrel of a gun pokes out from behind a tree up on the ledge. Then, a gunshot. And another, and another, and another, and another, all in rapid succession, until the rifle clicks empty. The distant sound of Maverick shouting pierces the cacophony.

Go home.

His words hit my ears, dull, like walls of glass separate me from him. Ethereal, too. But if the command is for me, I can't follow it. I brace for the impact, for agony, for death, because there's no way in hell every one of those shots missed.

The hit never comes.

The bushes rustle and stones go skittering down the incline as the sniper makes his escape. I look down, expecting to be riddled with bloody holes, but there's nothing there.

There should be blood by now.

And there is, flowing down the trampled bracken from uphill. I drag my gaze up, heartbeatless, to where Maverick stands stretched out and crooked. Eight bright flowers bloom on the front of his shirt, a ragged hole spills red from his neck.

Horror floods in, cold enough to burn. He didn't, that *idiot*. That stupid, psychic idiot.

"What did you do?" I choke out.

Red leaks out the corner of his trembling lips.

Sorry... Take care of them.

His words are whispery as his powers fade. As he fades. He sways, falls, I jolt forward to catch him. His dead weight crashes against my arms, toppling us both. It's sheer luck that keeps us from crashing down the steep hill.

"Don't you *dare*, don't you blazing dare die," I demand, it comes out more like a plea. I cradle him to the ground and press my hand to the wound on his neck to stop the flow of blood. Air rattles in his lungs, the bullet holes in his chest pour lifeblood freely onto the earth. No, please, please no.

His fingers find my elbow for the briefest of seconds, then he exhales, and his chest doesn't rise again.

"Come on, man," I say, tapping his cheek. "Get up, come on." But there's no answer. And there's no answer. And there's no answer. His hand falls away from my arm and when the pressure is gone, the realization finally hits home.

Maverick is dead.

I clutch him close. My teeth grind against a blinding, bone-shattering spasm. A scream dislodges and forces itself out. Screeching agony works through me. I swallow it. Drag in breath after breath. Lift Maverick. Red, red blood stains his shirt, his chin, my hands.

Up, over the edge of the ridge.

I have to get him out of here.

I have to.

I have to.

My legs buckle at the top of the ridge, the precarious hold I have on him with my one good arm slipping. Looking down, all I can see are the neon bright splashes of red marking the path from there to here. Even now, with my ears ringing too loud to think, there's a part of my brain telling me this won't work.

Think of Elle, the blood will lead them right to her. And the body, how am I supposed to show her that the only other person who cared for her died like this, torn to shreds and choking on his own blood?

I cradle him closer, he's already growing colder. I want to scream again. *We were supposed to be free.* Instead, I look to the sky, but even that offers no relief The blue blotted out by billows of oily smoke rising out of the camp.

There's a war raging below. Cracks of guns. Claps of thunder.

There's silence here. No breath, no movement, no future.

I don't remember the decision to move. The only thing inside me is instinct and a vague notion of where I'm going. I do my best to point myself in the right direction and stagger forward. Sharp pains shoot down my right leg from my knee with the slightest pressure. I slow down to ease the stabbing, but not too much.

Stab. Stab. Stab. Stab.

Like a knife that won't come free.

Stab. Stab. Stab. Stab.

The pain works its way up my pelvis, my spine, down my arms, sped on by exhaustion. I'm about to stop completely, to give my battered body a rest, when I spot a flash of ginger hair that could only belong to one person. Too numb to feel relief, I limp towards the bobbing head. The branch of a huge pine tree scrapes my raw skin as I push out of the way and enter a small clearing. Sky faces away from me.

"Bloody hell!" He jumps when I come up behind him, bolting to the other side of the clearing. He whips around to glare at me. "Don't do that!"

Elle is snuggled in his arms, her face shielded by his hand. His glare softens when he sees I'm alone. Elle squirms free of his grasp and flings herself across the clearing into my arm. Alive, safe, warm. I fold myself around her and lift her onto my hip. She throws her arms around my neck. I wish I could hug her back, but my other arm still persists on not being in its socket.

"*Tengo miedo*," she whispers in my ear.

"*Está bien.*" I whisper back, burying my face in her tangled curls. "You're okay now."

She's alive, she's safe, she's warm. Around us the forest is still and silent, a pocket of calm after all the chaos. If I could hide inside this moment forever, I would.

"You're bleeding."

Mud from the fight cakes to my legs, mixed with red. Blood is splattered across my shirt and a quick swipe of my face comes away smeared with drying blood.

"No, I'm not bleeding, it's—" I catch myself, the rest of what I was about to say slithers out as a sigh. "It's not mine."

Not my blood. I wipe my palms on my shirt, but that doesn't accomplish much except smear red on my sweater.

"Where are the others? Where is Maverick?" Sky asks tentatively, almost as if he's afraid of my answer. I bite my tongue and shake my head, dropping my eyes to the forest floor. How do you put something like that into words?

He reaches for me, and I must flinch because Elle's grip tightens, and he stops, hands up.

"Want me to look at that arm, mate?"

Right, my arm. "Okay."

"Jacket off," he instructs. I set Elle down and peel the too-tight soldier's jacket off. It's sticky, reluctant to come free. One of the seams tears and finally it drops to the ground. Sky takes my limp wrist and lifts my arm, studying it. He circles me. Pushes my shoulder experimentally.

"I think I saw, I mean, I think Piper must've come down when he heard the commotion. I saw him when I went past, he was… they—they shot him," he says.

Another person dead.

His touch lingers on my shoulder, like the reality of it all is sinking in.

"Who's Piper?" Elle asks.

Sky makes a strangled noise. "Sorry," he says, "sorry for this, too." And he clunks my shoulder back in. The pain is brief and dull, a drop in the bucket. I flex my fingers while pins and needles scatter down them.

"Thanks."

"You right?"

"Hm?" I try to focus on him, on his question. I feel far away.

He shakes his head, "never mind."

We sit on the ground, Elle curling up in my lap. Her curly hair is a mass of tangles, so I set to work finger combing it. She's alive. I have to keep reminding myself, keep checking her pulse and her breathing, she's alive.

The moment of peace shatters when a twig snaps out in the forest. Both Skyelar and I are on our feet in a flash. Elle is bundled in my arms. She squeaks as I squeeze her too tight too fast, but that's the least of my worries. If there are soldiers nearby, I'm in no shape to fight them, and there's no telling where Sky's loyalty lies now that his friends are dead.

The same pine tree I brushed past rustles, a low-hanging bough bends, and Delilah staggers into our midst. Her hands are up, fingers curled into claws. When she realizes it's just us, she sighs and doubles over to rest her hands on her knees. She's panting like she ran a marathon, fresh blood mats her hair and blinds her left eye. There's too much to tell where the injury is. She doesn't question us, which means she must have seen the bodies on her way out.

"I killed him. The *ublyudk* that killed my husband," she says, and nothing else.

Elle wiggles out of my grip and walks over to Delilah. For the first time, I notice that she is barefoot. Of all things, she's missing shoes, the one article of clothing that I can't give her.

"*Sígueme.*" She guides Delilah by the arm towards the sound of a burbling stream. I follow and dip my arms in the frigid water while Delilah crouches to rinse the blood from her hair and face and clean the wound it came from: a shallow slice on her crown.

When all the pink-tinted water has washed downstream, Delilah speaks again. "We can't stay here forever."

"Well, what are we bloody supposed to do? Wander?" Sky pops in from behind. His hand jerks agitatedly. The snap of his fingers hitting his palm echoes in the clearing. My heart speeds up to keep time with the sound.

"We could stay for the night" I suggest. It might be a selfish suggestion, motivated by the way everything is too fuzzy for me to recognize and how every part of me aches. Then again, if we stay, the soldiers could find us.

Delilah nods in agreement. "It's almost dark, and if King made it, he knows he's supposed to come here," she says. Right, Bakari, there's a chance that one more member of our group made it out alive. Delilah did, but she wasn't a half-step away from a heart attack.

Sky considers this for a moment, staring back the way we came from as if waiting for soldiers to come peeling out of the trees. He worries his lip and snaps his fingers but doesn't say anything.

"Unless they can control fire, there won't be enough soldiers for them to spare to come after us," Delilah adds. "The camp was in blazes by the time I got out."

Finally, that's enough for us all.

"Okay," Sky agrees.

We set up a camp in the clearing. I pull an armful of bushy pine branches from a tree as quietly as I can manage. They'll make half-decent bedding Better than the dirt, at least. It's getting warmer as spring grows on us, but the night will bring a chill, I layer them on the ground; two to lay on, and one exceptionally large one to crawl under.

"Okay, *chica, vamos*," I say, lifting the top branch. Elle loops her hand around Delilah's and pulls her along too. Her skin shifts in the pattern of the leaves under her feet, gold sparks in the corners of her eyes.

"What about those people?" she asks.

"I'll stay awake this time," I assure her.

"And fight them?"

"Yes, and fight them."

Satisfied, she crawls under the bough and motions for Delilah to follow her. Delilah does after only a moments' hesitation. Out of all of us, she seems the most convinced that the soldiers won't catch up tonight. Still, she pokes her head out and says, "I want second watch,"

The sun dips below the horizon, casting an orange glow on the trunks of the trees, and inky shadows dance along every surface. The breeze returns to tickle the tops of the trees, and the stream burbles soothingly. When the sun is set and a crescent moon has risen, Sky inches under the pine bough, and I prop myself against the nearest tree to keep lookout.

14 | Fever Fairy Wings

My head is fuzzy when I wake up, five days isn't long enough for the withdrawal symptoms to be completely gone. At least I'm not puking. There are prickles all down my side from the pine needles, and if I'm blunt, that's as painless as it gets right now.

The sun rises to a fog-filled morning, casting a dim sheen of light for me to see Elle is not next to me anymore. But before I can panic too badly, she reappears. If I had paid attention, I might have noticed the slight indent on the boughs where she lies. I deflate with a slow breath of relief and smile at her. She smiles back. The skin of her arm still blends with the flattened pine needles.

"Hendrix?"

"Yeah?"

"Who were those people?"

Good question, Elle. If only I had a cut-and-dry answer.

"Bad guys," I decide, Anushka's profile wavers in my mind. "Mostly. They were soldiers."

"Oh." She tilts her head. "They liked my horns."

"Did they?" I prop myself up on one elbow, careful not to jostle the top branch too much. Elle nods.

"They touched my horns a lot. One of the nurses even cut holes in the shirt they gave me, so it fit better, see?" She rolls onto her stomach to show me. Sure enough, two ragged slits have been cut into the thick green fabric of her shirt. A dark brown horn pokes out of either opening, the blunt tips curve up. I tweak the tip of one of the horns, and she rolls back over, then rolls again so her nose skims the front of my shirt. I feel the heat coming off her from here. She must be running a fever.

"Tell me a story," she says, tilting her head to look up at me. In the dim light she almost looks like she could be healthy. Except for the fever heat rolling off her in waves.

"Okay, let's go out there so we don't wake Delilah." I lift the top boughs, and she squirms out to sit beside the pile. It takes me a little longer to escape the pine bed, one of my sneakers tangled in the branches during the night. Eventually I escape and find Elle wandering around the small clearing. She stops when she sees me and lifts her arms.

"It feels nice," she says, either fog or sweat glistening on her bare arms. The morning is cool, borderline cold, but she doesn't seem to mind.

Skyelar is pacing the perimeter, arms crossed. His eyes are rimmed in red and glassy. He pulls his goggles down and keeps pacing. I leave him be.

Elle gags suddenly. Her hands fly to her mouth, and she stumbles to the side where a tree is the only thing to keep her from collapsing.

I squeeze my eyes shut for a second before hurrying over to her, biting back against the twisting of my own stomach. I've been off the Savella for a week now, the withdrawal pains have peaked, but they aren't gone yet.

"Sit down, put your head between your knees," I say, rubbing her back. "It helps."

She sinks to the ground, her hands still pressed flat against her mouth. I notice, not for the first time, how knobby her fingers are. Her joints look swollen and the spaces in between are nothing but skin stretched tight across the bones. I could count all the thin ligaments that run down the back of her hand and bulge when she flexes her fingers. I only hope that she doesn't throw up, she can't afford to lose whatever tiny bit of food or drink she might have in her, and I have nothing to replace it with if she does.

"*Un cuento*," she whispers, asking for a story with her head resting on the top of her knee.

"Which story?" I ask, sitting down next to her. Cold dew soaks through my clothes wherever they touch the ground. Is this better or worse for her fever?

"The one about how I got my horns," she says, lifting her head to lean it on my shoulder. Her eyelids are half-closed. Permanent purple shadowing and webbed veins make her eyes look more sunken than they are.

"Alright. Once upon a time, when you were *una poco nina*, you found a fairy circle and you knew that if you waited long enough inside the fairy circle, a fairy would come and grant you a wish."

"And I told you," she interrupts.

"You told me," I say.

"And you didn't believe me." She gives me a reproachful stare. I flick her ear playfully. "Hey!" She swats my hand away.

"Do you want me to tell the story or not?"

She makes a noise in the back of her throat and takes her head off my shoulder. There's a brief gap of chilly air before she curls into my lap, slouching to snuggle up closer. Her horns dig into my diaphragm, forcing me to shift away. "Ow, kiddo, watch those pointy horns."

"*Lo siento*. Keep telling the story," she says.

"Okay, well, you waited in the fairy circle for days and days, and eventually a fairy did come along. The fairy saw how patient you had been and decided to give you a reward. She granted you one wish. You were very careful with your wish, you saved it until you knew for sure what you wanted, and one day you were sitting in the fairy circle again, and you saw a flock of migrating birds, and you knew what you wanted—."

"To fly!" she says, smiling from ear to ear. I can't help but grin at her excitement. This is one of her favorite stories to hear, and my favorite to tell. Maverick and I came up with it to cover up the real history of her horns. A tattoo over a bulging scar.

"That's right, and the fairy granted your wish. You don't remember them, but you had very pretty wings." And she did—have pretty wings I mean. They were sleek and white and downy, like the birds that fly overhead when the seasons change from warm and cold. "But one day a bad fairy came along and saw your wings and became jealous, so he stole them. The fairy who gave you your wings found out and felt sad because you had waited so nicely for your wings and they had been stolen. She wanted to give you another pair, but she didn't have enough magic left, so instead she planted two baby horns where the wings used to be, and one day, when you're big and strong, she'll come back and turn those horns into wings again."

Elle's breathing has become slow and even. She's asleep again.

The true story about her horns is a lot less magical. In reality, some starry-eyed idiot Whitecoat tried grafting wings onto her. Where they got wings that huge, I'll never know, but I guess she was much smaller then, so maybe the wings only seemed freakishly large. At any rate, it nearly killed her, and in the end the Whitecoats cut off her wings and cauterized away the infection.

She doesn't remember any of those long weeks. She spent most of them delirious with a raging fever. A year later, about a month after they started irradiating her skin, nubs sprouted from the scars where the wings had been attached.

"Hendrix…" Elle shifts, her voice thick with sleep.

"Hm?" I watch her skin swirl in patterns of brown and green.

"I don't think I'll ever be big or strong."

I push my glasses up my face, then tuck a loose strand of hair behind her elfish ears. "Don't be silly. Of course you will."

All of a sudden she lurches, her hands fly to her mouth and her back curls. "I don't feel so good," she groans. She twists out of my grip onto her hands and knees and vomits dark brown chunks. Damn it. I hold her hair back with one hand, and steady her with the other while she heaves again, and again, and again, until there's nothing left coming up except mucus and bile.

The racket wakes Delilah. She crawls free of the pine boughs, muttering something about building a fire. The thick morning fog will cloak the smoke nicely. We share concerned looks across the clearing as I rub Elle's quaking back. She gags and retches more, and nothing comes up. Spent, she collapses against me, still dry-heaving and making weak choking noises. Her body doesn't seem to realize that it's empty. I wrap my arms around her frail, shivering form, ignoring her horns jabbing my stomach. It takes too long for her gagging to diminish. By the time Delilah has cleared a small part of the forest floor, she's still lurching. Though it could be hiccups now. Could be.

Skyelar joins us with an armful of small rocks. He drops it by Delilah. The clatter makes me flinch, though I can't place why.

"Good morning, citizens of the fog. Today's forecast is cold fog, more cold fog, and"— he rubs both his cheeks— "the start of a patchy beard. Man, the Whitecoats could have at least given me the ability to grow a good beard."

"Because that would solve so many of your problems?" Delilah says.

"Of course."

Elle squeaks, when I glance at her, green unnaturally bright spreads across her cheek like a cartoon. She's shivering and sweating all at the same time. I hug her closer, willing my warmth and the heat from the fire to chase away her chills.

"Wanna see something cool?" Sky asks, holding up a flat river stone. Elle nods, eyes glued to the stone.

"Okay, ready?" He smashes the rock between his hands, then holds up empty palms.

"It disappeared." She smiles weakly.

"It's magic," he says, wiggling his fingers.

She holds up her own hand and displays the stone etched into her palm. "Magic," she repeats.

Sky shows her a few more magic tricks, each one fascinates her. I try to focus on it, too, and find it increasingly difficult. Brain fog and tight, prickling skin distract me. Delilah snapping twigs nearby sounds louder than it should. I catch myself twitching at the pops of the breaking sticks, and lace my fingers together to keep from accidently grabbing Elle too hard. A twig snaps, a bird takes off in a flurry of wings, and suddenly I can't be here anymore.

I lean down and place Elle gently on the damp ground. She stares up at me with a question in her eyes.

"I'll be back in a minute, I'm getting some firewood," I explain. I smooth her hair back from her forehead, my hand comes away slick with sweat that isn't mine. I stand, turn to where the pine I stripped down last night once was, and walk away.

Behind me I hear Delilah say, "let him go, Sky."

Stab. Stab. Stab.

There goes my knee again. At least the hot iron is generously absent. After the last few days, the universe damn well owes me a good pain day. Except it's not really a good pain day, because there are iron bands crushing my ribs.

The stream burbles cheerily. The path of some wild animal is worn into the earth beside it. That direction looks promising, easy to follow back, few tripping hazards despite the saplings choking the bank and the sharp curve away from the stream the path takes. I follow it for a little way, scanning either side for a break in the tangled foliage, but the soil by the stream is rich and soft and thick with plant life. Fresh air is abundant here, it's just not making it to my lungs. I reach the curve in the path to discover that it's not actually a curve. A particularly thick grove of poplar saplings has sprouted, cutting off the trail.

Beyond the small grove is a shallow, thicket-less cove. It's a small gap in the underbrush, surrounded on three sides by towering trees and bushes approaching full bloom. A few saplings sprout from the leaves and needles littering the ground. The north side opens to the stream. Sunlight dapples the forest floor, and there are even little clusters of flowers here and there. A cool breeze rustles the branches of the saplings and shakes a few fragile leaves from their places. I watch a pastel green leaf fall. It comes to rest on the ground.

There, finally, I crack. I don't mean to, I don't want to. It blindsides me, stealing my mind, my body, my control, like a wraith. My legs give out, I land on my hands and knees. A rough slab greets my palms, and I have a moment to register that it is a large, flat rock before the visions start.

Sergeant Tatyanin crumpling forward, a hole in her head, blood in her hair.

I strike the rock, pummel it with both hands fisted.

Maverick, falling, bullets in his chest, red rivers pouring out his neck.

The skin on each knuckle splits open, but the rock slab holds steady, refusing to give. I punch it harder. Get them out! Get them out of my head!

Piper. Bakari. Dieter. Five people are dead. Five. I didn't even know four of them. They all had families, friends, they could have had kids for all I know. They weren't rubber dolls, they were real, and now they are stone-cold dead.

Maverick's last words echo in my head.

Bullshit, Maverick, I call bullshit. You're not allowed to be dead. You're not allowed to be sorry. You're my best friend, you bastard, come back.

I pound the slab one last time with my balled, bloody fists, and finally, it breaks. Spiderweb cracks radiate from ground zero.

Sharp edges shred my hands as they burrow in the rock, and shards break off to imbed themselves in the back of my knuckles. My glasses, all black plastic and too-heavy lenses, fall from their perch on the end of my nose. That's when I notice that my face is wet with tears.

Ripping my hands open on the rock seems to have knocked me back into myself. I tell myself that the bright, stinging pain is the reason behind the salt on my cheeks. Logically, I know that's not the reason, but I'm afraid that acknowledging it will bring back whatever the hell just assaulted me.

I wipe under my eyes with the heel of my palm, then search the broken ground for my glasses. They land face down on a cushion of wet leaves. I hope they aren't broken. As I reach for them my fingertips brush a leaf, and the glint of something metal catches my eye. I pick up my glasses and squint at them.

They're dirty and scratched, but thankfully not broken. I wipe the lenses with the hem of my tank top, place them back on my face, then skim the ground for whatever it was that caught my attention a moment earlier. Nothing is there. I rake my fingers through the leaves and… there. My fingers meet with a thin metal chain. I pinch the links and hold it up to get a better look. Clinging precariously to the end of the short string of tiny silver beads are a pair of dog tags. I slide the tags back up the chain and fasten the simple clasp to keep them from escaping.

There are letters engraved on both of the oval tags. One has the words Марся Татьянин etched in flowery Cyrillic cursive that plays tricks on my eyes. Below that is a string of numbers; 12.23.81. A birthdate maybe, or an anniversary. The second tag is stamped with ВС РОССИИ 22-428686.

I wish I knew what they said, I wish I knew what these were for. Tears blur out the letters. They won't stop even though the stinging has settled to a mild prickle. Shaking grabs ahold of me and an awful ache pulsates in my chest like some important part is missing and there's nothing there to replace it.

My mind flashes back to the cave under the ledge, with Anushka curled up and repeating the same three sentences over and over and over again. I think I've figured out what she was doing.

I clutch the dog tags, careful not to crush them, and suck in a lungful of spring air.

"My name is Trick." It comes out as the barest of whispers, only there to prove that my lips are giving shape to these words, making them real, tangible and true.

"I'm nineteen, I am a lab experiment." The pulsing ebbs, the shaking subsides. "I have a little sister. I will protect her."

The symptoms aren't completely gone, but they're better. I don't feel like I'm packed too tight inside my skin, at least. I give my eyes one last swipe with the heel of my palm and stand. Headrush makes me dizzy for a moment, but when that passes, everything is fine. Well, mostly everything. The backs of my hands are gouged with ragged, shallow cuts, seven out of ten fingers are bruised and torn, and dirt is caked under my nails and in every cut. I kneel beside the stream and rinse off in the frigid water. None of the damage is too extensive, which is extremely lucky. You don't normally come away from a fight with a rock without a broken bone or two.

After cleaning up, I lumber to my feet and return to my search for firewood. Sky appears at the edge of the grove, a small furry thing dangling in his hand. I ignore him as I walk past. He decides to follow me.

"You're limping," he says.

"Go figure," I mutter. We reach a stump, and I hobble down the length of the fallen tree until I reach a section near the top that looks like a good place to start.

"Are you hurt?" There is an apprehensive undertone to his question. I resist the urge to roll my eyes and settle for giving him a dead look instead. He ignores it, reaching down to strip the branches off a section of the tree.

"I'm fine." I lift the tree and crack it down over my bad knee. *Sun and stars.* I end up on the ground, clutching my knee as searing pain lances through the bone. By the stars, that was a *bad* idea. My breath hisses through gritted teeth.

"You right, mate?" Sky crouches beside me.

"Yes." I answer past a clenched jaw. I ease my aching leg straight and pull up my pant leg. A huge blue-purple bruise stains the knee, it radiates from the soft point right below the patella, the perfect spot to wreak havoc on the bundle of nerves tucked in there.

"You're definitely fine," he comments with more than a little sarcasm.

"It's just a bruise." I press gingerly on the edges of the bruise. It feels a little swollen, but considering I dropped a tree on it, the swelling probably isn't something to worry about. I get to my feet, balancing all my weight on my good leg, and bend to pry the tree from its place on the ground again. I notice with a measure of satisfaction that the top of the tree is broken off. I shift my weight to my bruised leg and crack the next section of the tree across my other knee. That hurts a hell of a lot less.

Skyelar purses his lips. I can practically see the wheels turning in his mind. He takes the first chunk of tree I break off.

"No sign of King," he mentions out of the blue. I grimace, cracking off another section of tree.

"Yeah."

"He should have been here by now. I don't think he made it out of the camp." His nimble fingers tear vigorously at the small twigs. His eyes dart as rapidly as his hands, always a step ahead of where he wants them to be. As the browning pine needles flutter to the ground, I find myself reminded of Maverick falling. Again. My heart clenches.

Snap goes the next chunk of tree. Snap, snap, snap, until the entire trunk is a pile of sizable logs. More than we need. More than enough to put a matching bruise on my other knee. Not enough to drown out the ache in my chest. Sky stops to pick at his palms, but soon gives up on his effort to dig all the splinters out of his calloused skin.

"We need to hold a funeral," he says as he hefts a log in each arm. I scoop up the remaining five, and we head back to the camp.

"Yeah," I agree. We may be freaks but our dead deserve respect. I tilt my head back to stare up at the mosaic of leaves against the steely sky. Black smoke stains the sky above the camp, remnants of the massacre last night. They deserved better than that.

Nobody says it, but it takes longer to build a fire without Piper. Delilah strikes the flint at least a dozen times before a weak spark catches on the kindling. Even then, the fire is little more than smoke and a thin orange outline spreading towards the edges of the pile. The fog pressing in doesn't lend itself to a healthy fire. Delilah puffs on the smoking bundle while Skyelar and I try to skin a squirrel he caught. Delilah is the first to voice the concern we all have.

"What do we do now?"

The question lingers in the air above our heads. Yesterday morning, the answer would have been simpler. Yesterday morning we had seven fighters, we had a plan, sort of, and we had a leader. Today, everything is different.

Nobody answers. I stare at Elle. She's lost in the folds of the sweater. She's managed to tuck her knees up inside the billowy fabric, and she sits with the hood up and her hair falling like a curtain over her face. She keeps her gaze leveled at the fire, but I know she's eavesdropping. Her fingers ripple with the colors of the flames, laced with shades of skin that aren't hers. Delilah's and Sky's in places, but most often Maverick's.

I push my glasses up and run my fingers through my hair. My hand comes away greasy and my hair stays standing up on its own. Turning back to the squirrel in Sky's hands. He holds it up by its tail and pulls a face. We haven't been very successful with skinning it. A jagged river rock isn't exactly a perfect tool.

"We can't beat them, we barely escaped last night when there were... more of us," I say. Elle finally looks up from the fire. Her skin has settled down. A red flush paints her cheeks but that's from her fever, and her gaze looks unsteady. A trickle of sweat runs down the side of her face.

"The buggers will probably have search parties out," Sky adds, tugging on the maimed squirrel tail.

"Delilah?"

She looks uneasy.

"I don't know." She lifts a shoulder and drops it in resignation.

Sky jumps to his feet.

"More squirrels," he says before darting off.

I get up as well, and kick around the edge of the clearing. Somewhere along here are the remnants of Anushka's supplies. We should have dug them up last night, but we were all too dazed and exhausted to remember. I've gathered most of it by the time Sky returns.

There's a knife, a firestarter kit, and a canteen with a tiny bottle of iodine clattering inside of it. There's also a miniature first aid kit, which Delilah promptly puts to use.

Through much trepidation and determination, she tweezes every last splinter out of Sky's palms and, not without protest on his part, soaks all of the teensy entry punctures with disinfectant. She raises an eyebrow when she sees the state of my hands, but she doesn't comment when she picks shards of rock as well as wood splinters out of my split knuckles. In return, I make her let me clean and bandage the cut on her crown. I also check her for a concussion, though she insists that she's fine.

Included in the first aid kit is the best thing of the entire load; a nearly full bottle of Tylenol. I take it and skim the label. I'm pleasantly surprised to find that there is an English translation on one side. It states that the medicine can be used for fever. Perfect, I'll give a pill to Elle when she wakes up. I check the label again. It's adult, extra strength. Okay, so maybe I'll only let her have half a pill.

I unscrew the cap and shake four of the red oblong pills into my waiting palm.

"Bit much, don't you think?" Sky comments from his place by the fire, he has a couple of dead squirrels and a questionable rodent-like creature by his side.

"Not nearly," I reply, and down all four Tylenol dry. He's probably right, in terms of taking them right now. Four pills on an empty stomach is practically begging for ulcers.

"Thought you said you weren't hurt." He wrestles with the squirrel's skin. I shrug, screw the cap back on the pill bottle, then toss him the knife. I'm not hurt. Not any more than the rest of them. It's not injury that's making my spine feel like it's forcing its way up out the top of my head. Not a new injury, anyway.

"I can't carry you if you keel over again." He jabs the knife at me before slashing a squirrel open. The sloppy contents plop onto the fire. Blood splatters against the charred bark.

I sigh, "I won't."

He peels the skin off, shakes it a bit, then places it on the glowing coals of what is left of the fire. Now that the sun is higher in the sky, the fog is clearing out, and we can't risk the smoke from building up the fire again. "Then what's with all that?"

Delilah returns from the creek then with the bottle swinging at her hip. "All what?" she joins in, dropping the bottle at Sky's feet.

"Four Tylenol!" Sky flips his wrist at me.

Reading the look on her face, I hold my hands up in surrender and try to wave off her question before it comes.

"Four?" she asks.

"Yes, four. I'm not gonna die. I'm not hurt." I aim that last part at Sky. He crosses his arms and worries his lip. "I have fibromyalgia, that's all."

"Fibro-what-ia?" His expression turns puzzled.

"It's chronic widespread pain, the Whitecoats gave it to me." I get up and bounce on the balls of my feet, testing the extent of the Tylenol, the pain is lessened. Free to move, I bring Delilah iodine for the water.

"On purpose?" Sky inquires.

"No, they used to mess up Experiments all the time. Kinetics got killed the most because they were the most difficult to change. Elle and I were both pretty lucky, they decided to turn us into Enhanceds," I explain. Sky gives a low whistle. Lucky is a stretch.

"And here I was thinking they had this whatever-percent success rate," he muses.

"Ninety point five, this year," Delilah intones. "Increased from eighty-seven last year, and seventy percent three years ago. The Whitecoats talked about it all the time. I think they forgot some of us could understand them."

"Wow, three years ago. So I would've been sixteen..." he trails off. He has to think back, recount when the cross from normal to experiment happened. "That would have been about the right time," he concludes.

"Four years ago they took me, and Chastin was there a year before that," The attention turns to Delilah, she's preoccupied rescuing the smoking squirrel from the coals, holding the squirrel in one hand and the water bottle in the other. Funny how I never met Chastin or Delilah before. Sky's absence makes sense, but five years ago? I wasn't that much of a hermit yet.

Delilah sharpens a stick with the knife and splashes a bit of water over the skinned squirrels to rinse the blood off. While she's doing that, I scrounge for utensils. The firestarter kit has a hard, plastic spork that is completely useless against the tough squirrel meat. We resort to passing the cooked rodents on their skewers, taking bites of them like they're shish kabobs.

"Why do you think they did it?" Sky asks around a shin bone toothpick.

Delilah looks up from the pine needle tea she's trying to make with the iodinated water, "What's that?"

"Why would the Whitecoats go through all that trouble? What were they planning to do with us, I mean, all we ever did was run test after test, you would think they wanted something more, eventually." He spins the spork between his fingers for a moment before jabbing it into the dirt.

"Dueling was an awful lot like culling, if you think about it," Delilah muses.

Sky begins to snap, fingers jittering. "Not much more of us to cull, hey?" he says it like a joke, lighthearted, until Delilah shoots him a cold glare.

"Why would you say that?" she demands. Sky ducks, hair falling to hide his expression.

"I didn't mean it like—" the snapping gets faster. He stands abruptly, startling everyone except Elle.

"Where are you going?" Delilah asks.

"Nowhere. Away. Um, headstones," he stammers out. The next instant he's gone, a rustle in the bushes the only indication he was ever here. Five seconds tick by, and Delilah sighs.

"Oops."

"Oops," I agree. "He'll come back."

She turns her head to skim the forest in the direction of the rustled bushes. "I'm never quite sure he will," she says.

I guess I'm not either. If I could run like that, I wouldn't come back.

When Elle wakes, she forces down a rodent drumstick and a half a pill from the Tylenol bottle. When I ask how she's feeling, she smiles at me.

Skyelar doe return, and he shows us the headstones he found. They are large, smooth rocks, five in total, each a different color. Black, blue, red, green, and white.

We clear the campsite, hiding evidence of our brief stay as well as we can. The pine boughs are tossed far into the bush, the coals are doused and scattered, Delilah sends a mini tornado across the site to bury our disturbances under debris. I catch Elle clinging to a tree at the edge of the clearing while she pukes. Blood speckles the ground under her.

"I'll be alright," she insists, pinching her bloody nose. I wish she were telling the truth. She needs her treatments. Delilah comes up behind us, wielding a travel cup of pine tea, and the other half-pill of Tylenol. She coaxes both of those into Elle, and this time they stay down.

Sky gathers the rocks, I carry a backpack in my arms, and Delilah shoulders the last pack, then we're on our way. It's mid-morning, and all the fog is burned away. I lead the way down the animal path and show the others to the cove. When we get there, the three of us each take a rock or two and stack them in the dent I made earlier. Elle watches us work for a moment, then wanders a little ways away. She's careful to remain in sight.

Sky packs clay from the stream into the cracks, sealing the stones together. He touches each one delicately, with the very tips of his fingers.

"I tried to pick their favorite colors." He trembles.

Maverick's I recognize, he always liked the color red. Pointed it out when birds with red bellies landed in the pine by the basketball court, or when he spotted a flower out in the wild grass between the fence and the woods to the west of the Compound.

The others don't come so easily. I didn't know them the way Sky did. I kneel beside him, hovering my fingers over the blue stone, I turn to him in question. He places his hand over mine, I can feel the vibration from his trembling.

"Bakari," he says, and guides my hand to the green stone, "Piper, Maverick."

He hesitates over the white stone. "I didn't know Dieter's or Anushka's."

I turn my hand over to lace my fingers through his. Elle returns then, cupping wildflowers. She sets a blossom in the cracks by each stone, lingering at Maverick's. She knew him, he was her friend. He came with me to visit her in the infirmary and kept an eye on her when I couldn't. She places the last flower with care.

She traces the edge of the headstone, adopting the same red shade onto her own skin. There are tears streaming down her face when she spins around and slams into me, burying her face in my chest. A sob shakes her entire body. I wrap my arms around her, kneeling on my good knee to hug her closer. She cries.

"You didn't tell me, you didn't—" She sniffles and breaks into another sob. "They're all dead."

"I know, I'm sorry, I know," I murmur.

Elle shakes, her tears soak through my sweater. She's a kid. She's not supposed to cry like this. She's not supposed to know what having dead friends feels like. I press my face into the side of her head, her hair covers my eyes, her sobs echo in my ears. She's just a kid.

16 | Soldier Blood

"Are we walking much farther?" Elle asks. I glance down at her, trudging along at my side, her bare feet sinking into damp soil. The red hue has washed out of her skin, along with all other color.

"I don't know," I answer.

"Oh." She presses her lips into a thin line.

I shoulder-check for signs that we might be being followed. Slender branches bounce where birds have taken flight, swaying treetops from the ever-present wind, but no crunching footfalls. We're following an animal trail. Dirt and old floppy leaves wind ahead and behind through the easiest patches of bramble. I face forward again, searching for…something, I don't know. We're lost, we've been lost since the moment we set foot outside the Compound. The threat of the military camp forces us to keep moving, but we have nowhere to go.

We stop for a breather. Elle kneels, taking advantage of the short break. The hood of the sweater slips off her head, and she squints at the sudden brightness. Her eyes are swollen and red from earlier.

"Piggyback?" I offer Elle. She glances up from the ground and shakes her head.

"I can walk," she says. "'Sides, your back is all messed up." I run the tips of my fingers over the fresh scar. Only the center, where the explosion hit worst, needs a bandage now.

"It doesn't hurt," I lie.

"Time to go," Sky announces, bouncing on the balls of his feet. He swivels his head left and right, searching the gaps between the trees for signs of the military. He hasn't calmed down since he came back from zoning out. I don't think he can. Suddenly he freezes, muscles tense.

"We have company," he says, pointing at a gap in the trees to the east. A cluster of domed helmets is bobbing through the trees. The faint murmur of conversation carries on the wind. The sun glints off the tip of a rifle, they must be soldiers. They could be looking for us. My breath catches as the soldiers freeze.

Sky reacts first. He takes off like a bullet, crashing through the underbrush towards the group of soldiers, too fast to be anything but a blur. The shiny rifle tips disappear into the bush. A second is all the time I'm given to grab Elle and drop to the forest floor before gunshots shatter the air. Elle screams, covering her ears and melting into the dead leaves. But there's no blood. There are screams but not blood, not anywhere from anyone. That won't last long, Sky is going to get himself shot.

"Go, run!" I urge, scooping Elle off the ground and shunting her to Delilah. "Go!"

Delilah's instincts are almost as quick as Sky's. It's only me passing Elle to her that keeps her from going after the soldiers. It's clear in her eyes that she wants nothing more than to fight, but I can't risk both of the last two people Maverick got out of the Compound in another gunfight. With Elle clinging to her and me already turning to go after Sky, she doesn't have a choice except to clench her teeth and bolt.

Gunfire splits the air again before I reach the soldiers, splinters spray from shattered tree trunks. I flinch after each one, expecting the hit, expecting Sky's ginger head to halt, anticipating the spray of blood instead of wood chips. By some miracle, only one person is on the forest floor by the time I reach the soldiers, and it isn't Sky.

The body on the ground is breathing, alive but not conscious, and not bleeding. Three soldiers are still standing; two men and a tall woman, all with long black guns pressed to the inside of their shoulders. The barrels of the guns sweep side to side as the soldiers try to aim at Sky. He crashes through the underbrush, old foliage crunching underfoot. It sounds more like a herd of fleeing deer than one slight man, and it drowns out the noise I make creeping towards them. With Sky's distraction, I manage to sneak up on the nearest soldier before any of them notice me.

I grab his head from behind, fingers scraping on the rough stubble on his chin. I squeeze just tight enough to keep him from squirming. The other soldiers are quick to train their guns at me. The woman barks out something in Russian, her finger tightening on the trigger.

"Don't!" I say, pressing the soldier's head, turning it towards me as if to break his neck. The other soldiers hesitate, and over the shoulder of the woman I spot Sky.

"Leave us alone," I say to the soldiers. I can only hope they speak English. "We won't hurt you if you let us go. We didn't do anything wrong."

The woman stares but there is no recognition on her face. She doesn't understand a word I'm saying, and her aim doesn't budge a single inch. The soldier worms in my grasp, glaring at me out of the corner of his eye.

"Leave us alone," I say again, slower. This time, the only response is a metallic click. I glance down in time to spot the silver handgun the soldier I'm holding draws. His finger is tight around the trigger as he whips the gun up. He makes it halfway before my reflexes kick in.

His head twists in my grasp, the bones in his neck snap with a hollow pop that makes my stomach flip. The light fades from his eyes, and he's dead before his gun hits the ground.

The woman reacts the quickest, her aim is steady despite her dead teammate dangling from my arms. I duck to hide my head behind the body, forcing myself to breathe through the nose while my heart rate skyrockets. I killed someone. My head spins, something that tastes like copper and electricity coats the inside of my mouth. I killed someone and there are armed soldiers trying to kill me, and I don't know if this dead body is a good enough shield to keep me safe.

Suddenly Sky is in the clearing, snatching something from the woman's hefty utility belt. His arm flashes in front of her and blood sprays from her side. She screams, swinging her gun to fire at Sky.

He skims past the last soldier as the woman squeezes the trigger. The crack of the bullet sets my ears ringing all over again, blood mists the air and Sky staggers to a halt. In front of him, the soldier collapses, a bullet in his neck.

One soldier left. My grip loosens around the neck of the dead man and with my moment's hesitation past, I throw him. The living soldier has her gun up and aimed at Sky. She squeezes the trigger the same moment the body crashes into her. There's a shot and a gasp in quick succession, then the soldier hits the ground hard, her gun goes flying and the body pins her down.

I scramble over to the pinned soldier. She writhes under the weight of her teammate, snarling vicious words at me. A solid kick to the head is all it takes to knock her out. Good thing too, I'm starting to shake and it's not from pain.

"Watch out!" Sky shouts, the click of a gun reaches my ears a second too late. It's followed at once by a wet squish and a garbled yelp that can only mean one thing. I turn to see the soldier who was lying on the ground unconscious earlier is on his knees. His gun is still half-raised and pointed at me, but his grey eyes are so unfocused that his pupils are two different sizes.

Sky stands in front of the soldier, his sweater and pants are soaked and the pommel of the blade he grips is glistening red. He looks from the soldier to the knife, disgust curling his lip. There's something eerie about the way he's holding himself, as if he's forgotten to breathe. Except I can hear him breathing, loud and shaky over the rustling leaves.

"Are you hurt?" I ask, making my way over to him. He jumps at the sudden noise, and I regret speaking. He whips around to stare at me, flecks of blood mingle with his freckles and under all the dirt smudges, his face is pale.

"A graze," Sky says at last. He looks down as if to find the injury, and catches sight of all the blood coating his clothes. Horrified, he presses the back of his hand to his mouth, muffling a sharp groan.

"It washes out," I say, repeating the same words Mav said to me the first time I came out of the dome unsure of whether the other person had survived. It's the only thing I can think of. This is a Maverick kind of situation, it's not something I know how to fix. Sky lifts his gaze to me, uncertain. "It washes out," I say again, putting my arm around his shoulder. He leans into the touch, ducking his chin to look at the blood again.

There's a moment where he wavers, something dark flickering behind his eyes. "We're messed up," he sighs, resting his forehead in his palm, the darkness winning out.

"You're okay." I rub his back. He pushes his fingers through his windblown hair and heaves a shuddery breath.

"Of course," he says, trying on a smile that wobbles despite his efforts. When he breaks away, he shakes himself out like a wet dog and clears his throat. "We should take their backpacks, they'll have stuff we can use."

"Good idea," I say. Sky nods but doesn't turn around. The knife in his grasp spins and he gnaws his lip nervously. "Why don't you go and find where Delilah and Elle went, I'll grab the packs."

Relief is plain across his face as he agrees. He darts off before I can say another word, and then it's just me and four bodies in the wilderness.

Only two of the soldiers have backpacks and I pick through them, sorting out what could help us most. There are food packs, medical kits, two knives, two blankets that crinkle when I touch them, and some other things. I leave behind one of the blankets and anything like flares or bullets that we won't use. Everything else gets crammed into one backpack. By the time I finish packing it all up, the unconscious soldier is stirring. I stand, hefting the backpack, and as a precaution I go around and bend the muzzles of all the rifles. No use taking chances. On my way out of the clearing I wrestle the olive drab jacket off the soldier with the broken neck. It's the cleanest one.

With the backpack snug on my shoulders, I head the direction Sky went. When I've gone far enough that I can't look in any direction and tell where the soldiers were, Sky shows up by my side.

"We're not far. We found the cave we stayed in before and holed up there," he says, his cheeks and eyes are red.

"Here," I toss him the jacket. He catches it with ease and slips it on. Zipped-up, it hides his bloodied shirt well. There's nothing to do about the spray of blood down his pantlegs, but this is a little better at least. He rolls his shoulders and tugs on the sleeves.

"Thank you," he says quietly, smoothing the front of the jacket. "This helps."

"Yeah, no problem," I reply. "Are we really so close to the cave?" I scan the surrounding area and find that some of the terrain does look familiar. That doesn't necessarily mean we're in the right place. I was delirious with fever the last time I was at the cave.

"We travelled a lot faster going downhill than we did going uphill," Sky explains. "Plus, nobody had to drag you." He shoots me a wink to show he's teasing.

"Ha, funny," I snort, ignoring the creeping sense of guilt in the pit of my stomach.

Sky leads the way, walking at a normal pace for once. He shoves his hands in his pockets, the sleeves of the jacket bunch up around his wrists. True to his word, it isn't long before we're rounding the last boulder to the mouth of the cave.

Weak smoke leaks out of the entrance, the source is a decrepitly small fire farther in. Delilah crouches by the fire, feeding it scraps of grass and funneling the smoke away. Elle sits beside her, legs folded to her chest and elbows on her knees, shivering. When she spots us, she jumps to her feet, a smile spreading over her face. She sways dangerously for a moment, but the spell passes, and she runs the short span of the cave to crash into me.

"You're back!" She throws her arms around my waist while I drop the backpack. "I was worried."

"Me too, *hermanita, es bueno* now," I say, rubbing her back. I can't help but notice that she's shivering and sweating at the same time, obviously symptoms of withdrawal.

"Oh," she huffs, pushing away, hands flying to her face. Blood leaks between her fingers from her nose.

"Did you bump your nose?" I ask. She shakes her head, sending drops of blood flying. With nothing else to wipe the blood away, I pinch her nose with my bare hands and tip her head forward. Warm drops splash on my palm in time with the crackle of the fire. We're used to her getting nosebleeds, it happens a lot, but two in the same day seems excessive.

"If you start to feel dizzy sit down, okay?" I say, eyeing the puddle forming on the floor.

"*M'bueno*," Elle says around her pinched nose.

"What's that mean?" Sky asks. I glance over to see him watching us, his fingers are snapping out an unsteady rhythm, the real source of the crackling that I thought was the fire. "*Bueno*, I mean, you say it a lot to each other,"

"It means 'good' or, um," Elle hesitates, her voice is garbled but steady. "'Okay,' like *estas bien*, is 'you're okay.'"

"What language is it?" Sky asks, rocking forward on his toes. The trickle of blood from Elle is slowing, she should be okay in a few more minutes.

"*Español*," Elle answers.

"Espanol," Sky repeats, murdering the accent. Elle corrects him.

"*Ñol.*"

"Nee-ol." He props his chin on the back of his hand. She takes her hand away from her nose to flap it at him, it looks like her nosebleed has stopped at last, and Delilah tears her stare away from the flames in time to see me scrubbing the trails off Elle's face with the corner of her sweater.

"You two." Delilah points to Sky and me with a smoking twig. "Go get me something to feed this fire, and Elle, you come back over here and sit," she instructs.

Elle obeys right away, with the way she's shivering, I'm not surprised. She folds up like a pretzel, as close to the fire as she can get without toasting herself. Holding her palms out to warm them, the pattern of the flames flickers up her skin, making it look like her arms are burning.

"That's cool," Sky says. Elle beams at him, the flame pattern engulfing her neck and licking at the edges of her face. I smile a little. It's nice to see her in better spirits after this morning.

We make our way outside to gather kindling. The air is sharp but not bitter cold like it was a few days ago, the sun shines brighter too. Maybe not warmer, but definitely brighter.

"Did you have any siblings?" I ask Sky as I pick a nearby pine tree and begin to scrape the flaky bark off it. There were lots of siblings at the Compound. Cousins too. I think most of them were sold into it, like Elle and me.

"Nah, I was an only child. I always wanted a little brother though." He picks dead twigs from the barren ground. There's some stringy green stuff hanging off the branches of the pine. They're dry to the touch, I take a handful and add it to my clump of bark.

"What about you, Delilah?" I call, catching her attention. She's beside the backpack now, picking through the supplies. Elle tends to the fire, poking at it with a half-burned twig and puffing on it occasionally.

"Hm?"

"Any siblings?"

She pauses with a shiny package in either hand. Her brow crinkles above her nose as she tries to remember.

"Yeah, an older sister. She lived in Nizhny Tagil, I wonder if she's still there." She digs out a pot from deeper in the pack. Her forehead is still crinkled, like she isn't sure of her answer.

"I bet we could find her," Sky says brightly. "All we have to do is make it back to civilization and from there it's a tip of your hat and off you are to the rest of the world."

I take the bark and add a few small branches to the mix. We return to the cave to surrender all the kindling and fuel to Delilah. Sky snaps his fingers almost silently the moment he's free of the bundle of twigs. Elle scooches out of the way, choosing to curl up beside a ripple in the cave wall. She rests her head against the rock and watches Delilah feed the shrinking fire. It takes a couple tries, but she catches a flame on a curl of dry bark, and from there it's a matter of time before the fire roars to life. Heat and light wash over us, carrying the scent of smoke.

Certain that the fire is happy and healthy, unlike any of us, I grab the bag in search of the food packs. At the sight of the green-brown packaging, Sky's stomach grumbles loud and clear.

"Hungry?" Delilah teases.

"Cook the food already." He snatches the package from me and starts prying it open. He fumbles with the tabs but eventually manages to tear it open and dump it on the ground. Plastic-wrapped crackers and spoons scatter on the stone, heralded by the clunk of metal tins. "Is this the same as the stuff before?" he asks, even as he's ripping into one of the tins. Red sauce drips on his fingers. "Guess so."

"Hey look, it's almost as bright as your hair," Delilah smirks. Sky rolls his eyes.

"Wow, so original," he says, squeezing the last bit of sauce from the second package into the pot. "What's next, we gonna call Trick 'four-eyes' and drop a spider down your shirt?"

"I am not afraid of spiders," Delilah declares, but she narrows her eyes at Sky nonetheless.

"You were," Sky says to the floor, eyebrows up like he doesn't believe her.

"And then I found out there were worse things than creepy eight-legged bugs," she retorts.

"Like the soldiers," Elle says, her voice barely carrying over the crackle of the fire. I glance at her, biting the inside of my cheek.

"They won't get you again," I promise, forcing myself not to clench my fists and instead gather the crackers. I can only imagine what they might have done to her in that camp, how afraid she must have been. I'll never let that happen again, I should never have let it happen in the first place. "You're safe."

She nods absently, her hair falling over her face in a curtain. I lay the crackers at her feet for her to take when she's ready.

"I've been thinking." Delilah prods at the fire, feeding it a whisper of air. The tongues of flame waver under her care. Sky taps a spoon against the rim of his tin.

"Well, don't keep us waiting," he urges. All eyes train on Delilah as she sits back and tucks her hair behind her ears.

"Is it safe for us to go back home?" she poses the question, and silence creeps up after it. Sky presses his lips into a thin line. The normally smooth skin over his blue eyes crumples like a wad of used paper, and he stares hard at the fire. I, for my part, can't help but look over at Elle's resting form. Russia is a long way from the island, even if it weren't, would I… could I take Elle back there? Her skin shifts in time with her breathing, taking on the texture of the fabric in patches along her face, and the color of stone across her spindly fingers. My parents will never have their son back, that's for certain, but do they deserve another chance with their daughter?

Nobody can come up with an answer to Delilah's question. A small paper packet rests outside the ring of firelight. I pick it up and turn it over while I'm thinking. It's not until I poke it and feel a hard lump that I realize it's not a napkin.

"What's this?" I pass it to Delilah. She holds it up to the light, squints at the writing, shakes it a bit.

"Multivitamin." She passes it back, eyeing Elle as she does.

"Hendrix." A low groan snaps my attention to the corner where Elle was resting. She's sitting up, her hair is a limp halo around her hollow cheeks, her head is clenched in her clawed fingers. I'm by her side in a moment. "My head hurts," she whispers, as if talking makes the pain worse. I kneel next to her and scoop her into my lap. Her head rests on my chest, and I rub her left temple. Headaches already. I bite my tongue and press the back of my hand to her forehead. She's burning up, even hotter than before, sweat all but pouring off her head.

"I'm going to throw up," she mumbles, moving only her lips.

"Let's go outside."

She nods microscopically and unfolds her legs. I help her to her feet and bend to wrap my arms under her shoulders, she leans all her weight on me, but she's so light it's like supporting a feather. Elle bows her head so her hair hides her face when we pass the others, I squeeze her shoulder gently, it's the most reassurance I can offer. Neither Delilah nor Sky look up from what they're doing, they carry on a hushed conversation until we're past.

We make it a half-step to the left of the entrance before Elle starts heaving. I hold her hair back while she clutches her stomach. A pained expression scrunches her face. She doesn't lean over quite far enough the first time and the top of her sweater gets soaked. Red so dark it's almost black splatters the rocks. The stench of decaying blood fills the air and makes her gag again.

She's puking up blood. *That* isn't part of withdrawal. Cold fear runs down my spine, sending goosebumps across my skin. The moment she stops heaving I'm on my knees, pulling up her shirt to look at her stomach. There's no bruising anywhere on her torso, no puncture wounds, and no swelling.

"Does it hurt when I press on your belly?" I ask, pressing right below her ribs to feel for anything I might have missed.

"No."

I let her shirt fall back into place, rocking to my feet. She wipes her mouth on her sleeve and looks at the mess on the front of her sweater.

"Sorry," she croaks, meaning the sweater. In the fading light she looks washed out, purple splotches circle her bloodshot eyes like bruises.

"It's fine," I assure her. "Let's get that off you." I tug the slimy sweater off her and discard it. It's useless now. With only a thin shirt acting as a barrier between her skin and the chilly wind, she shivers. I guide her back inside where it's warmer. She walks a few steps on her own and plunks down by the fire.

"Here, we ate." Delilah holds the half-empty tin of soupy cabbage-meat-mix out to me. I take it gratefully and offer a spoonful to Elle.

"No thanks." She hugs her knees closer to her chest, shivering. She squints at the fire, the light must make her headache worse.

"You should eat a little," I say.

"I can't," she says, turning her face away from the heat of the fire and closing her eyes. "My stomach still hurts."

Even this close to the fire she's trembling. I rub her arms, running through her symptoms in my mind. She's got the shakes and a fever, headache, stomach cramps, and with nothing substantial in her stomach, I don't know if I can give her any more Tylenol. Can I? Should I try to let her sleep it off? What if it can't be slept off, what if it gets worse? For a fleeting, horrible moment I wish we were back at the Compound. At least the Whitecoats could give her the right thing to stop her pain. I don't even really know what's wrong.

"Here, you look cold," Delilah interrupts my train of thought. She offers a grey hoodie to Elle. The tank top she escaped in hangs looser than it did a week ago. Her shoulders are thinner, but still squared. Elle eases into the sweater, thanking Delilah for it.

"Just returning a favor," Delilah replies. It's the same sweater I gave her the last time we were in this cave. Our eyes meet across the fire, and I know we're both thinking the same thing; last time we were here, there were a lot more of us.

Elle leans her head on my shoulder. "*Dígame un historia?*"

"What's that mean?" Sky asks.

"Tell me a story," Elle whispers, tilting her chin to face him.

"Trick tells stories?"

She nods, completely serious. A glint appears in Sky's eyes that I don't particularly like.

"It helps me feel better. Want to hear one?"

"Absolutely." The mischievous glint spreads to the rest of his face. I bite my tongue only because Elle sits up a little straighter, and the crease between her eyes gets a little shallower.

"Which one? The fairy one? The tree one?"

"The Compound tree one?" he asks, looking to me. "Mav said all of the older Experiments did."

I shift uncomfortably, reaching to let my fingers skim the edge of the burn scar. Sky's right, I know the story. An Enhanced told it to me and Maverick when I first arrived, back when the story circulated regularly. Then the guards started punishing anyone who told it, and the Enhanced vanished under uncertain circumstances. I nod once, to confirm Sky's suspicions, and hope he doesn't press for more.

A moment passes, then a weak smile crosses Delilah's face. "I was married under that tree," she says.

The tree in question was a towering pine on the far side of the crumbling basketball court, beside the fence. The 'coats hated it, the rest of us saw it as a sign of hope. It stayed longer than any of us, which was a feat in itself considering some of the chemicals they dumped on the poor thing. But the real reason we loved the pine was the legend of who put it there.

"Can you tell us?" It's Delilah who asks.

The room is slowly getting hotter, there's a tightness in my chest, sprung by all this discussion of the pine tree's secret legend. I fiddle with my glasses to buy more time.

"I don't think that's a good idea." All I can think about is the Whitecoats, waiting for me to mess up, wanting me to tell a forbidden story so they get the chance to toy with Elle. The hairs on the back of my neck prickle in anticipation. I know it's all in my head, but old habits die hard. I scratch the edge of the burn until it stings.

"I could tell you," Elle chimes in. "I know all about the pine, Drix and Maverick told the story to me." She grins up at me, proud of the fact that she knows the story and unmarred by the awful deaths the Experiments suffered. We should never have told her, but we were less careful back then.

"Okay, go ahead." Sky folds himself beside the fire. He rests his chin in his palm, a look of interest on his face. Delilah leans back on the cave wall, wearing a similar expression. Elle rubs her hands together deviously and takes a dramatic breath. She links her fingers and holds her hands up as a projector screen. The silhouette of a pine tree appears over her knuckles.

"Once," she announces. "There was a girl. She was brought into the Compound years and years ago, and she loved to cause trouble. She was *una fierabrás*." She pauses, fishing for the right English word. Her eyes are bloodshot. I roll her word around in my head for a moment for the right translation.

"Spitfire?" I say.

"A spitfire. She didn't listen to anybody, not even the 'coats. She didn't just cause trouble, she breathed it. So when the Whitecoats enhanced her, they made her florokinetic." She puffs her chest and scrunches her face when she mimics the Whitecoats, her hair turns white and her skin greys.

"I've never heard of 'florokinetic'," Sky interrupts.

"Never?" Elle's brow crumples.

"They only ever made one," I explain. Lei Kikira was the Compound's first and last Experiment given the ability to control plant life. She was gone long before any Experiment still alive showed up. She caused more damage than she was worth to the Whitecoats; Elle only knows the tame version of the story.

Elle continues with a curt nod. "The girl was miserable for months, she couldn't control her power very well, but she practiced. She grew grass during breaks and stuff, kept it real secret so everybody thought she was still useless. Then one day, she snuck over to the basketball court and found a sproutling near the fence. Witnesses say all she had to do was touch the sproutling and poof!" Elle jumps abruptly, hands thrust into the air. I lurch to keep her steady. The sweater sleeves flop to her shoulders and pattern of pine green complete with interwoven dapples of light and chipped bark climbs up her extended arms, giving them the appearance of pine boughs.

"She climbed over the fence on a branch and ran off, never to be seen again."

With the story finished, Elle heaves a huge exhale and returns to her place cuddled in my arms.

"Good story," Delilah says, "do you feel better?"

"*Sí.*" A smile brightens Elle's tired face, and, exhausted, she lets her eyes close.

Delilah stretches her arms above her head, yawning. Her back pops all the way up to her neck. "Ow," she mutters, rubbing the back of her neck. "Damn, I feel old."

"You are old," Sky teases. Delilah scowls at him.

"Go fetch more firewood for your elders, young man," she says.

"But—"

"Go!"

While Sky slinks out to collect more wood for the fire, I slip Elle off my lap. In the span of time between her finished story and now, she's fallen fast asleep. Good, she needs it.

I crouch by the dying fire to feed our remaining bark and twigs into the embers to get the fire blazing again. The coals crackle and hiss at the slightest touch. Most are buried under a thin layer of powdery white ash. Delilah flicks her fingers to help coax the embers back to life. The small flames come reluctantly and sputter. When at last the fire crackles happily, I plunk back and make a face at it.

A quiet creeps over the land, ushered in by the end of the story and the setting of the sun. Sky returns with an armful of sticks. He feeds them to the fire while he hums something melodious. We drink all but the last of the water we took from the stream yesterday and eat our fill of the little packaged meals. Outside, the shift from evening to night is coming to an end.

"Delilah, can you pass me the Tylenol?" I point to the bag. A warning ache is worming at my hips. Forget feeling old, my joints creak like actual grandma bones.

"Already?" She looks dubious, but she fishes the bottle from the side pocket anyways. She lobs the bottle, and I catch it with my free hand. It rattles louder than it did earlier. I brace it against my thigh to get past the child lock without shattering the plastic and pick out two red pills. One sticks on the way down but doesn't stay. The threat of pain almost has me reaching for more, and I have to remind myself to ration the pills. Who knows when I'll be able to get more, who knows if Delilah or Sky will need some, I can't go eight a day like I did at the Compound.

I set the Tylenol to the side and check on Elle. She's fast asleep. Gently, I lay her down in my lap, so she won't wake up with a weird crick in her neck.

Sky stops humming, and I look over to see him watching me.

"What?" I ask, perhaps a little defensively, remembering his earlier reaction to the Tylenol. He shrugs.

"You're different around her," he says.

"A good different," Delilah adds. She leans back against the cave wall, her hair is gathered on one side and her fingers work to braid it into a single rope. The cut over her eye is healing well.

"Oh," is all I say. What else am I supposed to respond with? I push my glasses up my face and stare at the fire. Outside, a night bird sings. I listen to it, the thoughts swirling in my head all boiling down to one thing;

What's next?

Long into the night, everyone except Elle is still wide awake. Delilah has rebraided her hair five times, and the fire has been reduced to glowing embers.

"I bet it's World War Three," Sky stands, finally bored of sitting still for so long. he announces. "All it would've taken were a few more countries, anyways, we were all in a big, bloody battle three years ago."

"We were?" No matter how hard I try, I can't remember any fighting between countries. But I guess I've been gone longer than Sky, and besides, no one tells a twelve-year-old brat that the world is about to be blown to pieces. Nobody even told me I was leaving home until it was a done deal.

"Yeah, I remember hauling tons of rice from the store and big cases of water, and my dad always had the news on some channel that showed all the places fights were breaking out." He swipes at an invisible bug near his ear. "Really fun stuff."

"Who was the fight with?" I ask, leaning back on my arms. Elle stirs slightly but stays peacefully asleep. The sheen of sweat on her forehead seems permanent at this point, and so does the shaking.

"America, mostly," Sky answers. "Buggers got greedy."

Delilah raises her eyebrows at him, lips pursed.

"Okay, more greedy. You know there was all that stuff in the history books about places like Syria and Iraq, and after so long everyone thought it was over, but I guess the big USA had different ideas." Sky flashes a mirthless smile.

"And Russia?" I ask,

"Russia promised to ally with America, but in the end we stood down," Delilah enters the conversation. "That military camp we saw shouldn't have existed."

If what Delilah says about Russia is right, then where does that leave us? And what reason would they have to stay out of the fight if they had the weapons and an ally like America, why stop unless… I think back to what Maverick said the night before he—before we went to get Elle. *Heavy shit has been happening… we're right in the middle of it.*

"Maybe it wasn't a stand-down, maybe they were stalling," I suggest, "maybe, they needed better weapons."

"To build us," Delilah says, realization dawning on her face.

"Bingo, why go nuclear and bring about death of your own country when you can." He waves his hands in the shape of a banner for effect. "Kidnap some children and turn them into your own personal supersoldiers."

"I guess that explains the military camp," Delilah says, her brow is knit. "And why that man was so eager to get his mitts on us."

"No kidding, and they're probably coming after us," Sky concludes. "I mean, if we were meant to be their ticket to winning a war, there's no way they'd let us slip through their fingers."

"Mm." Delilah bites her lip. "So we're fugitives now."

"We always were," I say. Some of us, like Sky, have been on enemy soil since the day we were first taken. Some of us, like Delilah, became hushed secrets when the first incision was made. Either way, we've been fugitives for a long, long time.

"Oh well," Sky mumbles around a yawn, "Now that we've discovered that, methinks it's time for some shut-eye." He stretches, wheeling his arms and rising on his toes. He makes a sound like a dying pterodactyl, then plunks down on the stony ground. Delilah crinkles her nose, smothering a yawn behind her elbow. She lays down with her back curled to the wall and rests her head on her arms.

"I can't decide," she murmurs with her eyes closed. "Whether this rock is more comfortable, or less now that I'm not drenched in the stuff. In the sky water."

"Rain." Sky yawns, eyelids millimeters from closing.

"What?"

"It's called rain."

Delilah cracks her eyes long enough to stick her tongue at him. "Sky water," she says again, and this time no one corrects her. Minutes pass, the embers grow dimmer. A snore comes from Delilah, and a quick glance at Sky confirms that he's dropped off too. Sleeping, he looks his own age. Luckily for us, there are no bugs out this time of year, the temperature still walks on the edge of too cold for them to survive.

I cradle Elle in my arm and add a couple dry branches to the fire to keep the embers alive. Outside a soft wind passes by. I still can't sleep, too much happened today and yesterday. I can't stop thinking about how fast Elle is going downhill. She's sick. She's so sick, and what do I have to help her?

A bottle of Tylenol and a ratty sweater.

Elle shakes in her sleep. I inch closer to the dying fire, hoping to feed her more warmth. I don't know what to do, I don't know how to fix any of this. I don't. I was built to break others, not repair them. My thoughts spin faster and faster, my shoulders getting tenser with every passing breath. If Mav was here he'd tell me to ice it. I bite the inside of my cheek hard enough to draw blood, the taste of it rings in my skull. If Mav was here, he'd have a plan.

"My name is Trick," I breathe. "I'm nineteen. I'm a lab experiment. I have a little sister who's sick. I'm going to get her help." I finish. I feel calmer now, it worked. I'm beginning to understand more about the Sergeant.

"Neat trick." A soft voice says. I look up to find Sky watching me. I wonder how long he's been awake, or if he was ever asleep to begin with.

"Yeah."

"I'm glad I came back," he says, sinking lower against the cave wall. Suddenly he's more interested in a hangnail on his thumb. "I almost didn't, that first day out? Mave told me to follow the quad. It felt so good to run like that, without any walls or fences or 'coats. I could've kept running forever."

"Why didn't you?"

He bites off the hangnail, stress-lined eyes wandering over the splits in the glowing embers.

"Ah, well," he says after a long pause, "I guess Maverick looked out for mee too much in the Compound. Wouldn't've been right to leave him out to dry like that."

And now he's dead.

Heaviness drags over the insides of my chest, clinging to the meat between my ribs and making my heart lag. Orange and yellow flicker over Sky's face, deepening the shadows under his eyes and a new hollowness in his cheeks.

"You can run now, if you want," I say.

He shakes his head, "don't say that," his voice catches, he clears his throat. But I have to say it. He deserves to know he can leave, he can't be held here by the ghost of someone who I got killed. "Don't say that, if you do I might do it."

"You should." It's a difficult thing to get out. With Sky gone we will be that much more alone. Who knows if Delilah will stay. Who knows what 'staying' means for us. Sky snaps his fingers. "It's okay, don't worry about us."

"Don't worry about us," he mouths, gaze lost in the flames. He gets to his feet, snapping, shifting from foot to foot. He won't look up from the fire, but I can see on his face that he wants to run. That the thin line tying him to us is stretching thinner.

He looks up, meets my eyes, and I can all but hear the thread break. His chin wobbles, but he reigns it in and is gone before I even blink.

I stare after him, gnawing on the inside of my cheek, then I take off my glasses and rub my face furiously. Blazing stars, I'm so tired of this mess.

I wake up to the sound of crying. In the sleepfog that coats my brain, it takes a minute for my heavy thoughts to recognize the cold spot in my lap where Elle should be. Instead of light pressure and the heat of a feverish kid, there's empty air. She's not camouflaged, this time she's gone.

I bolt upright, suddenly wide awake. Not again, not again. It would kill us all. My frantic gaze lands on a small form right outside the dim circle of light cast by the fire. Delilah is already awake and kneeling beside Elle's small body, her expression is crumpled. The awful, choked sobbing is coming from Elle. I scramble to my feet, pins and needles humming up my rudely awakened left leg, and limp across the cave.

"What's wrong? What happened?" A pang runs up my back as I kneel beside Elle, reminding me that there's a time limit on the effect of the Tylenol.

"I thought it would pass, I didn't want to wake you," Delilah says, retreating to make room for me. Elle is hunched over, her fingers are splayed and clawing her head so hard the tips are white. Tears and snot run down her face into her twisted open mouth.

"It hurts," she cries, pressing harder on her skull and rocking. "Make it stop."

"Tylenol," I say, ask, demand. I put my hands over Elle's and brush her wet cheeks with my thumbs. I hate seeing her in this much pain, it scares me more than I want to admit. "Listen, Delilah is getting you painkillers."

"I'll just throw them up," she whispers, light bounces off the tears building up in her eyes. Her breathing is labored. Suddenly she droops, and a scream wrenches free of her.

"My *head*," she gasps. "Make it stop, please, Trick it *hurts*."

Sobs wrack her tiny frame. Delilah hands me a pill. I tip Elle's head back.

"You have to eat this, it will help." I press the pill to her lips. Reluctantly, she takes it and swallows it dry. A shudder goes through her, and she falls against me, shivering and trying to hold in her sobs.

"It's exploding," she cries into my shirt. "I think I'm dying."

"Don't say that," I say firmly, wrapping my arms around her.

A niggling voice at the back of my mind says that this has gone beyond a headache. I ignore that voice.

Pebbles skitter right outside the mouth of the cave, alerting us to intruders, Delilah jumps to her feet, palms out and ready to fight. Thankfully, it's a friendly face that enters.

"What's going on?" Sky asks. He stands in the entrance, sweat plastering his ginger hair to his forehead, gasping for breath. Behind him, the sky is a shade lighter, the sun about to begin its slow rise. "I heard screaming."

Delilah motions to Elle, Sky tracks the movement. He takes in Elle's trembling hands, and the tears glistening on her face and presses his lips into a thin, hard line.

"Headache," I say in answer to his question.

He comes further into the cave, his hand trails on the wall. When he stops, his fingers start to drum. In the fire, a spent coal collapses into a pile of ash. Elle has stopped sobbing but tears still spill past her half-closed lids, and she sniffles periodically. Her hands open and clench into fists, one bunching the fabric of her sweater, the other squeezing my own hand.

"We should go back," Sky says. Tension rips through the cave, cutting us to our bones like a chill winter wind. My blood solidifies to ice in my heart, and I hold Elle closer. Delilah recoils, too. Silent now, gnawing on her lip. Fear and memories flash through her pale eyes. She looks closer to the Delilah who held her dead husband on their first day of freedom than she has since escaping the military camp.

"It's empty, abandoned, but I'll bet there are supplies in the unburned buildings. We can get warmer clothes." He tips his head at Elle. "Medicine."

"How do we know it's completely abandoned?" I ask. For all we know, the Compound is swarming with army people, just like the camp.

"I was there," Sky says. His answer shocks me, but only for a second. We're so close to the Compound, if I could move as fast as Sky I would check on it too. "It's burned, mostly, not a soul in sight. The fence isn't live."

He pauses, considering something, then his attention is caught by something outside the cave. "The sun is rising."

We all turn to watch the sliver of sunrise that's visible from the cave. The turquoise-tinted sky brightens in increments, a rosy swatch slowly gains more and more space and the tip of the sun peeks over the horizon. In a different situation, it would be a beautiful scene.

As the frosty landscape brightens, Elle drifts off into a restless sleep once more. Her shallow breathing is the loudest thing in the cave. There's not much conversation to go around, even Sky seems subdued. The prospect of returning to the Compound is a grim one. Too grim. If there's any other option, I'd rather take it, but I'm afraid there isn't.

The last of the flames hisses out, a thin curl of smoke rising from the ashes. It's time to go.

"Kiddo, time to wake up," I say, shaking her shoulder. Her head lolls with the motion, her eyes stay closed. Yellow sleep dust is crusting in her eyelashes and salt tracks dry on her cheeks. "Elle, come on, rise and shine." I nudge her harder. Nothing. No response. I can feel a crease forming between my eyebrows. I give her another shake, panic worms into my head and spreads fast.

By now, the others have noticed what's going on. Delilah kneels next to me.

"I can't wake her," I say, pressing the back of my hand to her forehead. Her skin is searing hot and damp. Delilah puts two fingers to Elle's throat.

"Sky, how far away did you say the Compound was?" Delilah asks, reaching for Elle's wrist, too. Impulsively, I take her other wrist between my fingers and my thumb. Her pulse is weak and fluttery.

"Not far, less than a day if we hurry," Sky answers. He stomps out the fire hurriedly.

I scoop Elle up. She's ragdoll limp. Is this because of the Tylenol? I didn't think a single pill would do this, if anything it should have affected her stomach, right? Not her head.

Avoiding the Compound is no longer an option, she's too sick.

18 | Metal Skeletons

The Compound is a blackened shell. The fence, with its rows of chain-link laced with barbed wire, still stands. There are three man-sized holes ripped through the chain-link. The inner buildings are husks, charred cement walls and twisted, half-melted metal skeletons are all that remains. The outer buildings faired better, one storage house is completely untouched save for a spray of bullet holes. What happened that night? Who were the Whitecoats fighting?

The infirmary looks toasted. Black crawls up the walls, the right branch is warped and buckling. I recall the flames bursting from the windows and can only hope that the damage inside isn't too extensive.

"You guys should check out the storage buildings, see if there's stuff we can use. I'm going to check out the infirmary."

"Be back here in an hour?" Sky suggests. He's jittering, bouncing from foot to foot nervously. His eyes won't stop moving. With the packs hidden back at the cave, there's nothing to weigh him down or keep him from bolting up a tree at the faintest noise. Delilah is fairing better, or at least she's hiding her fear better.

The three of us split. Sky darts off to the farthest of the outlying buildings, Delilah heads for a nearer one, and I pick my way through the rubble to the infirmary.

The front doors are blocked by debris. The glass is wavy and coated in thick ash. It's not much of a problem, but it would have been nice if the wheel tracks were functional. I throw a cursory glance around me. Something about this place makes me feel watched. Someone else might call it paranoia, but I am less optimistic than that.

"Trick." Elle's head rolls, her eyes flutter. My heart jumps to my throat.

"Elle, hey." I kneel in the ash and prop her on my knee. "Elle, can you hear me? Can you open your eyes?"

Her eyes open slow, she winces at the light. It takes her a full twelve seconds to lose the unfocused glaze, and the whites of her eyes are dark and bloodshot. She mumbles something, like thick word soup leaking out the corner of her mouth.

I look around for a crevice that's not layered in ash and find a place on the ground that has been mostly shielded by a large chunk of displaced concrete. I lay Elle there, helping her lean upright against the stone. She struggles to keep her head from sagging. "Hey, hey, hey. Look at me, *mirame*, tell me how you feel."

"They let you come today," she whispers, doing her best to smile. "I didn't think they would." Her skin bleeds ashes from her scalp, her arms look like the rubble they're propped on.

"What?"

Instead of answering, she lifts her arm to examine it and frowns at the gritty pattern.

"My head hurts," she says, letting her arm drop.

"I know, stay here. I have to go open the doors, then we can get your medicine." I give her a quick pat on the knee and jump to my feet. She's awake, it should relieve me, but instead I feel antsier. I don't think she knows where we are.

Walking back, I notice that the dust is lighter in areas, as if it's been disturbed, especially around the melted door. Clouds of ashy dust settle into the spots where I've walked, the thick motes falling back into place. I check behind me, tracing the path I made. The pattern there is strikingly similar to the one around the door. My skin itches, I want to shake out of it, like I would if this were a fight. But I need to stay entirely me, I need to be able to recognize the medications once I'm inside and Robo-Trick can't do that. Besides, I pinch the back of my hand and flex my fingers a couple times, I can't be around Elle like that. I don't trust myself.

A few mounds of drywall and brick from the upper level are collected inconveniently against the doors. I prod one pile with my toe, but it refuses to budge. I nudge until the jostling shakes loose a couple bits, but the rest stays put. On closer examination, I discover that the tangled mess of wall is fused to the warped glass. Bubbles of the once-clear window must have oozed over the bundle of wall chunks and solidified. Again, not a problem, but it would be nice if things weren't as difficult as they could possibly be for once.

I smash my heel on the connection where wall meets door window. Glass shatters, ash explodes into the air, and the wall bundle rattles. The ash dries up the back of my throat, and I hold back a cough. I crouch and jam my hand under the debris bundle to lever it the rest of the way free. When my hand jerks up, it meets a corner of jagged glass and the skin tears.

"*Que mierda,*" I swear under my breath, staring at the blood welling in the cut. I wipe it off on my shirt and hold my hand up to examine the wound. It doesn't look too deep, does sting like hell though. I wipe it off again and return to un-sticking the wall bundle. One more shove and it rolls free.

I work free a few more piles of debris that melted into the door and kick them out of the way. The ash and dust are swirling like mad, and it finally looks like there's a chance the door will open now. I wedge my fingers into the seal between the two sliding doors and pry them apart. They squeal and groan as they grate open on the warped wheel track. The right side snaps with a loud pop, and the door jams into the remaining chunk of wheel track. A hard shove and the wheel track crumples as the door rams to the side.

The second set of doors is already open, and stuck that way by the looks of it. Some important-looking wires hang limp from a fried panel above the door. Nothing inside looks like it's on the verge of collapse.

When I return for Elle, dust has settled all over her hair and face, making her look even more washed out than she already is. She staggers to her feet with my help, and with her holding tight to my arm, we creep into the infirm. Past the mangled sliding doors is a lobby that looks remarkably untouched. A fine, silvery powder coats everything, except for random bare patches on the floor. A few have puddles of black ooze, a few are human-shaped.

From the outside, it looked as though the right branch is on the verge of collapse, which is good because as far as I could ever tell things like treatments are kept in the left branch. That was the direction the nurses who got my refills always came from. I pick a hallway on the left and make my way around the patches to the entrance.

The hall is dark, darker than I'm used to it being in here. The glaring fluorescent lights are all dead. The first section of hall is devoid of doors, but the first turn reveals a long stretch of them. I walk along, Elle trailing behind while I kick each door open. The wood doorframes splinter and the doors all bang into the wall. Most of them fall open to operating rooms, there's an x-ray room at the end of one long hall, the sight of that equipment brings to mind the conversation I had with Elle, about the boy with the glowing eyes. I almost ask her if she remembers him, she was lucid when she was talking about him. But the idea that she might not remember now is enough to stop the question before it starts.

At the opposite end of the hall with the x-ray room, a flicker of movement catches the corner of my eye. I stop dead, my eyes dart around the small space, my ears strain for even the faintest sound. One second passes, another, ten, fifteen. Nothing happens.

"Come here," I motion to Elle, who stopped at the last door. She says nothing while I guide her past the melted equipment to the little cubicle the machine operator used to sit in. The thick glass pane between cubicle and machine is soot-stained but not warped, and inside the cubicle looks undisturbed. An array of dead computers, a locked file cabinet, and a lone worn stool stare at us.

"Hide under the counter," I tell Elle, "don't come out unless I come get you even if it gets noisy, okay?"

She blinks at me, eyes glassy.

"What did I just say?"

"Don't come out," she whispers.

A loud crash from the hall startles me, Elle shies deeper under the counter. The scare knocked loose my self, I can feel it slipping away like old skin.

"Stay here," I whisper. "Use your camouflage, I'll be right back."

With Elle as hidden as she can be, I push my glasses onto the bridge of my nose and step out into the hall. To the right, the direction I came from, there is no one, only a crumbly chunk of brick laying on the floor. I edge further into the hall, trying to get a better look at where the brick came from.

The silence that was welcome before is eerie now. The hairs on the back of my neck prickle like the air is charged. I stop a good distance away from the brick. It looks like it belongs to the top of the corner, where there's a gap in the stone reinforcements. I creep down the hall towards an intersection that feels vaguely familiar, the way recurring dreams feel when it's been a while. A hazy, unplaceable sort of déjà vu. I turn slowly, searching for 'coats. The hall is empty, but a metal door sunk into the wall clicks a memory back into place. This must be the wall bordering the dome. I've been brought through that doo a few times. Concussed, broken boned, whatever. Placing it clears my head a little. There's no one here after all, that chunk of brick was just a chunk of brick, probably knocked loose by me banging doors open. I allow myself a sigh of relief, and that's when I hear it.

A low, quiet voice that says, "Hello again, Trick."

Not 'Experiment', not feminine, not British: Not a 'coat, Delilah, or Sky. I spin fast, fists up, ready to deflect a blow. When I see who stands behind me, I freeze.

The person at the other end of the hall, shrouded by dim shadow with a small tablet tucked under his arm, is supposed to be dead.

"Welcome back to the Compound," Dieter says.

"You're alive," I say, it comes out more like a question. It doesn't click. Even with him standing in front of me. Dieter folds his arms over his chest. He's dropped a shocking amount of weight in less than a week. He's still round, but it's much less pronounced than it should be. He has the look of a house pet that's been left to fend for itself too long.

"I am." He runs his tongue over his top lip. "Find that girl of yours?"

Instinctively I edge over to block his view of the storage room door. He watches me with almost lazy interest.

"I'll take that as a yes," he says, his s's drag. A sneer breaks the casualness of his expression, his upper lip curls back, revealing cracked white teeth. "What was the cost of your pathetic rescue mission?"

Half-shrugged out of my skin as I am, I don't understand what he means. He doesn't talk much like Dieter. There's something dark swimming in his words, something cracked. The other Dieter—the one we lost in the forest—was just scared.

"How many people died?" he clarifies his original question.

"Five," I breathe. "Not including you."

He makes a thoughtful noise in the back of his throat. The sneer warps. He lifts a newstab like the ones the Whitecoats carry around and pokes at it. His eyes wander over the screen as it lights up. "Five or… twenty-eight?"

He has to be pulling that number out of thin air because even that first night on the side of the hill there weren't twenty-eight of us. Alright, so he's out of his mind.

"You attacked them." He flings the tablet at me, it bangs into the wall and the screen flickers. I glance at it just long enough to catch a giant headline on the screen.

WIND WITCH KILLS DOZENS

"What the hell?" I mutter.

"You don't remember? It was only a day ago, is your memory that bad? Is it worse than mine? Does it hurt to think?" he seethes, molten hate bubbled on the corners of his split lips. Spit flies from his mouth. He's worked himself into a rage, red face and clenched fists and all. "They were doing their jobs!"

More and more of me sloughs off as the argument continues. I can't cool it enough to drag my mind back to its proper place.

"Since when did you side with them?" I ask, narrowing my eyes at him.

"Since they showed me I didn't have a choice." He tugs the collar of his shirt down to show off violent red welts encircling his neck. His lips part in a wide grimace, revealing the ruined teeth that fill his mouth. Electric shock torture, and starvation, disorientation. The Whitecoats brainwashed him.

There were a few other Experiments they tried brainwashing on, troublemakers, one or two who tried to start a gang. After, those Experiments spent their time staring at nothing with blank eyes. It was freaky, but at least they kept their mouths shut. Dieter can't seem to stop chatting.

His expression drops, unsteady eyes fixing on something behind me. Turning, I find myself face to face with another ghost. Blazing stars, he'd better not be brainwashed too.

"Trick," King rumbles. His teeth, or what I can see of them, seem normal. Then he lifts his hands to show off the narrow black bands clamped around both of his wrists. Old-school shock restraints. "How is Delilah? Skyelar?"

He doesn't ask about the others.

"Alive," I answer, and that's enough for him. He nods once and shifts his attention to Dieter.

Dieter stands with his head cocked so far to the left it's practically sideways, eyes narrowed. A string of drool drips from his grimacing lips.

"You're not supposed to be in here, Dieter," King says, borderline delicate in his tone. Dieter reacts like he pulled a gun. His expression morphs into terror, mouth gaping. He claps his palm over his ear and his eyes bug.

"No no no no no," he mumbles. "No no, I'm going, no worry, no need." He turns on his heels, a motion interrupted by a stagger to the side. As he hurries away down the hall, he wrenches his free arm behind him and flaps his hand in what might be a signal to King. In turn, King clears his throat, pulling my attention back to him. He tugs at his ear, or rather, at something hooked over his ear. A slender wire ending in a smooth, flat disc pops free and he holds it up as explanation.

"You shouldn't have come back. They're using us to hunt each other." He lifts the shock restraints again. "They sent me to get you."

I open my mouth only to fumble for words. I'm spiraling down and down and down and my skin is peeling apart. he motions for me to go on while he's tucking his transmitter back in place.

"We thought you died." I say for the sake of making noise. My voice sounds distant, but it grounds me a tiny bit.

"I almost did, but the 'coats aren't that nice. The exits are blocked, you can surrender, or I can drag you back to a cell."

I nod, popping my knuckles. Now that the Whitecoats know I'm here, there's no way they'll let me walk. I'm a liability, a danger.

"Where's the girl? I'll steer clear."

I tip my head toward the hall that leads to the x-ray room. He grunts in confirmation. I appreciate the gesture.

"King."

"Yeah?"

"I don't want to duel you." It's true. To win I might have to kill him, knowing he was part of Maverick's group. Maybe I didn't know King well, but Mav did, Mav trusted him.

"You could come willingly," he suggests, rubbing the back of his neck.

"Not a chance." He will drag me to the Whitecoats bloody and unconscious, or not at all. I bounce on the balls of my feet, shaking out tense muscles. A humorless grin spreads across his face.

"Good, consider this a *screw you* for getting Maverick killed." He jackhammers his heel onto the floor. The linoleum cracks and a spike of grey stone rockets towards me. I dive out of the way, ramming the door full-force. It pops off its hinges and clatters into the room beyond.

The dome rises up in front of me like a leering mountain. Shiny and beckoning, strange from this new angle. I wrench one of the aluminum rods from its anchor to create a spear of sorts. The metal comes away jagged on both ends. A rock clips my ear. Hot, stinging.

My opponent kicks more fist-sized hunks of concrete out of the smooth floor to hurl. I duck and roll. Not quick enough. One of the chunks catches me by the stomach. I tumble over and let momentum carry me back onto my feet, breath knocked out.

I dodge another barrage, lunging closer with every step. Closing the gap. Taking away whatever advantage he has. Another step and I'm close enough now for the metal spike to be useful. With a shout, I drive the rod into his shoulder. He screams through clenched teeth. Stone rockets up, striking me hard. Vomit rockets up to the back of my throat. That's gonna bruise. I grunt. The pillar shrinks and I stagger. Dizzy. Can't breathe.

I swing before another can erupt. My fist connects, weak, but enough to make him stumble. Blood soaks his shirt, dripping on the concrete floor. Beyond him, a wraith made up of matchsticks and spring curls wobbles over the broken door.

What—

what—

what—

Shit. I plant my left foot and kick up sharply with my right, catching Bakari across the neck. This time he goes down, bad planning on my part. A brief motion from him sets a ripple across the floor, knocking my feet from under me. My head cracks on the stone. Heat bursts across my temple. I roll to my feet, ignoring the twinge of what's probably a broken rib. Blood runs down my eye and I swipe it away, scouring the dome for Elle. Terror turns my nerves to ice when I find her swaying in the middle of the room, Dieter looming behind her. His bloodshot eyes glued to the back of her head.

I make it one step, and the concrete erupts, sledgehammering me into—through—out the wall. Stars explode in my eyes, ringing fills my ears. For a solid three seconds I must be as close as you can get to passing out without collapsing. When I come to, the first thing I hear is my own groan. Rubble crumbles off my aching body.

"Dude!" Sky skids to a stop at my side, eyes wide.

"Elle," I gasp. He tears into the building. Scrabbling to my feet, I list hard to the side, tripping on broken slabs of concrete before I catch myself. I drag myself through the hole in the wall in time to see Sky hit the wall head first and collapse to the floor. Dieter strolls towards them, broken teeth clattering. Bakari has hesitated partway to the hole in the wall, watching Dieter like he's deciding whether to stop him or not. I make the decision for him, by turning him into a Bakari-shaped missile. He smacks into Dieter, sending them both tumbling across the wide open room.

I drop to my knees beside Sky. He's out cold, half-curled around Elle, but still breathing. Blood mats his hair where he hit his head. Elle clings to him, chest heaving too fast. She screams. An invisible force clips my shoulder, ripping through it and striking her head-on. She hits the wall, slumps, eyes closed. Whipping around, I see Dieter swipe at the air. Seconds later another wall cuffs my left side. What the *hell*.

These attacks feel different from aerokinesis, but I don't know what else it could be. I can feel the walls ripple through me, buzzing my muscles and bones like electricity. A third wall strikes head-on, sending me to the ground.

"Like it?" Dieter leers. "I'm the world's very first magnokinetic. Neat, huh?"

I don't grace him with an answer. I get to my feet, mind racing. The room spins. Blood still pours from my nose and the blood loss is beginning to make me lightheaded. The adrenaline rush that helped keep the pain from my ribs at bay is wearing off fast. Dieter swipes his arm again, and I brace for impact while I scrape my brain for a way to get to him.

A gust of roaring wind collides with Dieter, slamming him through aluminum webbing. He manages to cling to the lip of the dome and drag himself back up with an indignant shriek.

Bakari smashes his heel into the floor, enveloping Dieter's arms in stone.

"Stay *out of it*, Dieter," he snaps. The reprieve is short-lived as Dieter works up another ear-murdering screech and the stone casing explodes. Shrapnel splatters the room and red drenches his arms from elbow to fingertip.

"I've got Dieter," Delilah says, raising her own arms as she strides past.

That leaves King for me. I close the space between us, grab him. My fist sinks into his gut and all the air exits his lungs with a whoosh. He tries to stagger back, jamming a pillar between us.

"That was nothing, we're doing fine," he coughs into his transmitter. "A few more minutes and I'll be done." I catch him by the wrists and slam him into the wall. It swallows one of my hands up to the heel of my palm, and he whips his head forward, smashing his forehead into my nose. For the second time stars blind me. I release King, hand jumping reflexively to my broken nose. Copper floods my mouth, blood gushes out both nostrils. He ducks under my arm and escapes, but I hook my foot over his ankle to trip him. He catches himself, curling to avoid my next kick.

Wrenching my hand from the wall, I stalk towards him. Sweat rolls of his temple. Veins bulge in his neck, his breath comes quick, shallow, and ratty. He can't quite scramble to his feet fast enough. My first punch bruises his ribs, my second punch breaks them with an audible crack. I grab him by the shoulders and wheel him around to crush into the wall as hard as I can, the impact leaves a deep dent.

He slumps, gasping for breath that won't come. He's fighting to keep his eyes open. With one hand holding him up by the chest, I grab the side of his head, pull it back and crack it against the wall. His legs buckle as he loses consciousness. My hand clutching his head keeps him upright. All of me screams to beat his skull into the wall one or two or three more times until it's finished for good.

I'm so close to doing it.

A high-pitched cackle wrenches me away from King. Dieter teeters on the edge of the dome, blood dripping from both arms while he leers down into it. Delilah is nowhere to be seen. The rage in my chest is hot and living as I cross the space, fists clenched. He's too enamored with the inside of the dome to notice me. A kid watching a trapped bug. I pull back to strike him, but he lurches before I ever lay a finger on him. The wind bumps him and down he goes. He hits the bottom with a resounding crack. Well, there's that problem solved. I peer over the edge, find Delilah on her knees at the bottom of the dome. A metal rod spears her arm, that hand sags limp at her side. Dieter stirs, pale face flushing magenta. He lifts his hand to throw a magno-blast, and in one quick motion Delilah rips the spear from her arm and brings it down on his head. He crumples, unconscious.

Breathlessly, she drags herself to her feet. Sweat drenches her forehead and she clamps a hand over the gash.

Without a glance up, she turns toward the door and says, "I'll meet you outside."

Get out of here, right. I shake loose my fist and head over to where Sky is sitting up.

"Can you walk?" I ask, picking up Elle.

He slurs an incoherent sentence. His eyes won't stay in one place. I grimace.

"Right. Okay, come on." I shift Elle to one arm and loop my other arm under his shoulders to help him to his feet. He leans heavily on me, which is bad because the light-headedness is making me wobbly. We stumble over the debris and through the hole into the ashy open space. Delilah meets us at the edge of the Compound with her sleeve torn off and wrapped tight around her wound. As we escape over the spiky remains of the chain-link fence, we hear shouting behind us. The Whitecoats. They must have discovered their pawns in the observation room. The commotion urges us farther, faster, we go west instead of south this time and soon the Compound is blotted out of sight by loose-knit forest.

The sun is low in the sky, a breeze plays in the tops of the trees surrounding us. I slowly wrestle into my skin, cramming all the pieces I can find back into place as we all stagger on. Nothing feels right, and the horror of what I did to Bakari—what I was going to do—sticks to my skin like slimy residue.

I am becoming less and less human. The idea, or rather, the knowledge, scares me less than it used to, less than it should. Not for the first time, I wonder how many more times I can do this before Hendrix Sanchez is gone forever.

Sky has lost all color under his tan complexion. He's walking on his own now, but not in straight lines. Every once in a while he lists heavily off course and one of us has to grab him to keep him on his feet.

Elle hasn't woken up. The only sign that she's alive is the shallow rise and fall of her chest. Every moment that she spends unconscious is more terrifying than the last. A thought keeps niggling in the back of my mind, and I keep trying to smother it. What if she doesn't wake up? What if she never wakes up, what if she's too far gone? All her medicine is back at the Compound, there is nothing I can use to help her.

Among other things, we're also out of water, food, and any medical supplies we had except for the Tylenol in my pocket. We could circle back, if any of us recognized any of the terrain. At the rate we're going, it'll only be a day, maybe two, before we succumb to whatever kills us first, especially if we can't snatch more sleep than the few hours we've had between last night and now.

"Sorry," Sky apologizes after I pull him upright again. "The ground's still moving." His words are slurred, but less than they were at the Compound.

"I think you have a concussion," I say. He wobbles, missteps, regains his balance.

"Really? What was your first clue?" Ability to walk? Gone. Sarcasm? Just fine.

"Focus on walking," I retort.

"Walking where?" Delilah poses the question we're all thinking. We have two options: Wander the Russian tundra until we die, which will probably be soon, or we could locate civilization.

"To find a city." The words tumble out of my mouth even as I decide the chances of that are invalid. We haven't seen so much as a dirt trail this whole time.

"That's our best bet," she muses.

"Minor detail," Sky says, patting the trunk of the tree he almost walked into. "Which direction is the city?"

The corners of Delilah's mouth turn down. We all come to a stop. Sky leans his head against the tree, his eyes closed, grateful for the momentary break.

"Here." I fish the Tylenol out of my pocket and pass it to him. He takes two dry and hands it back.

"Thanks," he murmurs. We wait for a while longer, nobody really has the motivation to move, Sky least of all. When at last he lifts his head from the tree trunk and squints at the surrounding area, a grimace wrinkles his nose. "This tree is the only thing not spinning right now," he says miserably, and presses his forehead to the bark again.

He tries to take a step and trips over his own feet. This time Delilah catches him and loops his arm over her shoulder. He droops over her, boneless.

"We could find your sister."

She hesitates before responding, "… we could."

"Tell us about her. What's her name?" His concussion seems to be affecting his mood, or maybe the swings are a result of sleep deprivation. Delilah considers his question, her lips pursing thoughtfully. I wonder if she remembers, memories from before the Compound are weird. Sometimes I know with absolute certainty that my middle school classroom had one chair, in the left back corner, that didn't squeak. Other times, I can't bring to mind my *mamá's* face—brown eyes or green? Wavy hair?

"Amiah," Delilah says at last. "Her name is Amiah Tsinknova."

"Ah-my-yer," Sky repeats slowly.

Delilah shakes her head and corrects him. "You're saying it wrong, it's ahm-ya."

"It's the accent." Sky shrugs.

"It is not."

"Hey, so, what's the first thing you guys are doing when we reach civilization?" Sky changes the subject with a hiccup.

"Find a hospital first," I say. I was headed there anyways. If the Compound had worked out, Elle might've gained a little more time, but what she needs are real doctors. Now, between Sky's concussion and the wound that Delilah is hiding under a few strips of ripped fabric, it looks like all of us need an ER visit.

"Right right right, okay, after the hospital?" He waggles his head. One of his pupils is dilated more than the other. The effect might have been slightly less disturbing if his irises weren't so light.

"Finding a real bed and sleeping for a long time," Delilah says.

A real bed. I dare to imagine sleeping on a mattress, not cement, not dirt, not a gurney. An honest to suns mattress. I might do the same as Delilah, minus the 'find my sister' part. It hits me, not for the first time, that I don't know what I'm doing beyond the hospital. Panic starts to swirl around my broken ribs. I breathe and crush it down. I can't afford to deal with that right now.

"I haven't slept in a real bed in seven years," I say to keep my mind in the present. I angle my head to look at the sky, where the sun is well into its arch towards the horizon. It will be dark soon, and we have nothing to light our way or give us any heat. My shoulder aches dully where Elle's chin rests, I shift her to the other side. The grey of my shirt ripples across her skin like monochrome fire, giving way to lighter shades of green and yellow.

"Seven years is a long time to not have a bed," Delilah says with a hint of wistfulness. Beside her, Sky snorts out a short laugh that earns him wary stares from both of us. He hiccups again and rolls his eyes with a shake of his head.

"Sounds like a song title," he chuckles.

"I think you might have more brain damage than a concussion." Delilah's tone is light, but worry lines her dirt-stained forehead. Considering how hard he hit that wall, I'm worried too.

"Hey!" He scowls and ends up tripping over his own two feet. This time, Delilah smirks, which only riles Sky more. I tune their bickering out for the sake of my pounding headache.

We walk and walk and walk. The trees all look the same, blurring together into a mass of green. I should be more vigilant, there's so much to watch out for. But I blink and the world takes several seconds to return and moving one foot in front of the other feels like slogging through cement up to my thighs.

"Trick, we have to run," Delilah whispers, grabbing me. Fire shoots down my shoulder, locking my hand in a spasm. I almost drop Elle. "They're going to see us, we have to run."

My heart drops. It falls out onto the dirt when I see who she's talking about. Dieter's platinum hair bobs between the trees, accompanied by five bright red coats. In that second when my gaze skirts over the group, Dieter turns his head and his cold eyes meet mine. He flashes a mouthful of broken teeth at me, and I bolt.

Sky clings to one of my arms while Delilah holds his other side. We barge through the brush as the forest breaks out in chaos. The first bullet blows a hole in a tree trunk, spraying me with splinters. Another gunshot, and Sky yelps. Blood hits my face but we can't stop. If we stop we're all caught. I choke back panic. We're nowhere near anything, we have nowhere to hide. But I cannot stop, I would rather die than let them take me back to the Compound.

I can't stop. I can't stop. Sky is bleeding, dragging his feet. Delilah is wheezing and coughing. We're slowing, another bullet wings us as we spill through a break in the trees. Out in the open. A black rock splits the forest.

The double lane road winds as far as the eye can see. Narrow ditches on either side bear few trees and thick dead grass half-flattened by the weight of melting snow. Racing down the road towards us is a truck.

"Hey!" I shout, Delilah shouts. We all duck when the Redcoats fire again, and Sky doesn't stand back up. He kneels in the grass, hands pressed to his neck. The truck isn't slowing.

"Delilah, Del, take her." I give Elle to Delilah and limp as fast as I can into the middle of the road. Right in the vehicle's path. The horn blasts and all I brace for the hit.

Damn, I hope this doesn't break any more bones.

Tires screech as they skid on the asphalt, the truck swerves hard into the ditch, screeching to a stop. The drivers' side door bangs open and a woman with a pinched face storms out screaming Russian. Then she pulls a gun.

Howling wind hurls her into the cab of her vehicle. Her head smacks the window. She raises her gun but Delilah flicks her fingers and it's like the words are sucked out of the woman's gaping mouth. Her eyes bug, she drops the gun to claw at her throat. Harsh Russian leave Delilah's mouth. The woman squeaks, her face is turning purple. Again, Delilah snarls something, the look on her face is pure murder. I back away, leaving her to scoop Elle off the ground and haul Sky to his feet.

"Get everyone in the back," Delilah says.

The Redcoats are upon us, their bright red jackets too close. One stops to aim his gun, and I jerk to the side in the nick of time. I drag everyone to the vehicle all but throwing Sky over the side of the truck bed while Delilah shoves the woman into the cab. I climb up with Elle slung over my shoulder. It starts backing up while I'm still climbing, and I fall the rest of the way in, landing on my back. I can't help the cry that punches out of my mouth.

"Trick!" Delilah calls as we bump onto the pavement. She sprints for us, arm outstretched. I lurch over the side, reaching for her. Our hands meet and I haul her into the bed even as the force of the truck jolting forward bashes me into the tailgate. The tires leave black marks on the road and Delilah and I collapse on the bottom of the bed.

"Elle?" I rasp, my vision is static.

"She's fine," Delilah answers.

"Sky?"

"M'okay," he mumbles.

Good, okay. No gunshots chase the truck.

I lay in unspeakable agony while the sky goes from blue to orange. Hurts too much to move. Think. Tylenol couldn't touch this. The driver hits a speed bump and that's finally too much. I claw myself upright to puke over the tailgate.

Sky is curled in a ball on his side, the gunshot wound on his neck is a bad graze but not fatal. Elle is laid out beside him, shivering in her sleep. They're both still breathing. Delilah looks several shades paler and blanches grey when she applies pressure to her re-opened injury, but she looks at me and says:

"She's taking us to a hospital."

I close my eyes and nod. Night has fallen, I shrug against the cool wind while the truck shudders forward. The idea of a hospital brings to mind sharp scalpels and reeking chemicals, it's not a place I'm going to enjoy spending time in. But it is a place that can help Elle, that can help us all.

Sooner rather than later, we reach city limits. Delilah cranes her neck, skimming everything with lettering on it in search of a sign of where we are. On the other side of the bed, Sky groans whenever we hit a bump. Streetlights loft above us, and the buzz of electricity fills the air. I stick my finger in my ear to make sure they aren't ringing. The city. We're here, we made it.

The truck rumbles deeper into the maze of concrete. Buildings made of glass and metal tower above us, the night sky reflected in their shiny exteriors. Some of them have bright lights glittering out from the inside, but most are dark. Every few feet or so, a tree or a signpost with chipped Cyrillic lettering pokes out of the slush-covered sidewalk. After a while of driving under the trees the road meets with more and more roads, and the truck starts taking turns. The motion makes my head spin, and I close my eyes to shut out the rising nausea. Motion sickness. Great. I don't remember having this. The cool breeze from travelling so fast helps ease my stomach.

Thankfully, not long after the twisting and turning starts, the truck slows. There are a couple more turns, and then it slows more, and inches into a well-lit, cramped parking lot. The hospital rises five story's in the air. Light pours from the ground floor and many of the upper-level windows.

The vehicle rumbles to a stop and rocks with the impact of the driver slamming her door. Delilah hops out first, circling around to the cab to meet the woman while the rest of us crawl out. My feet hit the pavement, and I grimace at the creaking of my joints. Sharp tingling races up and down the back of my legs and swells over my hips. It could be worse, but I'd rather it wasn't there at all. Sky slithers off the tailgate onto unsteady feet. He makes a truly valiant effort to stay upright and keep his breakfast, clinging to the truck with eyes screwed shut.

At the front of the cab, the driver shouts at Delilah. Curses, I'm sure. Human-sized shapes form beyond the glass sliding doors of the hospital as the commotion reaches a fever pitch. I wait for Delilah, watching them watch us. The truck door slams again, rattling the truck. The woman caws something from behind the safety of her closed window, flapping her hands, then wrenches the steering wheel about and rumbles the truck out of the parking lot. Robbed of support, Sky sways. I catch him before he collapses and manage to pull him so his head rests on my left shoulder and Elle is draped over the right.

"I've got him," Delilah says.

"I can walk," Sky mumbles, sounding exactly as wobbly as he looks. He picks his head up with determination. Then drops like a sack of bricks.

When Sky hits the asphalt, the hospital doors open with a whoosh reminiscent of the infirmary and spit out a dark-haired man in threadbare clothes. His eyes sweep over us as he jogs our way. Over the old crusted stains and the newer, brighter blood, and the bruises and the dirt and the torn, ragged clothes. He stops midway and I can practically see him re-considering the decision to come near us. He has a child with him, a little girl with a red snotty face and green eyes that wobble like little squishy marbles. Her white-blonde curls stick to her tear-stained cheeks. For some reason, she looks familiar. Maybe she's related to someone from the Compound, who knows, it doesn't matter.

Something Russian comes from his mouth. Delilah, kneeling beside Sky, answers him.

He retreats back into the hospital, child in tow. The moment his back is turned, Delilah smacks my leg, sending sparks down to my toes. I'm almost too tired to feel it, certainly too tired to complain.

"That's Anushka's kid," she whispers, "she looks just like her."

That's it, that's why the kid looks familiar. Not an Experiment's relative; a soldier's. That was Marsya. That was a toddler, a four-year-old at most, and her mom—images flash in my head. Bullet holes and caves and blood and falling and falling and falling.

"Trick," Delilah says quietly.

"Hm?"

She glances pointedly at my arm, where my fingertips are turning white from how hard I'm gripping it. My bone creaks when I let go. The outline of a bruise is already welling in the new sore spot.

The doors whoosh open and release the man, followed by a small woman in nurse's scrubs the color of pine needles. She pushes an empty wheelchair, her auburn hair swinging to the beat of her quick steps.

"You need to tell him to run," I say. "Remember what Anushka said when we found her?"

What I'm doing is traitorous…they will try to hurt her…

She nods, eyes glued to the man. They're halfway to us. "What if he's here for the kid?"

My heart stalls. If he's here for the kid then he knows what happened at the camp. He knows Anushka was a traitor, he knows the four specters in the parking lot are escapees. And if he knows, then this a trap.

There's no time left, and no way to run. The man and the nurse are on us. So I do the only thing I can think of, and dig the broken dog tags from my pocket and hold them out to the man.

It only takes a second for recognition to dawn on his face. And then, tears. In spite of everything, relief trickles through my system. That is not the face of a man here to punish a child for her mother's crime. He takes the tags delicately in one hand, holding Anushka's daughter close with the other.

"*Pochemu u vas est' metki Anushki?*" he whispers. I look to Delilah for answers, and at that moment, a siren wail splits the air.

The man's head jerks back to search the dark sky. He hoists the little girl onto his hip, taking a few unsteady steps toward the hospital. Delilah reaches for him, takes him by the arm. At the same time, the nurse taps me. I must flinch something awful because she yanks her hand away with a startled expression.

"This is bomb siren," she says, motioning to the hospital. "Inside now, inside."

She bundles us towards the hospital, somehow managing to both push the chair with Sky, and herd both Delilah and me. Light pools in front of the hospital, a beacon. We're short a body when we reach the doors. Somewhere on the trek across the parking lot, the man and Anushka's daughter vanished.

"I told him," Delilah says, barely audible over the wailing siren.

Inside; chaos. A crush of bodies seethes through the small lobby. I have a spare second to take in the cramped quarters, mouth turning desert dry. *I can't do this*, I think, and the lights cut off. There's a moment of dark, a shroud hanging over the impenetrable black silhouettes. Then dim red emergency lights flicker to life and someone shoves me inside.

The crowd disperses slightly, only to swarm back in and cut off escape. There are too many of them. Too many. I hit a wall. Cover Elle's head. I'm cornered. Clammy sweat drips down the back of my neck, an arm pops up in my peripheral, and I shy away, batting at it weakly. *Whitecoats with cold hands*. There are hands on my shoulders, on my head, on my legs. *My legs, my legs, my legs*. Sharp shooting pains. Crushed.

"Trick!" For the second time this evening, Delilah dredges me halfway out of an ever-more familiar spiral. "Snap out of it. Help me with Sky."

He's on his feet, sort of. The wheelchair and the nurse lost to the crowd. I don't know if I can hold his weight. A breathless kind of pain is working its way up my body doing its damndest to paralyze me. I loop my arm around his waist anyways.

"Where—" that's as much of that sentence as I can get out. She points deeper into the hospital, in the direction the crowd is flooding towards. A pair of double doors are pinned wide open, the space beyond nothing but dark. Bodies pass over the threshold and sink down. That's the entrance to a basement.

My broken pinned-together legs stall out from under me. "Del, I can't."

At once Delilah's fist is balled in the collar of my sweater. She glares down at me, not furious, but something I could mistake for fury if I hadn't seen what it really looks like to receive the brunt of her anger.

"We do not have any other options. Get down those stairs or I will *throw you down them*." She bites out.

The crowd grinds my bones into dust as we creep down the endless stairs into a pitch dark, windowless dungeon. Other people's sweat mixes with mine and stings in open wounds. Sky's weight across the back of my neck digs in like an anchor, a concrete block, and I feel it down in my brittle hips every time I limp down another step. Any second now, my bones will snap and crumble, and Sky and Elle and I will smash to the bottom of the stairs and get trampled into dust.

Delilah, holding up Sky's other side, forces us all the way down to the bottom, where the walls are close in. The people are too close, it's suffocating. I can't breathe and I want to scream. The door at the top of the stairs slams shut, plunging us all into the shadows. Now we're all trapped in a dark, crowded room, and my claustrophobia creeps in. The cramped room spins, my heart feels like it's spinning too. My shoulders hunch and I tuck my chin to my chest, drawing my arms in as if squishing my body smaller will make the room bigger.

"Get against the wall." I can't connect the voice to the person. I shuffle to a wall, my feet drag on the concrete, I can't pick them up all the way. The alarm blares again, startling me, and I find myself curled up on the floor with my knees to my chest and a sharp ache shooting up my spine. Elle's horns press into my sore legs. I have to stuff my fists in my pockets, a fragile imaginary line keeps me from putting my arm through the wall pressed against my back.

It's too dark, it's too small. I can't see, I can't breathe. I can't breathe, I can't. I can't stop my thoughts from racing and they ricochet too fast off the inside of my skull.

We're going to die. This hospital is about to explode with us in it and we're all going to *die*. And if that doesn't happen I'll suffocate in this tiny room. Elle won't have a chance to wake up if a bomb goes off now.

Somewhere between my own hyperventilating and speeding thoughts, I hear crackling.

A bomb. Do bombs crackle? No.

Sky is sitting beside me. His fingers are snapping, the rest of him is shaking. His eyes are wide and his lips are pressed together so hard they're white from lack of blood. He's snapping faster than any normal human being can. Someone's going to notice. That won't matter if we all die in the next seven seconds, but if we don't die that will be a problem.

"Sky." The word can't make it past my too-tight throat.

I pry my hand out of my pocket and reach out. My hand closes over his, muffling the snapping, then stopping it completely. Sky grips my hand. I feel him shaking into pieces right next to me. The alarm blares, and Sky jumps, his hand squeezes mine, I can't squeeze back for fear of crushing his bones.

"*Está bien*," I hiss like a deflating balloon. Spanish works better than English. "*Está bien, está bien*." Maybe if I keep telling him that it will come true.

Somewhere around the fifth alarm my skin falls off.

It's strange, losing myself when there's no one real attacking me. There have only ever been short moments before and after duels when I floated like this. Hollow and numb, save for the sense of being wound too tight.

Wherever the rest of me went, it took my thoughts with it. I'm sitting now with nothing except the aches and pains to fill my headspace. Sky's hand in mine acts as the only contact point between me and the real world.

Delilah says something, her voice sits in the air like film. I know it's there, but I can't hear it. She speaks again, Sky answers. Him I can hear.

"It's very very very very tight in here," followed by, "I know, Dels, I know. But I'm trying very hard not to cry right now, please just give me a bloody minute."

The bodies press in, blocking out all the air. My shins are more bruised with every touch, my knees ache harder with each passing brush of a finger. I turn into a cage around Elle. An unbreakable metal shield.

Two-point-nine.

They're crushing me.

Two-point-nine. The bodies clear out. It's better, but I can't move. My muscles are locked up. And I can't breathe. Air is entering my lungs, but it's not enough. There's not enough oxygen in this tiny tiny space. I'm going to suffocate. I'm going to die.

"Hello."

My name is Trick. My name is Trick. It's not working. I'm still hyperventilating. Still shivering. My name is—my name—

"Hello, can you look at me please?"

English. Someone is speaking English to me. Badly accented, but at least I can understand it. It takes effort, but I manage to pry my gaze off the floor and find the source of the voice. It's the woman with red hair from earlier, she's kneeling halfway across the empty room, staring at me. Her eyes are large and crystal blue.

"My name is Yana Karusev, what's yours?" she asks me.

"Trick—Sanchez-Fernandez," I answer, my breath hitches in my chest.

"How old you are, Trick?" Yana asks.

"Nineteen."

"What your favorite color?"

"I don't know."

"How about a favorite thing to touch? You have one of those?"

"I can't—breathe."

"You are having panic attack," she tells me. Is that what this is? It's awful.

"I'm claustrophobic." My voice won't rise above a whisper. My muscles are so rigid, clamping me into this balled-up position around Elle, that they all shake from the effort. Yana looks around the room, her short curls are pinned back with glinting bits of metal.

"Then this room is no good." She clucks her tongue.

"No." It's an unbearably tiny room. I hate it.

"Trick, focus. Take deep breaths." Her instruction forces me to become hyperaware of my rapid breathing.

"I can't," I gasp. My face is flushed, and my toes are numb, like all the blood in my body decided to defy gravity. "Can you— help—my sister?" I ask around periodic gulps for air.

"Is that who you're holding?" Yana asks.

Yes, and I'm afraid that I can't let go, and I need someone to pry her out of my arms before I crush her, and I can't say that because it's too many words for the thimble-sized bubble of air I'm sitting in.

"What your sister's name?"

"Elle," I answer.

"That is pretty name. You know her favorite color?" she asks.

I do. I think. It takes me some time to sift through a jumble of thoughts but I finally get to the answer.

"Indigo."

Yana nods, "A pretty color. She is younger or older than you?"

"Younger, she's thirteen."

"You are older brother then, protector, yes?" She doesn't know the half of it. I find my muscles are loosening, I can nod my head, albeit slowly. "You do good job. Can I see her?"

Yana reaches across the gap between her and I, her fingers hover closer to the scraped raw skin on the back of my arm, to grab, to pull, to pry. Someone else grabs her first, yanking her hand away.

"*Ne trogat'*," Delilah says, looming over Yana. She doesn't let go until Yana agrees. Yana folds her hands neatly in her lap, a smear of dirt on her otherwise clean skin. She doesn't have any scars.

"I know it is hard, but you try and let go. I look your sister. We see what is wrong," she says, slow and even.

Okay, let go. I have to let go. I can do that. With significant effort, I pry my arms from my knees and my knees from my chest, waves of pain roll over every bone in my body, and my old friend, the hot iron, is back with a force. I hiss out a groan, blinking to stop the room from swimming. The bruise on my chest feels more like a nasty dent.

"Maybe we should look you as well?" Yana suggests, closer now than she was before.

"Elle first." I shift Elle to face Yana, holding her head so it doesn't flop. I watch Yana's expression morph into open shock at the sight of the bundle of ashen skin and bones in my arms. She shakes her head, as if trying to clear it. With a glance at Delilah for permission, Yana takes Elle's limp wrist between her fingers.

"She does not wake up?"

"No."

"When did she pass out?"

"This afternoon."

Or yesterday. I don't know what time it is.

"She hit her head?"

"No, she's sick." The room begins to feel tight again.

Yana touches my shoulder lightly, laying Elle's hand in her lap. "I will get doctor and bed. Okay? You stay here a little longer, with your friend, I will come right back, okay?"

"Okay."

She retreats up the stairs, out of sight.

Out of the blue Delilah's hand is on my cheek, wiping away something wet and warm. A tear. I hadn't realized I was crying. And just like that, I snap back into myself.

I wipe the tears from my eyes. I wish I could pretend that they were never there to begin with. At least it's Delilah crouching in front of me, anyone else might have tried to say something nice. She only hovers there, one hand on my shoulder, until the moment passes and I can lift my head again.

"Where's Sky?"

Delilah grimaces, her uninjured shoulder shrugs up a couple of inches in reluctance.

"He's getting a head scan. The doctors are worried about his brain swelling," she answers.

"That sounds bad."

"It can be," Yana says, back sooner than I thought she'd be, a wrinkled old man at her heels. Delilah cuts them a sharp look.

"Shit," I swear. I run my fingers over the edge of the burn, then swear again. Can we not, for once, catch a break? Delilah doesn't try to offer a positive outlook. After so long, it's easier to be prepared for the worst than to be crushed when your hope doesn't follow through. Still, if Skyelar dies, I'll drag him back from the grave and kill him myself for putting us through that.

22 | All that's Left

The room they stick us in is quiet, save for the soft beep of machinery from the hall. I shake away the chill that goes through me. The space is too small. Blinds are drawn over the only window, thin rays of sunlight stream in past the spaces between the slats. There are two hospital beds, the one nearest the door is empty. Two chairs with cushions sit in the corners. Elle rests on the bed, chest rising and falling in time with the beeping of the heart monitor.

Someone hits the lights, bringing the room into sharp relief.

They've stripped Elle down to a hospital nightgown and an oxygen mask is secured over her face, opaque condensation clouds the translucent plastic with every exhale. Without the added padding of the sweaters, she looks unbearably thin.

Pain sears my chest, and I crawl up on the bed to kneel next to her. It hurts seeing her like this, worse than the chainsaw. It always has. I sit at the end of Elle's hospital bed and watch her heart monitor. The thin green line spikes and falls and spikes again and falls again.

Out of the corner of my eye, I glimpse Yana's red hair hovering near the IV pole. My skin prickles. Then Delilah appears behind her. Eight stitches, a bandage, and a sling holds her left arm in place, she has some nerve damage but I have no doubt she could put Yana through the window in a heartbeat if she tried anything fishy.

Yana has a tray full of plastic-encased medical tools. She rubs something into her hands and pulls on gloves. Plastic tears as she prepares the needle.

"What is she giving her?" I ask, I can hear the brittleness in my own voice. Both women look to me.

Turning to me, Yana switches to English.

"No worry, I don't know how to translate…" Yana slips back into Russian, turning back to Delilah.

"Delilah," I sound strangled. I feel strangled.

Spike, and fall. Spike. Fall. Spike.

"Liquid nutrients," Delilah answers.

Tension winds tighter and tighter over me. I've watched this same scene with Elle a thousand times. Latex-gloved hands, glinting needle points, Whitecoats handling her fragile skin. The needle sliding out. Delilah makes a small noise as the needle breaks Elle's skin. The cotton pad and bandage pressed over the bead of blood. I glance to the doorway—empty, to Delilah—she's facing the window, hunched over. I guess she doesn't like needles. Can't blame her.

The shivering is back—still there?—I run my thumb over the back of Elle's cold hand, watching the conversation. What I see when I lift my thumb makes my heart sink. A bruise is painted across her bony knuckles. I wasn't pressing that hard. I swear I wasn't. Flipping her arm, I look at the IV, and the dark purple bruise enveloping the crook of her elbow.

"What's happening to her?" I ask.

Yana reaches past me to take Elle's bruised arm. She examines it, a crease between her brows as she prods at the edges of the bruise. My heartbeat quickens as I follow her gaze to the newly forming bruise encircling Elle's upper arm, where the tourniquet had been tied. "Why don't we take history, it will help us help her."

She peels off her gloves and lays a soft hand on my shoulder. "It will be okay."

As if I could ever believe a lie like that. I slip off the bed, away from Elle so I can't bruise her anymore. Black crowds the edges of my vision for a minute, it doesn't quite fade away no matter how much I blink.

"Where you are here from?" she asks, "you do not look Russian."

"We're from Puerto Rico," I say.

The hospital around us buzzes with energy. The halls are full of people going every which way and that doesn't help with the way it feels like I'm swaying on a ship. I can't stop the glare that settles over my face when Yana doesn't back off fast enough.

"I'm so sorry. Were you traveling when it happened?" she asks, folding her hands together at her collar. I catch her gaze darting to the puffy pink scar tissue that creeps over the top of my shoulders.

"What do you mean?" I take a step back, reaching up to cover the edge of the scar. That whole area of my back is numb, not even the pins and needles spilling over the rest of my skin permeates the scar. Deeper down, where the muscle meets bone, hurts more than it used to though. I need painkillers.

"Were your parents at home? Is that why you and your sister are here alone?" she asks.

"At home for what? What happened?"

That seems to catch Yana by surprise, her brows draw together over her blue eyes. Her hands unravel from each other and slip into the pockets of her purple nurses' scrubs. "I think you should sit, please."

"No, tell me what's going on."

"You are sure?"

"Tell me."

"Trick, there is no more Puerto Rico."

Hm. I take my glasses off, clean them with the dirty hem of my shirt, and slide them back on with no hurry, stalling for time to figure out what she means.

"What?" I ask at last. Yana shakes her head, the bobby pins holding her hair back cling on, her hair sways with the motion.

With her lips downturned and a sheen of tears gathering in her eyes, she looks more upset than I feel.

"I will show you." She pulls a smooth, flat square from her pocket and taps on it. A news article appears on the screen, the block-lettered title all in Cyrillic. I reach back and tap Delilah. I need her to translate. She over my shoulder to squint at the report. I wince hard and resist the urge to fling her away. This is Delilah, she's not going to crush me. It's just Delilah.

At first she says nothing, then she takes the newstab from Yana and scrolls. The minutes of silence tick past, each one winding me tighter than the last. I watch her reach the bottom, and when she scrolls back to the top I know she's stalling. I should've kept my mouth shut. I duck my head to stare at the floor. My right shoulder cracks, the noise loud in the otherwise quiet room.

At last, she says, "The *Krovavaya Brigáda* bombed Puerto Rico six months ago, there were no survivors."

I think I do need to sit. I turn on my heels and walk away, the beat of my heart striking the dent in my breastbone too fast. There's nowhere to go except to the window, the walls are closing in and in and in. Nobody says a word for a long time. This new puzzle piece hangs in the air, absorbing into our pores, into our bones.

"I feel like I missed something." Sky's voice at the door makes us both jump. He leans heavily on the doorframe, as if he's seeing the world tilted. A clump of hair at the left side of his head is missing, the skin underneath split by a row of centipede-ish staples. "Look at you all, acting like I ran off without you," he quips, stumbling further into the room. He throws his arms out to steady his swaying, nearly knocking Delilah over the head as he does. She steps out of reach, narrowing her eyes at him.

"Should you be walking?" she asks.

"'Course not," he says without hesitation. "Any idiot can see that."

I catch him by the wrist, directing him towards the chair, "You must be a special kind of idiot then. Sit." Thankfully, he obliges with only a mild glare at me for the insult. Looking at him slouched in the chair, legs sprawled and fingers tapping the seat anxiously, I'm aware of how little we see him down. Compared to pretty much anyone at the Compound, he's a ray of sunshine.

"So, I'm not dying," he sighs, "just a major concussion."

"Don't act happy or anything." Delilah crosses her arms. He flaps his hand at her.

Eight stitches, a concussion, a bruised nose. It all seems a lot less fatal than it did last night. I perch on the edge of the empty bed, my gaze finding Elle. She's the only one who hasn't shown vast improvement in the last twelve hours. I need her to wake up, now more than ever. She's the only family I have left.

23 | Tattooed Over Scars

Delilah rouses me and shoos me off to the showers.

"You'll feel better," she says, "and I'll feel better because I won't have to smell you anymore."

The shower room is empty when I arrive. It's an echo-y space, rough yellow tile covers the floor and the lower half of the walls. A row of large mirrors lines the wall that separates the toilet stalls from the shower stalls, and a counter with sinks sits under the mirrors.

I don't recognize my reflection. My first reaction is to search the shower room for signs of someone else, the person the reflection really belongs to, but aside from me, the place is deserted. I push back all the doors to all the stalls, every last one creaks open to show an empty cubicle. No one is hiding in a corner, just out of sight, and when I poke my head out the main door, nobody who looks like the person in the mirror is there.

I return to the mirror, stand in front of it, stare. This isn't me. I raise my hand, the person in the mirror raises his hand. This isn't my face. I don't recognize this person. His black hair is greasy and lays flat, dried blood flakes off his chin and a black bruise dominates the bridge of his nose and his right cheekbone, square glasses settle below the bruise. I correct my glasses, wincing when they rub the bruise, the reflection mimics me.

"My name is Trick." My scratchy voice rings against the quietness of the bathroom. When I lower my hand I catch a glimpse of the reflection's shoulder. Puffy pink scar tissue shows, the burn from the grenade, mirroring where mine is. I touch the burn, and with my other hand reach out and touch the mirror. Little circles of condensation form around my fingertips.

How is this me? Why can't I recognize myself? What happened, what's wrong with me? What's wrong, what's wrong, what's—

I rip my hand from the mirror and turn away. My heart stutters and there's sweat on my forehead.

Reeling, I limp to the nearest shower stall. There's a hook on the stall door to hang the towel on, and a small metal bench for the clothes, I set my glasses on it too. A black contraption is anchored to the wall inside the shower itself. There's a small opaque window on the front, a word I can't make out without my glasses, and a lever near the bottom. When I press the lever, pink goo drizzles out and lands on the floor with a loud plop.

What the hell.

I press the lever again, this time sticking my hand out to catch the goo in my palm. It's slippery, and I swear I know what it is. I bring it to my nose to sniff it, it smells like Delilah did when she hugged me.

Liquid soap. That's what it is. I smear it on the wall and turn to the tap. I have been away from the real world for far too long. Water spurts from the tarnished showerhead, striking me like icy bullets. I don't bother to step out of the way, only turn around so it hits my back and lean my head against the cold tile wall.

What else don't I remember? Are there things that I won't ever remember because they don't exist anymore? The island doesn't exist anymore, not if what Yana says is true. My home is gone, bombed for no reason. My fist clenches, I press my knuckles to the wall.

My parents are gone too. I've spent so much of my life hating them for what they did, hell I've wished more than once that they died sad and alone. But now, after everything, the idea of them dead makes me feel even more like I'm adrift in a stormy sea. I don't want to want them back, but I do anyways.

I groan, the sound rising from somewhere deep in my gut and working its way loose. It's been growing there for a while. I resort to hooking my hands behind my neck to keep from punching something. This is all too much, too fast. There are too many things happening, too many things that need answers.

Where will Elle and I go after the hospital? We have no more home to turn to. How will we survive without money, without food, without shelter? How will we escape the reach of the Whitecoats and the military before they catch up to us? I can't find the answers, outside of the walls of this hospital, there are only blank spaces. "I'm nineteen."

Maverick would know what to do, he would have a plan.

"I have a sister."

I jab the soap lever. The water is scalding now, steam rises in thick clouds.

"I will find a way out of here."

I return to the room cleaner than I've been in two weeks. No dirt, no sweat, and no blood. It's an amazing feeling, and I'm glad Delilah convinced me to take a shower sooner rather than later. Everything still aches, but at least nothing itches or sticks. I pause to wipe the drops of water off my glasses, then enter.

Sky sleeps on the bed next to Elle's. Nothing else has changed, except the blinds are up and Delilah is standing in front of the window. Her good hand waves absently, gusts of wind swirl around the room as calm breezes. The sunlight streams in, and outside the window is the picture of a massive, sprawling city. Somehow, it doesn't make the space seem any bigger. Delilah looks lost in thought, so I leave her be, and drag a chair over to Elle's bed. The heart monitor beeps steadily, the best reassurance that Elle is alive. I take her cold hand in mine, trying to warm it up.

She's so still, even her skin doesn't shift.

The chair calls to me as a cramp hits my left thigh. It's been too long. I stop holding myself upright. One hand clutches my aching chest, the other presses into my forehead and I double over. I'm hot all over and my stomach roils. If not for the complete lack of food in me, I'd have vomited already. It feels like my intestines are made of white-hot metal rods. I hiss out a groan, my fingers curl tighter in my hair. My head throbs and I'm shaking now—this time it's not from a panic attack.

Breathe, in out, in out, slow breaths. In out, in out. In through the nose, out through the mouth. Try not to gag.

"Okay," I say to myself, "I'm good, I'm just gonna…" I straighten up slowly, bones pop all the way down my back. Ah, yeah, that hurts. Sighing, I lean over and rest my head on Elle's bed. Reaching up, I take her small hand in mine, her skin ripples faintly.

"Kiddo, it's time for you to wake up. There's a lot we need to talk about," I say, running my thumb over the bony back of her hand. "We're in a hospital now, they're working to get you better."

Pain lances through my breastbone, leaving me breathless. I rub my chest, grimacing. Hopefully they'll get me better too. This sucks. Bit by bit the edges are worn off the pain and my lungs start to work with only a dull ache. Able to breathe again, I talk to Elle. My gaze trains on her hand as I watch for signs that she's waking up. The patch of sunlight on the floor grows longer, then begins to dim, until there's nothing left but shadow. Delilah curls up on the chair in the corner and dozes off. Every now and then a nurse in lilac scrubs strides past, I whisper more quietly. There's something about talking to her that makes it easier to believe she'll come to.

Steadily, the dizziness and the aches grow worse, until my eyes burn and blur constantly and I can hardly see Elle's hand. There better be a bedpan nearby because I might end up puking regardless of how empty my stomach is. I'm certainly gagging enough. In the moments when my eyesight clears, I can see the beads of sweat forming on my outstretched arm. Still, I keep talking. I tell her about the city outside her window, and the flashing lights and shiny glass buildings that rise out of the ground like nothing she's ever seen before.

I tell her about Anushka and what the Sergeant did to help us rescue her, and about the little girl we met last night who is getting taken far away from danger right now.

And I tell her about the nurse who I hope isn't a Whitecoat.

"I think you'd—like her, as long as she doesn't end up—you know, evil." A sliver of moonlight has inched up over Elle's hand

"*Zradsti.*" Speak of the devil. Yana knocks on the doorframe once, twice before entering. "I come to check on you all, and I bring something for Elle she might like." She holds up a small glass bottle of indigo liquid. I don't see her initial reaction when she catches sight of my face but judging by what follows I don't think she expected to find me looking like death.

"What is wrong?" she asks, rushing into my field of vision. Her hand is on my forehead and her fingers are pressed into my neck before I can answer. Her touch is bruising but flinching away would hurt worse.

"Please don't touch me," I say, my voice hoarse from all the talking and the clenching in my chest. Immediately her hands retract, and she asks another question.

"Are you having panic attack?"

"No." I blink to clear away the now constant blur and manage to get a rough idea of her facial expression. It's not a happy one.

"What in hell's going on?" enter Sky, with an exclamation that makes my ears ring and my headache revolt. Oh well, good to know he's awake. He gets himself between Yana and me suspiciously fast. "What d'you think you're doing?"

"You are his friends? You tell me why he is ill so I can fix."

"Will you?" There's Delilah, sounding not at all convinced that Yana won't poison me.

"Guys," I croak from my seat. I understand where they're coming from better than anyone in this hospital, in this entire city. But right now, I need either painkillers or for everyone to shut up and leave. Sky, nearest to me, catches on.

"It's a pain thing, fibro-something, he needs painkillers," he says.

"Savella," I wheeze through gritted teeth. "I'm supposed to be on Savella for fibromyalgia. Is there somewhere I can get that here?"

"I will go see the pharmacy," Yana promises. She leaves, and I almost melt from relief at the idea of getting back on my meds, until an idiot pats me on the back.

"Ow, Sky," I mutter, scrunching my eyes shut.

"Sorry, sorry," he apologizes, "don't mean to make your dying worse."

"M'not dying."

"Sure, sure, you just look like a grim reaper used you as a punching bag." There's mirth in his tone, but there's also a waver that gets to me. The teasing on its own is fine, but I wish he wouldn't worry. I've been living with this for years, he's the one who cracked his head open yesterday trying to save my sister. I should be worrying about him.

Thankfully, Yana returns not long after. She hands me a tiny paper cup with two pills in it, and I swallow them both dry. One of them I suspect is Tylenol, and the other tastes like chalk. Now it's just a matter of waiting it out. Through bleary eyes I watch Yana lean over to check on Elle.

"What was that thing you brought?" I ask.

"Ah." She pulls the small glass bottle from her pocket and holds it out to show us. Viscous liquid, a deep shade of indigo shimmers in the lowlight. "Nail polish."

She lets me take it, turn it over, shake it. It's enchanting to watch swirl, it tugs my mind away from the all-consuming pain vortex just a little. Elle would love the color. "What does it do?"

"I show you."

She takes the bottle back and unscrews the top. First, she explains the polish, showing us all how it works. Then, as the night stretches on and she paints Elle's nails, the topics drift to other things. Delilah asks questions, and Yana seems more than happy to answer. Sometimes they slip into Russian but they both always bring it back to English for Sky and me. For the most part, though, we fill the space with idle chit chat. I don't know why she's bothering, I don't know why she brought the nail polish. I don't know if I trust whatever this is, but I can't convince myself to hate the way it smooths the sharp edges of tension filling up the room. Not completely.

The night takes a turn towards morning, the paint is dried and the conversation is drifting more and more into Russian. I pick up Elle's hand. The paint looks different dry, shinier. As I'm watching, the indigo on her pointer finger pools on the nail bed and drips down the side. I swipe at it, and Yana tuts.

"How I miss that," she frowns at the smear of color. I cover it, heart thrumming. My thumb came away bone dry, there is no paint dripping off Elle's fingernail. "No worry, I bring something to clean it tomorrow."

"Don't worry about it," I say, too fast. Delilah cuts me a sharp look. Her gaze drops to Elle, realization snapping into place.

"Is there a computer I could use in this place?" she asks, snagging Yana attention.

"Oh, *da*," Yana answers.

"Will you show me where it is?" Delilah slips off the bed. Moving towards the door, she invites Yana farther away from the danger of finding us out. "I know it's late, I'm sorry, if it's too late—"

But Yana is cutting her off with a dismissive flick of her hands, "No worry, we will sneak." She adds a conspiratorial wink, and hurries Delilah out the door. Out of sight. Away from Elle.

The moment their voices fade into the distance I tear my hand away from Elle's to check for the colors. Hope fluxes through me, a living thing. I saw it, I swear I saw it. A full minute passes with nothing but the muted beeps of the heart monitor and the wheezing of the oxygen machine. Her skin is as still as it was before and I begin to wonder if that smear really is dried paint. It's too easy to see how I could have imagined it. Didn't I hallucinate quicksand only a few days ago? I'm barely in better shape now. I feel myself deflate, so much worse because I believed for a moment that she was actually waking up.

There's a conciliatory hand on my back. I stand there, staring, for a moment longer. Searching for a sign. My fingers curl in the sheets, scrunching the course fabric like it's a lifeline.

Then, a ripple spreads up her skin. It starts in her fingers, a washed-out purple, and spreads up and out, one thin line of color crawling all over her. When it hits her head, her eyelids flutter.

"Elle?" I stoop, ignoring the ache in my shoulders that comes from bending like that. Her eyelids stop fluttering, and for a second I'm perched precariously on the edge of a blade, with no room to inhale for fear of pushing the steel through my skin.

Her eyes open.

The blade vanishes as relief washes over me. "*Buenas dias,* sleepyhead," I breathe, reaching out to squeeze her hand. She regards me from behind half-closed eyelids, a weak smile lifts the corners of her chapped lips, only to be pressed down by the oxygen mask. Confusion wrinkles in the corners of her eyes. She lifts her free hand to touch the mask and her gaze darts over the parts of the room she can see. As she begins to recognize her environment, her heart rate on the monitor spikes.

"It's okay. We're not at the Compound," I say hurriedly, "we got out, remember? Look, Sky's here too, and Delilah, we're all okay." That seems to calm her. More so when Sky pokes his head over my shoulder.

"Had a good nap?" he asks. Elle tries to answer, but her voice is muffled by the mask. She paws at it, her fingers forming weak half-claws as she makes every effort to get the plastic over the end of her nose. I tug it off for her, leaving it dangling around her neck.

"Yes," she whispers, her voice is hoarse and airy. She looks around some more, regaining more strength by the second. "*¿Dondé esta?*"

"A hospital, in a city," I answer. I shift my weight so I'm not leaning on my arm and start asking questions. "How do you feel? How's your head?" I press the back of my hand to her forehead. Her eyes are clear of the fever-haze. In fact, they're clearer than they've been in a long time.

"Trick," she rasps, clutching my hand with her cold one. "I'm going to die."

"No, you're not." I withdraw my hand from her head. "You'll be fine. You're already doing better."

"My wings," she mumbles, her bright eyes, sunken in shadows, drift closed for a long minute. As if it's taking all the energy she has to focus.

"Do your horns hurt?" I ask. They've never bothered her before, but she's been laying on them for a day now. She shakes her head once to either side, webs of heavy purple veins stretch across her eyelids from the ridge of her brow to the ledge of her cheekbones, holding them shut.

"I had wings once," she murmurs, a furrow appearing over her eyes. "*Recuerdo*, they hurt."

My heart drops down to my toes. I thought she couldn't remember that, Mav told me that all her memories from back then were too fuzzy to read. She licks her lips with a dry tongue. "I think my bones are too heavy to fly. If I got my wings back I would just fall and die."

I straighten up abruptly, pulling away from her. Why is she talking like this? She's not going to die. She's not. She's fine now, she's awake and she's going to get better with the right medicine. I run my fingers over the edge of the burn scar. This new version of Elle scares me.

"Elle…"

"*No ahora*," she whispers, the webbed veins weighing her eyelids down again. "*Estoy cansado.*"

"Okay," I replace the oxygen mask on her thin face. She's out by the time I finish adjusting the straps. Asleep so soon after waking up. But at least she woke up, I tell myself, and she'll do it again.

Towards the end of the night, the pain has uncoiled enough to let exhaustion squeeze in. The noises of the hospital become distant and blurry, fading away into a thin nothing-buzz as I get dragged down into sleep, too.

Late in the afternoon the next day, I find myself alone in the room with Elle and Sky while Delilah is away with Yana. Elle is awake, staring out the window at the city. Sky lays on the bed, one arm over his eyes, pretending to be asleep while I attempt to paint Elle's toenails with the indigo nail polish Yana left behind. She made it look so easy yesterday, but the sheer amount of precision it takes to get this stuff on only the nail is insane. Already there are drops of purple on the sheets and smears of it on the sides of Elle's toes. The brush is too tiny, and my hands shake too much. I'll have to practice some more, maybe Sky will let me do his.

"Hey, you want some nail polish?" I ask, not looking up. Sliding the brush across Elle's third toe, I silently rejoice when the polish leaves neither drip nor smear. Then a blob from the brush drips off and ruins the paint job.

When Sky doesn't answer, I glance up, the paintbrush poised over the next toe. "I know you're awake."

"You don't," is his muffled reply.

"Your hand is twitching," I say, turning back to the nail polish. I don't have to see him to know I'm right. The sound of his fingers snapping together rises above the beeps of the heart monitor, and he doesn't do that when he's asleep.

"Put the polish on my other hand then," he fires back, flopping his arm across the bed and tilting his head to look at me. "So how about that nurse?"

"Yana? What about her?"

"I think you have a crush on her."

This time the smear on Elle's toes doesn't come from shaky hands. I wipe at it with the pad of my thumb and only succeed in making it worse. "I don't know what that is."

"Oh, come on. You like her, admit it," he scoffs. I catch a glimpse of his conspiratorial grin out of the corner of my eye. I frown and shake my head, focusing harder on putting the paint where it's supposed to go.

"You have a concussion," I mutter.

"You have a crush," he repeats, sitting up.

"Stop saying that." I shoot a glare at him. Paint is glistening on Elle's toe. I stick the brush back in its bottle and give it a couple quick twists. The hard plastic cap cracks in two with a startling pop.

"Ice out mate, have some fun." He hops up to stand on the edge of the bed. His hair sticks up in all directions, almost hiding the bald spot. He snaps his fingers and points to Elle when she turns her head to look at him. He holds up his cupped hands. He has something, and he won't tell us what. He's been sneaking around with it in his pocket all day, only taking it out when he knows we can't see it. He's made a game of getting us guessing. I suspect he stole it, since there's no other way he could have gotten ahold of anything, but I don't know what he was stupid enough to steal.

"Is it a pencil or a pen?" Elle asks, propping herself up on her hoard of pillows. Her skin stays cool and her grip on reality is as solid as ever, it's all too easy to believe that she's improving. But there's a tray of food resting precariously on the bedside table, no different from when the nurse brought it in this morning, except that all of the foods have been mashed up and pushed around. She hasn't eaten a bite since she woke up yesterday and shows no interest in trying.

"Neither. Trick?"

"This is serious." I set the bottle of polish to the side and scoot off the bed so I don't accidentally smear more paint all over the place. There is a worldwide war going on right outside this hospital, no one has time for games or crushes, least of all us.

Sky shrugs teetering across the bed like it's a balance beam. "I agree. I mean, she's a bit older and way out of your league, but less possible things have happened."

"*Es esto?*" Elle holds out her hands, wiggling her fingers to show off the shiny indigo paint.

"Nah."

She stops wiggling her fingers but leaves her hands spread out in front of her. Light from the open window glints off the paint, the sheen is captivating. Elle tips her hands to get a better look at the paint, examining each nail with intense curiosity, as if she's noticing it for the first time. "What is this?" she asks, looking to me for answers. This is the second time she's asked, her memory hasn't been the best since she woke up.

"It's *pintar,*" I answer, for lack of a better explanation. She scrunches her nose, looking closer at her nails.

"Like what they put on walls?"

"Kind of, but made for fingernails." It's not the most eloquent way to say it, but it works. Sort of.

"And toenails?" She tilts her head, laying her hands on the bed.

I nod, "Yeah, toenails too."

"Oh, okay." She purses her lips, head still tilted. I can tell she still has a lot of questions, but instead of asking them she drums her fingers and watches the pattern of light across her purple nails shift. Her eyelids droop and her chin rests heavily on her shoulder. She's so tired for someone so young.

That's all right, I tell myself, she's got her whole life ahead of her to get up and go out and learn more about nail paint. As soon as she kicks this sickness we'll get out of here and find some way to live a normal life. I don't know how, but I'll find a way.

A disgruntled squawk from Sky shakes me out of my thoughts. I look over in time to see a newly returned Delilah scooting out of Sky's reach, his prized stolen item raised triumphantly in her hand.

"This is what you've been hiding? A toy?" She's tied her hair back into a tight braid, save for a few stray strands that float over her eyes and tickle her ears. She holds a tiny plastic man pinched between her finger and thumb, raising her eyebrows at it. The tiny man is orange and stands with both arms up by his face in a fighting stance, his paint is chipped in several places. Fortunately, Elle is distracted by a bird perched outside on the windowsill and misses the reveal.

"Give it back, you thieving mongrel." Sky jumps off the bed. He lands with a soft thud, snatching the plastic man away from Delilah. "Trick has a crush."

"On the nurse?" Delilah guesses, as if this is no news to her.

"I do not."

"He does."

"Skyelar." She sighs a full-body kind of sigh, and I can practically see her restraining herself from rolling her eyes. She catches me narrowing my eyes at her and lifts one shoulder in a half-hearted shrug.

"Hey Trick, any chance you're going to tell her?"

"Shut up."

"Are you doing alright?" Delilah pauses at my side, her hand is on my elbow, the touch just light enough to stay on this side of bearable. I can feel the Savella seeping through my body, dulling the effects of the fibro. It's not enough yet for the sand between my joints to be gone, or the creaking of my bones to stop, but the worst of the pain is controlled.

"Fine," I say when I finally work the words up from my belly. "Elle is getting better, everything will be fine."

"Good," she says, her gaze lingering on me for a moment longer. I can see uncertainty swimming behind her eyes, but we both choose to ignore it. She retreats to her chair in the corner by the window, digging a newstab from her pants pocket. Looks like Sky's tiny plastic man isn't the only thing she's stolen today.

"Why did you lie to them?" Elle's whispery voice startles me. "Trick, *¿por que mentiste?*"

She's sitting up in bed for the first time since she's woken up. The oxygen mask lays discarded at her side and her chapped lips press together in a thin line.

"I didn't," I answer. It's the truth, with all the advancements science has made, it should be no problem for the doctors to cure her. After all, look at what they turned us into. If they can give Elle the ability to change the pattern of her skin at will, they can sure as hell make her better.

Elle nibbles on the corner of her lip, looking unsure. I walk over and perch on the edge of her bed with one leg propped up and the other bouncing on the tile. "You'll get better," I promise, brushing a hair off of her narrow shoulder.

"*¿Cómo?*" she asks, hugging her knees to her chest. The indigo on her fingers has flushed up to her hands, I watch it creep farther up her arm.

"The doctors will help you," I answer.

"What if they hurt me instead?" the purple races up her arm, overflowing onto her neck and pooling in the crevices over her collarbones.

"I'll make sure they don't." I'll be there this time, I can ask questions and get Delilah to translate the labels on whatever medicine they give her. I won't leave her alone with any nurses or doctors. This time I'll get it right, this time she will get the treatment she needs.

Elle considers this for a moment, her chin dipping to rest on her kneecaps. Then her lower lip begins to tremble ever so faintly. She bites it hard enough to split her dry skin, bringing tears rushing to her eyes. It keeps trembling anyways, and she sniffles to hold back the tears.

"Woah, hey, what's wrong?" I lean forward, my forehead creasing. Delilah rises halfway but I shake my head at her. Nobody else can see Elle like this.

The colors come first. Thin lines of navy and black leak out the corners of her eyes, and spill down to her chin. Two swatches of soft yellow and pink streak either of her cheeks, swirling all the way up to her temples. She lifts her purple hands to wipe at her eyes and they come away wet.

"You're a good brother," she mumbles, red bleeding out of her mouth. I can't tell if it's blood from her cracked lip or a new shade from her shifting skin.

"Is that a bad thing?" I ask, forcing a smile onto my face in a poor attempt to lighten the mood. I have never seen her act this way before. She holds her hands out to me, flattening her legs to make way for my hug. I scoop her up, doing my best to avoid the IV lines, and hold her as tightly as I dare. She weighs nothing, I could crush her as easily as I snapped the lid of that nail polish, I could never forgive myself if I did. She burrows her face in my shirt, her arms pulsing red and gold and purple. A choked sob escapes her, followed by her muffled, barely coherent reply.

"I'll miss you."

The floodgates open for real now, she cries so hard she shakes. The colors are frantic, taking on forms, running into each other, bumping around between her tendons and veins like madmen. Her breaths begin to rasp and wheeze on their way through her lungs. It sounds like she's sucking air from a leaky straw, I think she should put her oxygen mask on before she drowns in her tears.

When I reach for it, she clutches me harder and shakes her head. A string of mumbly noises comes from her open mouth, but she's sobbing too hard for the words to form. Okay, she doesn't need it right away. I settle back, resting my cheek on her head, and rubbing circles on her back. The ridge of her spine juts out too far, and I can feel each individual rib my hand passes over.

The minutes pass marked only by the heart monitor and her dwindling sobs. Her shivering muscles relax as she loses energy, and she sags against me. Delilah watches us out of the corners of her eyes. Sky perches like a bird on the chair, his sneakers on the floor and his bare toes dig into the worn cushion for balance. He doesn't seem to be doing anything, just staring at the floor with the knuckles of his left hand pressed to his teeth. We all watch the door, strung on a razor-thin trip wire. I don't know how long it is before I suggest she lays down. She tenses at that, shakes her head again, but it's obvious she's barely holding on.

"Just for a while, you don't have to sleep, just lay down," I bargain, staring at the tendril of green that loops lazily around a shock of blue on her wrist.

"No, I don't want you to leave." She sniffles into my chest.

"If I lay down, will you?"

There is a beat of silence, save for her congested breathing, then she nods. Okay then, that will work. I heft myself the rest of the way onto the bed and ease onto my back. Her head now rests on my shoulder, my arm is hooked under her, and she finally relaxes. It's ages before she calms down enough to sleep, but eventually, she gets there. The last of the tears ebb, and not long after a quiet snore squeezes out.

Good. After all that, it's no wonder she's exhausted.

This isn't the first time she's cried herself to sleep. There were nights when the Whitecoats came banging on my cell door and dragged me off to stay with her because it was the only way to calm her down. There were nights when the Whitecoats had to do the same for me, a snotty thirteen-year-old screaming until they brought Elle to me.

"*Tengo miedo*," she whispers, startling me.

"You're supposed to be asleep," I remind her. Her eyes are barely open, swollen and red from all the crying.

"I'm scared," she repeats in English, quieter.

"You don't need to be," I say reassuringly, giving her shoulder a comforting squeeze. She tilts her head to see my face.

"*¿Promesa?*" she breathes. The blue and navy streaks from earlier are stained to her face, pools of the colors rest stationary all along her jaw and chin.

"*Prometa.*"

She settles down again, but not for long. Right when I think she's fallen asleep for good, she speaks up.

"Trick," she murmurs, sleep making her words slow and heavy, "*Te amo.*"

"*Yo también te amo*, Elle," I say, planting a kiss on the top of her head. A minute passes, then another, and ten more. After fifteen, I know she's asleep for real.

"Trick."

"Hm?" I blink, and for a moment I forget where I am. This is not the infirmary, the walls are the wrong color, the machines make the wrong noise. I blink again, and the pieces fall back into place. Yana stands in the doorway. A gentle smile lifts the corners of her lips, and a dimple appears on her chin that I hadn't noticed before. A ray of dying light from the window catches her across the face, shining over her left eye and rendering it a lighter shade of blue than the other. For a brief moment before everything collapses, all I can think is; if things change, could we be friends?

Then she catches sight of Elle and all the brilliant swaths of colors drenching her, and the moment shatters. Yana stops dead, the smile dropping off her face, replaced by a string of Russian that sounds suspiciously like cuss words. A file folder that I hadn't seen falls from her hand and explodes all over the floor with a startling bang.

Damn it. Before she can even begin to form the right questions, I know that this is the end of whatever safety we had here.

My heart is in my throat as I realize that after all that's happened, after all the running, and the fighting, and the death, we're getting dragged back down by a little bad timing.

"What this is?" Yana demands, the file folder and its contents lay forgotten on the floor. She reaches to touch Elle, and on instinct I lurch to stop her. My fingers close around Yana's wrist too tight, wrenching a startled cry from her. I let go as soon as I realize what's happening, but not soon enough to take back the damage.

She staggers back, holding her injured wrist gingerly. Pain contorts her face for a brief moment, and ugly red marks are rising in stark contrast to her smooth skin.

"I'm sorry." The apology tumbles out, I'm already rising, untangling myself from Elle. "Did I hurt you?"

"It's fine," she lies, tugging the sleeve of her scrubs up to hide the bruise. A neutral mask replaces her pain as she blinks away any tears that may have welled up. "You must tell me where you are from."

There are alarms going off in my head and a sinking pit in my stomach. That was wrong, she was defenseless, I shouldn't have squeezed so hard. There is something wrong with me. I find my feet, ignoring the pins and needles that all-too-happily dig into my calves, but I don't dare get closer to her.

"Puerto Rico, I told you," I answer.

"No, where you were before you came to hospital," she snaps, but there's no edge to it. I open my mouth, but nothing comes out and I can't find a voice to fill in the blank. There's no good way to put this, and certainly not one that will convince her to keep this all to herself. When the silence stretches on for too long, Yana decides to ask a different question.

"There were reports last week of America attacking a private warehouse near here, was that you?"

The fear in her is a raw and powerful thing, spitting from her mouth like acid. The pit in my stomach grows too fast to hold, the fear in me could squash a mountain if it could escape. Bands tighten around my chest, choking away my ability to speak, but that's okay because I can't get my brain unstuck anyways.

She spins on her squeaky sneakers and storms out the door to go report us to the authorities. To tell them we're secret American spies. To tell them to throw us in jail and take away Elle's medical care.

Skyelar slams the door, in front of her in a heartbeat. The doorframe bends from the force. She stumbles back, smacking into Delilah, who pins her arms behind her.

"Wait, wait!" My voice rams back into me, "let her go."

Instead Delilah drags her farther from the door. "She'll tell someone."

"There's a security guard coming," Sky hisses from the doorway. We're done if a guard catches us manhandling Yana. She watches us with wide eyes, body taut, her breath caught in her chest. She has the look of a trapped animal ready to bolt. The guard is getting closer, and my chest is heaving, and my toes are going numb. It's too late for secrets now.

I catch Yana's eyes and blurt, "the warehouse the Americans attacked was a laboratory full of kidnapped kids and if you tell anyone they're going to come and drag us back and kill us!"

The guard knocks on the door once. Opening it, he pokes his head into take in the scene. There's Sky perched on a chair, bracing to keep it from slamming back down on all four legs. Delilah with her hands locked behind her back. And Yana, standing over the scattered papers of the file she dropped. One word, and she could kill us.

The guard asks a question, she answers, and I swear the room turns into a vacuum.

How long do we have until the Compound comes for us? Days? Hours? I'm well and truly hyperventilating now, shaking, images of Dieter and his broken teeth and bubbled skin burn my retinas every time I blink. That's what the Whitecoats will do to me. That's what they'll do to Elle.

"Us?" Yana's question squeezes past the white noise. I look up, sometime in the last few seconds I ducked my head and pressed both hands to the back of my neck. She stands with her back to the door, staring at me.

"Experiments." Is all I manage to get out on the first try. I clear my throat, work my jaw, and try again. "Elle, and Sky, and Delilah, and I, were all taken to be experiments. There were a lot more of us but…" I trail off, unable and unwilling to finish the sentence. "When the attack happened, some of us escaped and came here. I don't know who caused the attack, but it wasn't us, and if you tell anyone we're here the Whitecoats will come and take us back."

And that can't happen.

"What you mean, *experiments*?"

"You saw Elle's skin," I say. She tucks a curl behind her ear and smooths it down, a motion that seems like it's meant for herself, her hand hovering even after her hair is set perfectly in place.

"How do I know you are not lying?" she says at last. "You all could be experiments made by the Americans to destroy our country."

Sky makes a rude noise.

"Elle is thirteen, and she can barely stand on her own."

"You could have kidnapped her," Yana argues, but she's sounding less and less convinced. Her anger is petering out, leaving room for the gears in her head to turn.

"For what?"

She folds her arms over her chest, being careful not to bump her bruised wrist. "*Ladno*, I believe you, but I want to know more."

We close the door again, shutting the rest of the hospital out, and settle down for what I know is going to be an awful talk.

Yana on the chair, and me and Sky and Delilah on the edge of the empty bed. We talk for hours. Sometimes I stop because the words vanish and my head spins, and when that happens Delilah fills in, or Sky. She doesn't get the entire story, but she gets enough that she can fill in all the gaps on her own.

At the end, none of us say anything, and Yana can't look me in the eye. She stands, smooths the wrinkles out of the front of her shirt, looks at Elle. The expression on her face is indecipherable, some cross between thoughtful and deeply sad and a fight not to show either.

"You should go to the news with this, tell them this that you told me," she says, still staring at Elle.

"What?" Shock ripples through me, kicking me to my feet.

"The people of Russia do not want this fight, but there are not enough of us standing against the government to do anything. You could get more people to rise up, you could help end the war."

"That would expose us to the Whitecoats." I nix the idea. This is not my war to fight, the only thing I can afford to focus on is keeping Elle and the others safe. Nothing can put that in jeopardy.

"We give you safety, keep you guarded here at the hospital," Yana pushes. She's drawn herself up straight and squared her shoulders. She reminds me of Delilah like this; determined and fierce. Of course, considering King could floor this entire hospital on his own, her offer isn't very convincing.

Sky tilts his head, considering her suggestion. She takes this as a sign to press on. "They have tools to spread the word across the nation, a story like this would rally the people against the Bloody Brigade."

"It's also dangerous." I interject.

"For you," Sky says, "I could go to the reporters, agree to meet them somewhere else. Hell, I could meet reporters all over the place, take the Whitecoats on a goose chase and keep them away from the hospital."

"And if they catch up to you?" I argue, but I'm grasping at straws. Sky bursts out laughing, it sounds a touch deranged.

"Right, they're going to catch me," he scoffs, then he catches the genuine concern on Yana's face. Clearing his throat, he sticks his hand out to her, "Skyelar Jones, Enhanced speed," he says, cracking a grin.

"Oh." Yana shakes his hand, the crease over her nose smoothing out. "Yana Karusev, normal nurse."

"Trick thinks you're a bit better than normal." He wiggles his eyebrows, the grin on his face turning mischievous.

"*Sky*." The only thing preventing me from smacking him is the idea that it might send him into the wall. And even that doesn't seem too bad at the moment. The growl works well enough though, and Sky has the good sense to duck his head and look the slightest bit sorry when he slides out of reach.

Delilah speaks up then, "what if it was just one reporter, and we knew that we could trust her."

"Yeah, right, let me pull one out my arse," Sky laughs, Delilah doesn't. The laughter fades from the air, "you mean it?"

Delilah takes her stolen newstab out. Casting a semi-guilty glance at Yana she says, "I was going to give it back."

Then she clicks it on and swipes the screen. An image capture zoomed-in on the article Yana showed us the first day we were here comes up. Delilah lingers on it. She clears her throat before speaking.

"I thought it was a coincidence, but Yana helped me do some research," she starts, flicking to a capture of a news site. The room waits, breath held. "My sister wrote that article. She's a political journalist and she lives here."

Sky flings his hands in the air, a huge smile cracks his face, "Dels, you found her!" He throws his arms around her, crushing her in a hug. A weak smile lifts the corners of her mouth.

"She doesn't know yet," she says.

"Well let's go meet her, tonight!"

Delilah hesitates, the smile fading into a ghost as she shrinks into herself. "I don't know, it's been so long, and so much has happened…"

"So?" Sky peels himself away from her, bright with excitement.

"So, what if I'm a monster to her now?"

There's a beat of silence, and Delilah blinks fast, rolling her eyes to the ceiling. In the dim light of the outside fluorescents, it's hard to see her as the woman who crushed a man to death. As Delilah the Wind Witch rather than Delilah my friend. I glance at Elle, skin rippling on the hospital bed. I can't imagine seeing her as a monster.

"Then you come back, and we figure it out from there," I say. It's not comforting, but I'm not a comforting person and Delilah isn't the type to want coddling.

She exhales. One more breath, and the moment of fragility is gone. "Okay, okay. Let's go."

Sky loops his arm through hers. "Right now?"

"Right now." She takes the newstab again, and flicks to a capture of a map.

"Perfect,'" he pauses just long enough to skim the map and glance between me and Yana. "You'll be right?"

"We're fine," I say, "go."

"Be right back." And he's gone with Delilah in the blink of an eye.

Yana lingers a few moments longer. She takes the time to adjust one of Elle's IV bags and check her heart monitor. In all the commotion of the past few hours, the hair that she so carefully tucked into place earlier is loose again. I realize I'm staring, and occupy my eyes and hands with retrieving Savella from my new prescription bottle to keep from giving in. This dose is a few minutes late, but that won't screw with my insides too much. I hope.

Two little pills go down the hatch. The pills themselves are a lower dose than the ones from the Compound, at least, according to the tiny number stamped on their sides. But with two together it makes for a higher dose than before, and it's working well.

I set the pill bottle down and turn in time to catch Yana watching me. It is inconveniently then that I remember I'm only meant to take two per day, not two per dose. Yana doesn't comment, and she looks away so fast I'm almost worried she's going to give herself whiplash.

"I will go now." She brushes that loose strand of hair back and hurries towards the exit, when she reaches the door she pauses, delicate hand resting on the dent in the metal frame. She doesn't look up. "I will come back and help. Whatever you choose, tell or not tell, I am on your side."

And with that, she's gone. The tip of her heel vanishes around the corner leaving the space she occupied empty.

"Thank you," I say to the sound of her receding footsteps.

Then it's just me and Elle. She's out cold, snoring faintly. The hospital could be collapsing and she would keep on snoring. I grimace, reaching out to pull the blankets up around her chin. That isn't the most comforting thought to have at the moment. Her hair is tousled, tears from earlier dried a few dark curls to her cheek, and the wild colors have faded out completely. But the dark circles around her eyes look lighter, and for the first time in ages, the tint of her dreams is soaking into her skin.

Grey. I lift her arm to get a closer look at the faint dappling of color. It doesn't match the sheets or the pillow, and while it could come from the silvery needles in her veins, I prefer to imagine it's from her dreams. Grey isn't what I would call a dreamy color, it's not even particularly pretty, but it is calming.

I sigh and turn away. Taking the chair, I amble over to the door and set up what will be my guard station for the rest of the night. As I curl myself into the chair to wait, an old, old tune worms its way out of the caverns of my memory. I can't place where it's from.

The sun is set by now, the night is well on its way and the hospital is settling down. This floor is never busy, at least, not as busy as the ground floor, and at night it is even quieter. I can hear a machine beeping somewhere down the hall and the soft patter of a nurse's shoes before she passes the door. She tips her head in acknowledgement as she strolls past, I wave back.

At some point, as time lumbers on, I start to hum the tune. It's a lullaby, I think, an old one. Something our *abuela* sang to put us to sleep, and something I sang to Elle during our first nights at the Compound. I can't remember the words anymore, but the melody is there.

I tilt my head to look at Elle, her chest rises and falls, her breath fogs the oxygen mask and her heartbeat pulsing from the monitor creates a matching tempo with the lullaby. I wonder why it's stuck in my head after all this time. I'll have to hum it to her when she wakes up and see if she remembers how it goes.

I wake up to the soft refrains of the lullaby being chased out of my head by a high-pitched keening noise. Sludge sticks to the inside of my skull. From the exhaustion, from adjusting back onto the meds. I wobble when I jump to my feet, too flustered to tell where the sound is coming from.

One of the machines.

One of Elle's machines.

A stampede bursts through the door, an old man leading the way at a run. The lights spring to life, searing my eyes with fluorescent laser rays. Whitecoats. My heart seizes.

But no, the old man in lead is dressed in toothpaste green scrubs, like Yana. Nurses bundle in with a cart. One of them presses me away from Elle's bedside. I fling her back. She hits the wall with a thud and a shriek and immediately the old man hits a button on the wall.

"What's happening?" I demand.

The last remaining nurse is climbing onto the bed, straddling Elle's listless form, and pressing her hands to Elle's chest.

All the blood drains out of the bottoms of my feet.

Two barrel-chested men appear in the doorway. The one in front points a finger at me and says something I wouldn't be able to understand even if I did know Russian. Elle's heart monitor displays a thin flat line. One of the barrel-chests grabs me and pulls me toward the door. My body moves out of sync with the rest of the world. Stuck in place. All I can do is watch.

The woman jumps off Elle while a younger man pulls the sheets out of the way. There's too much happening at once to keep track of it all. The heart monitor is screaming, one of the scrubs is wrestling with the oxygen mask, another is yanking a red carrier from the cart and throwing it open.

The mustached scrub grabs a pair of floppy white squares, shouts an order, and presses them to Elle's chest. Elle arches hard, then falls limp. Dull ringing fills my ears.

"Come on, Elle, come one," I say, but I can't hear myself so maybe I only say it in my head. This could be all in my head, I could be asleep. I pinch myself. The pain is sharp and brief but it does nothing.

Again, she jerks and falls limp.

Again.

Again. I pinch myself a second time, a third time. I want to wake up, I want to open my eyes and find that none of this is real. But no matter how many bruises I leave on my arm, the scene stays the same.

After the fifth try, the mustached scrub jabs at the red carrier and the woman climbs up to restart chest compressions. The green line on the monitor carries on, and I stare at it, willing it to spike. But it doesn't.

And it doesn't.

And it doesn't.

The woman stops her chest compressions, and I lunge forward, begging them to keep going. She flinches away, afraid that I'll fling her into a wall too. Both barrel-chests wrench me back.

Don't let my sister die. Don't let Elle die. I'll do anything, I'll take her place, please, don't let her die. Please, please, please no.

The mustached man grips me by both arms, looks me in the eyes, says, "Her time of death, three forty-nine a.m. I am sorry."

If I stay upright, it is only by some miracle of physics. The world switches off. It is pitch black and dead silent for an endless, dragged-out moment. I blink, and it all returns with a force. The scrubs are gone and with them the machines. The sheet is smoothed out and pulled up over Elle's face.

I drag myself to the edge of her bed. I pinch the edge of the sheet with trembling hands and tug it down. She looks tiny without the machines. Blocked-up sobs squeeze my throat shut, unshed tears blind me, the shakes wrack my entire being.

She can't be gone. She isn't. It's not possible. She was awake earlier, she woke up, she was doing better. I run my thumb across her forehead and nothing happens. There's no shift, there's no color to her skin at all, only a bloodless kind of pale.

"No." I back away, terror crawling under every inch of skin.

I hit the other bed, the force knocks me to my knees. A scream rips out of my chest as I slam both fists into the concrete floor. Dust explodes around us, the building shakes and the floor crumbles into a valley of bent rebar and broken concrete.

Shattered bits of floor stick to the side of my hands like splinters, a broken chunk of rebar tears a ragged hole in my pants. No, no, not Elle. Please not Elle, please. Bring her back, let me take her place. Let me die instead, not Elle. Not now.

Stinging dust fills the air. I cough hard, standing and picking my way through the dust and the rubble to stand by Elle's bed. Wrapping my arms under her frail shoulders and knees, I lift her as gently as I can. She is impossibly light, limp. Cold. Dry. There's no pulse in her chest. I sit in the crater in the floor with her in my lap, and cry.

I shouldn't have fallen asleep, I should have been awake and ready to keep this from happening. But I wasn't and now she's dead. Elle is dead. My sister is dead.

I press my lips to her forehead and rock back and forth. Her horns scrape my arm. Tears smear on my glasses, pouring down my face.

Her horns. Her wings.

She will never get her wings.

Sky finds me first, mere moments after I crumple into the crater. He races in, fists up, expecting a fight, but that changes when he sees Elle in my arms. He circles the crater in the blink of an eye, shakes his head, circles the crater again. Then he's gone, leaving nothing but a puff of dust to mark that he was there to begin with.

After him, there is nobody. The room is devoid of all life except the persistent beating of my own heart. I remain, stuck in the same, curled up, defeated position for so long that I am convinced all of my muscles have turned to stone. My arms are locked around Elle, my forehead is welded to hers, I'm incapable of moving.

Until the first rays of sunlight squeeze their way through the blinds, and I force my eyelids shut. The dark behind my eyes is the perfect background for scenes of violence to play out in full screen. Duels, riots, the snap of a guard's gun firing, the feeling of blood on my hands. It's all better than what's happening in the present world, I'd rather see this than her.

"Trick." It's Delilah, her voice is soft and I'm afraid of what her presence means. "I'm sorry, but we need to go. Sky took off hours ago and hasn't come back, it's not safe here."

I turn my head and rest my cheek on Elle's curls. Warm tears run down my face for what must be the hundredth time today. I don't have the ability or the will to stand up. I open my eyes and stare at Delilah, she's crouched in front of me. Sharp lines of exhaustion are drawn on her face, they make her look a hundred years old.

"Leave me," I croak.

"Can't, mate, too many people want to kill you."

Delilah starts at Sky's remark, relief smoothing out the lines for a brief second.

"You're back."

"Yeah." He sounds exhausted, his voice is raspy like he's been running all night. Delilah stands, and they both leave the room.

A while later they return, and this time it's Sky who crouches in front of me. His eyes are red, and his hair is blown back from his face. He doesn't say anything, only reaches out and takes Elle from me. I close my eyes and let him.

"Look at me," Delilah instructs. "Trick, look at me."

I open my eyes.

Sky is by Elle's bed, pulling the sheet up. Delilah holds two pills in front of my face. "Eat these, and then we have to go," she says.

I take the pills. They stick to the sides of my throat on the way down.

"Can you stand?"

No.

They hook their hands under my arms, one on each side, and lift me up. I manage to sort of get my feet under me, enough that I can shuffle, and we turn towards the door. This lasts all of three seconds, and as we cross the threshold my knees turn to water and a new sob crushes me down. If not for Delilah and Sky by my side, I would collapse on the floor and never get back up.

We make it out of the hospital this way. With Delilah and Sky supporting me on either side and me staggering, barely able to see through the tears. A mass of people wait outside the glass sliding doors, lights flash and a hundred voices all smush together, rising as we step out of the safety of the hospital.

Sky and Delilah elbow and shove past the mob. Delilah shouts at a few of the people. At one point a lightbulb explodes right in front of my face, leaving me dazed and blinking away stars. We break free of the mob and Delilah all but shoves me into the backseat of a car and shuts the door.

Removed of the support of Delilah and Sky, I fold over in my spot. My knees press into my chest and my head squishes against the back of the seat in front of me. Sky enters from the other side of the car and pats my back.

There's a man behind the wheel, and Delilah says something to him as she's sliding into the passenger seat.

The car lurches into motion, peeling away from the curb and making my stomach flipflop. It takes a sharp turn, and beside me Sky groans. I stare at the floor of the car and count the specks of dirt in an attempt to keep my guts inside of me.

After ages of lurches and twists that send my stomach up to my throat, we ease to a final stop. I hear the click of a latch and take that as my cue to get out. It takes two tries to find the door handle and wrestle the door open. When I do, I manage to summon enough willpower to stand up out of the car and stumble to the trunk. Delilah is nowhere to be seen, but Skyelar is waiting on the sidewalk with the palm of his hand pressed to his forehead. I stare at him a moment before bending over and puking all over the curb.

"What's wrong with him?" A voice I don't recognize asks.

"Motion sickness," says Delilah.

"What else?"

"His sister died."

I look up to see two Delilah's. One looks older and has shorter hair, this one is frowning at me. She continues to frown at me while her pale green eyes scan me up and down and up again. What does she see? There's an old bruise splashed across my face, and new bruises creeping up my arm and making my knuckles swell. My eyes are so bloodshot I can see the redness in the reflection of the car window, and I'm covered in dust from the crater. She takes this all in, then she sticks out her hand, "I'm Amiah."

"Hi," I rasp, and shake her hand.

"Come on inside before the reporters show up," she says, turning on her heels. "You guys were already live on the news this morning, it won't take long before someone sticks their head outside and sees you here."

Soon we're all situated around Amiah's table, drinking cups of some warm, oddly soothing liquid. I wouldn't be surprised, with the way Amiah was eyeballing me, if she drugged my cup. I wouldn't mind it either.

"Here." Amiah sets a stack of clothes on the table. "Shower is down the hall, you all need one." She plucks a bundle off the top and hands it to Delilah, who heads off to wash up. Amiah slides two other bundles of clothes across the table and pulls up a chair. Mumbling a thanks, I take the bundle nearest to me and set it on my lap without looking at it.

"I didn't think either of you would fit my blouses, so you'll have to make do with my ex's pajamas," Amiah says, not that any of us could possibly mind wearing pajamas. She sounds like she's joking, but I can't tell because I'm too busy staring at my cup of… whatever this is.

"I'm just glad to have a change of clothes. You have no idea how bloody long I've been wearing this shirt," Sky states, lighthearted. Amiah laughs and whatever ice might've been here before melts away. At least between them it does. I'm my own glacier, and I'm keeping it that way. I would rather not talk. Or think. Or breathe.

"Where are you from?" Amiah asks, "I meant to ask yesterday but then that whole thing about the Wind Witch came up and, you know."

"Oh yeah, yeah. I was born and raised in England, which got interrupted by, you know, evil Russian overlords. I mean, not that all Russians are evil, but the Whitecoats are" Sky trails off with a nervous chuckle. "But yeah, England."

Amiah hums in acknowledgement, "And you?" she says.

It takes Sky kicking my shins under the table for me to realize that the question was aimed at me. I glance up from my cup long enough to meet her gaze, "Nowhere."

It's technically true, my home is gone. Wiped off the map. It doesn't matter where I'm from because the island no longer exists.

"Trick was from Puerto Rico," Sky answers for me, breaking the stiff silence I caused.

"Oh," Amiah murmurs, and suddenly she has to clear the table of the empty cups. Not a moment too soon, Delilah pokes her head out the bathroom door.

"Shower's free," she says, her cheeks are pink, and she has a towel wrapped around her head. Sky pats my back.

"You go ahead. No offense mate, but you definitely need a shower more than I do," he teases, his voice is tight though, and everybody in the room picks up on it. Amiah leans on the counter, staring at me on my way past.

Amiah's small bathroom contains two big white cubes, beside them is a toilet, and beside that is a weathered bathtub. A sink with a mirror over it sits across from the cubes, and Delilah's old clothes are stacked on top of the highest cube. I strip down and add my clothes to the pile, running my hand over my face, I keep my head turned so I can't see myself in the mirror. When I turn to use the toilet, I notice a cluster of tiny glass bottles on a shelf at eye level. I pick one up. There's liquid inside, bright exit-sign red. Nail paint.

Carefully, I set the tiny bottle back in place and wipe away the fresh tears. I don't know how I'm supposed to live without her. I've spent my entire life protecting Elle, taking care of her, and now she's gone, and our parents are gone, and our home is a hole in the ground. I have no one and nowhere left to go.

I'm all alone now.

ooooooo

Later, I find myself sitting in the darkest corner of Amiah's living room. I tuck my knees up against my chest as I rock back and forth. There is a blanket made of thick fleece wrapped around my shoulders. I can't remember who put it there, I may have blacked out. I'm clean now but my skin crawls anyways and while I don't stink, I washed the dust covering up all my bruises down the drain. There's a cluster with ragged red centers up the edge of my left arm. I saw Sky eyeing them when I came out of the bathroom, I saw the wheels turning in his head and the realization dawning in his eyes.

He's pacing in the kitchen now, Delilah and Amiah are in there too, talking. I can't hear them, they're speaking in low voices. That, and my ears are ringing.

I blink, look around the room. Next to the door is a big square calendar, I'm too far away to read it. There's a saggy couch, a glass coffee table with coasters and a newstab on it, and a big window shrouded in half-closed drapes. Outside it's dark, the only light coming from a streetlamp at the edge of the front yard. I thought it was daytime, I guess that explains why it's so dark in here.

Amiah shouts, making me jump.

"Amiah—" Delilah slips into Russian, her voice is raised too, but not so much that I can hear without straining.

A moment later Sky's standing in the doorway between the kitchen and the living room, blocking the only source of light in the house. He looks me over, grimaces, and returns to the kitchen. After that, they lower their voices again.

Oh well, didn't want to hear anymore anyways. My fingers tighten over the blanket, pulling it closer around me. My skin itches, there are gunshots exploding beside my ears.

"My name is Trick," I mouth. "I am nineteen years old. I'm a lab experiment. The Whitecoats took everything away from me."

And again.

"My name is Trick." Rock back, rock forward. "I am nineteen years old." Sky darts in, darts out. Voices drone on in the background. "I'm a lab experiment." Images of the Compound flash in my mind, the tree, the basketball court, the cells, the dome.

"The Whitecoats took everything from me." Rock back, rock forward. Images, sensations. Being dragged away from our home in the middle of the night. Fear and pain. Elle sick. Needles, testing, running, dueling. Elle held over my head like bait for a fish; 'run faster and we'll save her', 'hit harder and we'll keep her alive one more day'. I feel the blood on my face, hot and sticky. Hear bones crunching, voices screaming. Losing my mind to pain. Elle is dying. I'm in pain, I'm in pain, I'm in pain.

Puerto Rico gone. Elle stolen. Anushka falling. Chastin falling. Maverick falling.

Falling, falling, falling.

I start again.

"My name is Trick."

It's night or very very early morning. Everybody is tucked away in bed, Sky has taken up residence on the couch with a blanket and a pillow. Amiah stuck a blow-up mattress beside the window in case I decide to lay down. I don't want to sleep.

I shuffle about the kitchen and living room. I find my battered sneakers by the door and a jacket that fits pretty well in the hall closet. I slip them on. The prescription bottle of Savella sits on the kitchen table. Into a coat pocket it goes, the zipper pulled shut. That's all I take. It was kind of Amiah to let me into her home, I hope she doesn't mind too much that I took her clothes. I start to leave a note on the calendar, but when the marker touches the paper I realize I only know how to write in Spanish, and not very well.

LEFT. DONT LUK.

I scratch out.

The kitchen clock reader three forty-nine as I slip out the front door.

Stars don't glitter above, too crowded out by the city lights. A slight breeze carries the night chill over the streets. It watches over me while I walk.

And walk.

And walk.

And walk.

The sky grows lighter. The roads become sparse. My fingertips are numb.

I don't stop, I can't. I force myself to keep moving, keep walking, to count the cracks in the sidewalk and recite the same four sentences until my lips are sore and my tongue is swollen. And in the moments in-between, when my eyelids start to droop and my breathing evens out, they come. Flashes of memory; Anushka, Maverick, Piper, Chastin, Elle. Falling, falling, falling, fallen. Every time I jerk awake, gasping. My eyes burn and it takes too long for the images to stop. Yana's wrist, Dieter's cracked teeth. The skin around my eyes feels raw from all the times I've rubbed until I saw stars instead of bruises.

Eventually, when the sun is over the tops of the skyscrapers, I come to an asphalt strip that snakes out of the city. The ache in my bones gets too loud to ignore then. I stop to take two pills.

More walking.

Down the asphalt snake. Towards the forest and the Compound. A roar startles me out of the stupor I've swayed into. The jolt, a kickstart to my lungs. I skitter into the ditch. Long grass itching my skin, pollen burning my eyes.

What the hell is that?

I crouch, scanning the long asphalt snake. Sun glints on something bright and quick, barreling towards me. I press myself lower, curling my hand into a fist. For a long second the world snaps into crisp, perfect focus.

Everything bright, loud, real.

A car races past, leaving a kick of dirt in its trail, the driver oblivious to my existence. I watch the shiny, oversized bullet shrink into the distance. My bones groan when I try to ease out of the crouch. Pain like knives to my Achilles' makes me wince. There's blood on the once white heels of my shoes. I guess that's what happens when you walk this long. Nothing I can do about it. I eat another pill and linger another few seconds. Then I start to feel all the blood all over my skin and the world goes blurry again.

More walking.

Stumbling along the ditch. Maverick walks with me, watching me, silent for miles. I guess I don't mind, except blood runs from the bullet holes riddling his body.

The sun sinks, turns red, and in the final moments of dim, oversaturated light, I reach the place along the road where the forest begins.

"Mav," I say, "leave me alone."

He blinks at me with cloudy eyes.

"Please," I beg. I can't look at him anymore.

He tilts his head to the side, as present as the grass and the trees I hobble towards. We breach the tree line together. A few steps in, when the trees obscure the road and blot out the inkling of stars above, I pause. Unsteady on sore feet. I take two more pills. The bottle lid bites my palm. When I look up from screwing it back on, Mav is right in front of me. I startle backwards. Heart in my throat.

"Come on, dude," I gasp.

My name is Trick.

He makes no noise as he glides closer, not a leaf rustles.

My name is Trick.

He reaches a red-stained hand towards me. Every part of me recoils, stomach churning.

"Mav," I say, "Mav, Mav."

I stumble back and the first step is the last straw. I crumble to the forest floor.

Falling, falling, falling.

And the tree branches spin up up up above my head. What time is it? What day? How long have I been wandering, dragging myself towards the only clear point in my head?

I roll to my side. Tuck my knees up to my chest. Press my hands to my ear and wait for the panic to subside.

28 | Hand Bones

It's cold.

My limbs are locked in place, the damp forest floor chill seeps into my muscles from below. Broken twigs and the zippers on the coat press indents into my skin. That side of my body is asleep. If I stay here forever, it wouldn't be so bad. I could go to sleep and never wake up. The bugs could eat my flesh. Roots and grass could grow over my skeleton. I would be a nameless, faceless, pile of bones at the side of the road. Just out of sight for the rest of time. Surrounded by ghosts.

A twig snaps.

The ice melts from my joints. Sitting up, I try to will the forest to stop spinning. Bile rises in the back of my throat, stomach clenching. I press my hand to my belly like that will appease it while I squint at the trees.

Glasses.

They're on the ground, a little scratched and beaded with dew. I wipe them on my pant leg and slip them on my face. A bush sways in the not-so-distance. It could be a wild animal but I'm afraid it's a Redcoat. How far are they willing to go to hunt us down? These woods could be crawling with them.

"Trick."

Something touches my shoulder. Like a spark to my system. I grab it and crush it. The thing I now recognize as a hand crunches, there's an ugly, hollow pop, and Sky screams. He twists, smashing my neck hard with his free hand, temporarily robbing my ability to breathe. Black floods my vision and I'm forced to drop his hand. His next blow lands square against my chest, knocking me into a tree with a thump.

"Sky?" I croak, staring in disbelief at his pale, hunched form. What the hell is he doing here?

His hand is contorted, the bones are buckled and when he tries to straighten his fingers a pained, weak cry escapes him. Hearing that, watching his lips shake and the pain flash in his eyes, puts hot coals in my stomach.

Shit.

"Damn, Trick" he shudders.

"Sorry," I say, "I'm so sorry, Sky, I thought you were—"

The tree between us shatters. Wood shards and splinters spray everything in a ten-foot radius. They burn like streaks of fire when they burrow under my skin. A shard clips my glasses off, barely missing taking out my eyes. Sky flings curses. He's a smear among the smears of trees, but he looks too close to have escaped the shards. I shove the glasses on right, ignoring the sting and the fresh new cracks in the corner of a lens.

Sky *is* too close, bleeding and yanking on the ground.

"Run, bunnies, run," A chilling voice crows. Dieter, swaying between the slender tree trunks I rock to my feet, keeping low, tracking his movements.

Watch his arms, those are the only reliable way to gauge his actions.

"Sky, can you get up?" I whisper.

"I'm working on it," he hisses back, yanking harder on the thing on the ground. "King has me."

I spare a glance at the thing he's pulling on. It's his unbroken hand, encased to the wrist in rock. So King is here somewhere, too.

Dieter whistles off-key and unsteady. He wavers closer. His arms stay at his side, limp, marionette-like and moving on a different beat than the rest of him.

Keeping one eye on him, I creep closer to Sky.

"Hold still, I'm going to break you out."

"Wait, wait wait wait," his eyes go wide.

"What?"

"Can you do it without shattering my other hand? I kind of need it." Right, important detail. I hesitate, Sky grimaces. "Right, let's—"

Dieter moves suddenly, the magno-blast ripples through the undergrowth. I lurch away from Sky. The blast punches my right side and screeches through my leg.

Sun, moon, and stars.

My vision spikes white, bright bright bright. I come-to on the ground, leg on *fire*.

What the hell. What the hell is that?

I have to clutch my leg to make sure it's there and not in a million tiny shards all over the foliage.

"Trick!" Sky calls, panic sharpens his tone. I have to get him out of here. I roll to my hands and knees, crawl, favoring my leg. Lower down, the foliage is thicker. I catch glimpses of Dieter, but more importantly, I can watch the otherwise invisible magno-blasts tear a path through the brush.

"Come on out, bunnies," Dieter coos, "come on, pretend you have a chance."

"Ice it, Dieter." King's voice joins the chaos. He sounds groggy.

"I thought you were busy," Dieter sighs.

Taking advantage of their brief distraction, I sneak closer to Sky. He's vibrating, kicking at the rock.

"You could at least let me stand, King!" He shouts, silencing their bickering. "How many 'coats are there, huh? We could take them."

Summoned by Sky's heckling, King comes into full view. Veins stand out on his temples as he crouches in front of Sky. Taking in the bandages and newly useless hand—curtesy of me— he shakes his head.

"Not likely."

"Come on, mate, we could be free."

King wobbles, he presses a fist to his chest. The tremble is subtle but present nonetheless.

"We tried that," he reminds Sky, "look at where it got us."

"Yeah, but—" Sky's whole body snaps back. A spray of blood mists the air. He collapses, boneless, with a groan.

I scramble to my feet, ready to dive for Dieter. King beats me to it the punch, his heel driving hard into the dirt. A pillar erupts from the earth and closes around Dieter's hands. The instant the rock traps him, Dieter flips a switch. Shrieks, thrashes. His head whipping harder than Sky's.

I wince, biting back the childish urge to cover my ears.

Never mind him, I limp towards Sky. A muffled boom threatens the pillar.

"Dieter, enough!" King stomps another layer over the pillar, rising from his crouch. He makes it halfway up, flushes, hits the dirt. Now is the perfect chance. I lunge for Sky. I'll have to risk breaking his other hand, the idea heaps more coals into my stomach, but it's the only way to get him out fast enough.

The pillar rumbles and cracks as my hand closes around Sky's wrist. I wind back to smash the stone, already silently pleading forgiveness when the blast strikes me square in the chest.

Cracked bones.

Weightlessness.

A tree cuts my plane impression short. Sandpaper bark. Dirt in my face. Glasses knocked loose. I claw for breath, my already broken ribs scream with renewed agony. I grip the tree I hit, put it between me and Dieter.

Okay, I think, *what is he?* A distance fighter.

I peek around the tree, only to stall out at the flashes of red uniform fast getting closer.

Sky is rolling groggily to his stomach, coated in his own blood. Beside him, King clutches at his chest, shoulders curved inwards. And Dieter… Dieter is cowering. In mere moments the Redcoats are on them. I can only watch in horror as a Redcoat taps a watch on his wrist and electrocutes King until he drags his foot weakly over the ground. A second 'coat hauls Sky upright, a third slaps shockers on his wrists. I shrink behind the tree, hiding from their hawkish eyes. Cowardly, I think, even as I stay rooted to the spot by fear.

Sky casts a glance back in the direction Dieter threw me, blue eyes full of panic even from this far away. Looking for me. I grind my fingers into the dirt. It's over, I can't win that fight. The Redcoats alone, maybe. But not the 'coats and Dieter and King and Sky, and the 'coats *will* make them fight me.

The Redcoats shove Sky, marching him, and King, and Dieter, back the direction they came from.

I watch until Sky disappears in the foliage, and then I crumble against the tree, panic seizing every muscle until my body is not mine.

It should have been me.

Sky was here for me.

And now the Compound has him.

I can't stay here. Propping myself up on the tree, I get my legs under me. My right leg still aches like it's been shattered all over again. Throwing a wary look around for telltale red, I limp for the road. The plan, if the numb-brained fixation that got me out here could be called a plan, has changed. I have to get back to Amiah's house.

I hit the asphalt and hobble as fast as I can. The luxury of time is gone, I can't take the whole day this time.

And I don't.

As it turns out, running—a close approximation of running—gets me places faster than sluggish ambling. Little houses begin to pop up. I come to the place where the single snake starts sprouting more snakes, and stall.

Where…?

I slow but don't stop, sticking to the snake. It keeps going, winding on and on, branching over and over. None of the landscape is familiar. Damn my foggy brain. Damn it!

A car whizzes past and I flinch half into some stranger's yard. The house is bright red, doesn't invite any memories. I think I've come too far down the snake. I would remember a house this color, right? Then which of the branches before here was the right one? My fingers work their way up to the burn. I'm wasting time. I step back towards the snake.

The right direction?

My skin breaks under my nails. It's not familiar. The other direction; not familiar. Where am I?

Movement in the corner of my eye wrenches my attention back to the red house. A crooked door set in the face of the house creaks open, a withered prune waddles onto the stoop.

"English?" I call to her, "*¿Español?*" Anything other than Russian? The prune plants her wrinkled hands on her hips and waddles back inside. Dead end, like every other cursed route in this cold, dead land! I whirl to the road, biting hard on a curse when my knee buckles.

"Ah! Boy!"

I turn back to the sound. A different withered prune shadows the stop now. "English." He juts a stern, wobbly chin at me.

"English," I repeat, "yes, do you speak English?"

He narrows his droopy eyes. Flapping his hands at me, he scoffs and shuffles into the safety of his home.

"Why would you ask if you don't speak it!" I shout after him. The house blurs and fades for a second, like a power flicker, and suddenly my breath is gone. Oh, ugh.

I blink away static. Coming back to the stable world, I see the second prune shuffling out into the open again.

"Boy, fight."

"Yeah, sure, I fight," I say.

A loud click announces the entrance of a rifle. The first prune steps out from behind her partner-in-crime, a long black gun that looks heavier than both her arms combined nestled in the crook of her shoulder. Aimed at me. I lift my hands above my head.

"No move," man prune says, "*Militsiya* come, you no move."

As if I time for this.

"Please, I'm not going to hurt you," I say, slowly, "I'm trying to find my friend."

Man prune crosses his arms, woman prune scowls. I don't know if they understand a single word I'm saying.

"I'm not going to hurt you," I repeat, searching for any inkling of recognition on their faces. I slide one foot back, and the woman prune barks an order, brandishing the rifle.

"Okay." I still. I don't think I'm supposed to be feeling my heart beating in my palms or seeing the edges of my vision blur in time with my pulse, but I am. The sun beats down on us. Midday, already. I look around the yard for something—anything—to use as a shield or a weapon. The best option is a tiny pointy… man… thing. I could kick it at them, if I reached it before the woman could squeeze the trigger. And I could swim on the moon, too.

Vehicles thunder closer, bright lights glinting off the metal shells. Red and blue. I hear the grumbling engines slow as they draw near. Squeezing my eyes shut, I focus for a moment on steadying my trembling hands.

What next? I have to wonder. Are the cars full of Redcoats? When I open my eyes, the man prune is waving to the cars behind me. The red and blue lights reflect off the house's windows. A car door slams, then another, and a couple more all in quick succession. The woman prune lowers her rifle but keeps her finger on the trigger, as soon as it's down I turn sideways. Prune and rifle to one side, flashing cars to the other. My heart seizes at the sight of other people, also leveling their guns at me. Their uniforms aren't red but that hardly matters. They look as determined to lock me up as any Compound worker.

One of them breaks from the others, coming closer to me. She says something, it sort of sounds like a question. The man prune barks a sentence that ends in "English" and makes the uniformed woman frown. Keeping her weapon trained on me, she reaches one hand up to a black box hanging off her shirt pocket and, bringing it to her mouth, speaks into it.

Almost immediately, the box crackles and spits out a gravelly voice. The sound of the static makes my skin crawl. Whatever the box voice says gets the woman to holster her gun, and she strides even closer, holding out the box instead. I shrink away. The static is loud loud loud.

"Hello?" The gravelly box voice speaks.

I glance from the box to the woman, she shakes the box at me.

"Do you speak English?" the box voice asks.

"Yes." I answer warily.

"Who am I speaking to?"

The answer is the first easy thing in a long time.

"My name is Trick, I'm nineteen years old, I—" the thing I'm about to admit sticks in my throat.

"Can you tell me what's going on, Trick?"

I work my jaw, my mouth is desert dry and the flashing lights turn my brain to mush.

"I don't know." My own words sound far away. "I need to find Delilah."

"Where are you from, Trick?" box voice asks.

A lab. Puerto Rico. Nowhere. Do they have to keep those lights on? The box crackles, I cringe.

"Can you hear me? I need you to tell me where you're from."

No, I can't do that.

"Hello?"

The uniformed woman waggles the box again, saying something.

"What?" I squint. The lights are too bright. Someone from the Compound could see them, it could lead them straight here. I step back, I have to run. The woman matches my step. The box voice scrapes at my ears, I don't make out the words.

"Don't come any closer," I say. I think I say. Wait, that's wrong. I should get her closer, I need her within arms reach. Like the soldier in the forest. Get her close. Grab her. Use her as a shield. Right?

The lights flash. Redblueredblueredbluered. Blinking makes it worse. Shutting my eyes isn't an option.

A car leaps as if from thin air. Suddenly there, roaring past, loud like a gunshot. I recoil hard, expecting the bullet, but it's my knee that betrays me. I hit the dirt, skin stinging.

The woman shouts. Suddenly uniforms are surrounding me. Guns in my face. Shouting.

Static. Static from the box.

I cover my ears. It's all I can do to make it stop.

One of them shoves me and he ends up on his back on the ground, wailing. His bone sticks out of his arm. The shouting gets louder. Something hard cracks across the back of my head and at once my face is in the dry, cold grass. And someone is on me. Wresting my arms back. I twist, throwing the uniform off. I don't know where he lands. I'm already reaching for the next nearest uniform. My hands close around a leg. Driven by panic, I yank.

Bang! Dirt explodes next to my face, biting, blinding. And the next thing I hear is ringing.

Just ringing.

The ground in front of me is nothing but a blur. There are hands splayed below me, palms down, tips pointed away from me like I'm laying on someone and their arms are spread out flat.

Ringing, blur. Touch the ground beneath my belly. Blur, ringing.

Something deep inside begins to ache.

Blur. Where am I? Blur. Someone must have handed me my butt in the dome. Or maybe it's them I'm laying on. I touch the ground underneath me again.

"Get up." The first sound to break the ringing. "Hendrix, you need to get up."

That's my name. I look up and realize the blur is because my glasses are somewhere not on my face.

"What the hell happened to you?" The voice. Delilah. I must take too long to answer because she says, "never mind, tell me in the car. Where are your—ah."

The glasses reappear on the bridge of my nose. Delilah is a little to the left, bent over to be face level with me. Although I don't remember sitting up. Her expression is pinched, like someone put their hand flat on her face and scrunched. Her eyes are stormy. Glinting. Redbluered.

"Broken bones?"

I shake my head.

"Stand up." She offers her hand and I take it. I don't ask where the uniforms went. It doesn't matter. Not here. In their flash-y cars, maybe.

I blink. We're in a car. Amiah sits in the driver's seat, watching me through the little mirror hanging off the roof. I catch a glimpse of my reflection. Blood seeps from hundreds of thin nicks, glasses cracked, eyes red. My right ear is a skinless sort of red. I touch it gingerly, snap my fingers next to it. Nothing but ringing. I try not to think about how close that bullet was to nuking my off switch.

"What are you doing here?" I ask.

Amiah lurches onto the road and taps one knob of an array of buttons and knobs.

"You were on the police station."

"I was on the ground."

Her reflection rolls its eyes.

Delilah nudges me to get my attention, "have you seen Sky? He went looking for you."

Her question hits like a sucker punch, crushing all the air out of my lungs. One look at me and any hope she had flees her expression. Dread replaces it.

"We have to go back to the Compound," I say, "the Redcoats got him and—"

And they were going to torture him like they did Dieter.

And he could barely stand on his own when they caught him.

And I mangled his hand.

"Trick?" A faraway voice speaks my name.

I blink.

The car is stopped.

I blink.

We're standing on the stoop of a quiet green house. Delilah follows me inside, the click of the deadbolt sliding into place is the last thing I hear before I collapse.

30 | KITCHEN KNIVES

Hyperaware of my heartbeat, my pulse in every tiny vein, beating blood to every locked-up limb. Static blankets my vision and crackles in my ears, blocking out everything except the wheezing of my own lungs. Beyond it: screaming. Endless, piercing screaming of someone in agony, making my blood run cold and my muscles spasm with shivers. My shaking legs ache under my weight, pressing into the floorboards with too much force, bruising straight to the bone. Tears sear my eyes, burning worse with each passing moment, and no matter how hot the tears get, they don't warm up the rest of me.

I can hear her.

I can hear her.

I can hear her.

Make it stop, make it stop, please make it stop.

My hands climb to my chest, where my heart fights to escape my ribcage. They reach my neck, then my ears, where one stays pressed with bruising force against the side of my head and the back of my neck, where the other digs in sharp fingernails as if that will help me catch my failing breath. No, no no no, no, no, no. All I want is for it to be quiet, all I want is some peace. No, no, no. I can't keep seeing them die, I can't keep watching them fall.

"Trick, can you hear me?"

I gasp at the intrusion into my cocoon of static and screaming. A warm, soft grip pulls my hand away from my jaw as easily as peeling paint off a wall. Empty, my fingers move of their own accord, clenching and unclenching jerkily until they're pressed against smooth skin. Little hairs tickle my palm, the ridge of something bitingly cold presses the edge of my hand.

"Open your eyes." Someone using Yana's voice tells me. I pry apart eyelids that I didn't know were closed, the static fades but tears blur everything in its place. "What do you see?"

I see shallow scratches on the hardwood floor, I see two sets of knees; mine, and a pair covered in thick yellow linen. I see curled hair, and crystal eyes, and a bent elbow attached to a hand attached to fingers that lace through mine, pressing an ice cube into the palm of my hand. I see the danger she doesn't know she's in, being so close to me when I'm like this.

Yana stretches out her arm to slip her fingertips over the precariously tight grip I have on the back of my own neck. "What do you see?" she asks again, while her fingers nudge mine.

"You," I breathe, fighting to stay perfectly still, to not accidentally squeeze too hard.

"And what does that mean, that you see me?"

"It means you're not safe," I rasp out, cold trickles of fear slide down my throat, my cheeks, my back. The bruises on my legs are growing still, soon all I will have is purple skin and dented bones.

"No, it means I am here to help you. You understand?"

"No."

"You are safe."

"I don't want to hurt you," I whimper, fresh tears shed from my eyelashes. I don't want to hurt anyone, I'm sick of it. I'm scared of it. Yana tilts her head, her forehead is mere centimeters from mine, I can feel her breath skirting my nose.

"You will not," she soothes.

Five finger-shaped bruises cling to the arm bridging the gap between her and I.

"I already have."

"It won't happen again."

I don't know how she can be so sure. I've never been less sure of anything in my life.

Scared and tired. Seated once again in Amiah's kitchen. Palms damp and cold from the ice cubes. That was a neat trick. Yana's lucky it worked. I'm lucky it worked. My hands are mottled and my fingernails are split and stained from scratching grooves in the hardwood. Voices buzz in the air over my head, hovering around so I can hear the words but their meaning is lost. It's a little disorienting, only hearing them on one side.

"We can't use my car."

"We need a way to get there."

"I'll get another car."

Yana's fingernails are painted indigo. The gloss catches in the sunlight while she pulls stitches from Delilah's shoulder with a pair of blunt, bent scissors.

"Are we bringing him?"

A pause in the hum.

Him. That itches my brain. Him. Me.

"No," Delilah says.

Yana brushes the pile of discarded stitches into her hand and gets p to deposit them in the trash.

"*Khorosho, da skorava*," Amiah says. The sound of bootsteps and a shutting door end that part of the conversation.

A cabinet door shuts, echoing the front door, and Yana straightens to wash her hands in the sink. She turns, notices me watching her.

"What you think about?" she asks, leaning her hip against the cupboard.

"Nothing," I say around a mouthful of sand.

"How do you feel?" she asks, looking at me. I manage to scrunch up my shoulders, one makes it higher than the other and the shrug ends up lopsided. It's a shock I can even manage that motion. It feels like splintery wooden spikes are being driven into my arm sockets, but more importantly, I'm still stuck outside of my body like some sort of ghost. "You look not well, dizzy?"

I am, I hadn't noticed until she mentioned it, but I am sickeningly dizzy and sweating hard despite the chill in the room.

"Mm," I grunt, tongue thick and heavy.

"Eat food first, then you have your medicine," she instructs.

"Hm," I grunt another time. Yana's presence, her talking to me, is dragging me back into myself and it aches. My bones are being forced apart to accommodate the parts of me that are being stuffed back inside, and it all stretches around the empty clawed-out space on the inside of my chest.

It's a slow process, uncurling myself from the chair. The spinning of the room alone is too much, and I stop after every lurch upwards to steady myself. Once on my feet, it's a little easier to keep going. I shuffle, one foot in front of the next until, twenty-seven steps later, I have a box of… cereal, I think.

The conversation carries on while I force down the dry cereal. I only hear snatches of it. Something about reporters, something about war. For lack of anything else to occupy my mind, I study the contents of the counter. Amiah is a tidy person. There is a machine with a clear bucket half-full of coffee attached to the wall, and on the other side of the flat-topped stove is a knife block missing only one out of a set of ten. The blade of one peeks out a teensy bit, teasing at a deadly sharp edge and sturdy metal. I stop studying the counter.

The front door explodes open with a deafening crack. Delilah jumps to action but before she's even halfway into a fighting stance, Sky crashes into the table.

His hair is matted, his clothes are torn, and worst of all, narrow black bands are fastened around his neck and wrists. My heart drops like an anvil. His hand is engulfed in the spidery metal prison of an external fixator. Pins burrowed deep into his flesh are soiled with grime and dried bloodstains.

They worked fast.

"Whitecoats—" His body goes rigid as the shock restraints fire. He convulses and falls to his knees gasping for breath. Yana lurches instinctively to help him, only for Delilah to yank her back when, with another ear-splitting crack, the front door flies into the room. It smashes into the opposite wall, chalk dust erupts into the air, but nobody has time to cough it out of their lungs.

Delilah and Yana scramble to get the window over the sink open, while Sky struggles to his feet, the shock restraint on his neck slipping to show agitated red skin.

And who should come strolling into the kitchen except a short, gaunt blond boy with swollen pink scars.

"Sorry about the door, somebody locked it," Dieter sighs, a slight smile on his pasty face. King enters a mere pace behind Dieter, his lip curled in disgust as he looks at the path of chipped wood and drywall dust. It's so different from the Compound out here. The walls crumble like they're made of paper. A shivering hand takes me by the elbow, nearly jolting me out of my body. It's Yana, her skin shakes against mine, but her grip is firm as she guides me towards the window. I stall. I can't leave without Sky, not after the forest.

The reluctance costs me. Dieter flicks his wrist, a wave of magnokinesis clips me, but thump and crunch of a body hitting the counter belongs to Yana. She cries out, slumping to the floor.

"Dieter, don't!" Delilah shouts. Another magno-blast whips her against the window she's trying to pry open. Fissures explode across the glass.

I crouch to help Yana to her feet. King pulls me away none-too-gently. I catch sight of the black band around his wrist, the raw wounds under it.

"Are you ignoring me?" Dieter demands, shoving his face so close to mine I can smell the rot in his teeth.

"Yes," I say, and reach over to snap the bracelet on King's wrist. Dieter flinches at the sound of the plastic shattering and flings his hand up as if to slap me. I can make out the faintest ripple of invisible energy exploding from the back of his hand all the way down to his elbow. It doesn't come towards me, it flies back, straight into Yana. The force knocks her hard into the solid lip of the counter, for a second time she yelps and crumples to the floor.

The anger that razes through me is instinctive and messy, possessing me like a living thing. I don't even realize that my fist is up until it's trapped tight in a column of stone.

"Sorry, man," King mutters, shoving me down until I'm kneeling, both hands stuck in pillars of rock above my head.

"I can't help but notice," Dieter purrs, pacing deliberately up the length of the small kitchen, "that someone is missing."

He pauses beside the knife block, turning his head to look at it. A string of drool drips from his chapped lower lip. A thin crust of dried blood lingers beside his ear, either a by-product of the shock torture or from Delilah dropping him on his head. "She's dead, isn't she?"

"That's not why we're here," King says, a warning clear in his tone. Dieter turns sharp on his toes, glowering. Then the harsh frown lines clear, and he shrugs.

"Just, checking. Wouldn't want to miss one of them, would we?" He wipes the drool from his chin. Then he flips his arm, sending off another wave that hits Sky square in the chest. Sky crashes against the corner where the wall and the hallway meet, the air leaving his lungs with an audible whoosh. "Don't think I didn't see you," Dieter says.

"Let's go," King says, he lifts his foot to release me, but Dieter knocks him off balance with another magnetic pulse.

"Not yet. You know, Hendrix, we're only supposed to gather you lot, bring you home. But there's nothing in the instructions about bringing you back alive." He draws the biggest knife from the block, and turns it over in his hand, examining it. He presses the tip of his finger to the glinting point of the blade and smiles when the skin breaks and a bubble of blood wells up. He sticks his finger in his mouth, slurps, and the blood leaks back out, diluted in a thick string of spit. "Maybe you'll have an unfortunate accident."

One, two, three steps to stand in front of me, wielding the knife. My heart races, my lungs are shrinking, and the static is creeping back into my eyes.

"We would have made it, if not for you and that girl. We would have been far out of reach by the time that storm hit, we could have hidden in the mountains and the Whitecoats would never have found us." He presses the blade to my neck, the point bites into soft flesh, and nobody except me is in any condition to stop him. I can feel it in my muscles, how I could kick out and knock his legs out from under him. But he's right.

He's right, about all of it, he's right. I forced Maverick's hand, I knew he wouldn't leave me to find Elle on my own.

I killed them all.

I blink, the floor is falling away. I see their faces, I hear their screams. I will never be able to close my eyes without this nightmare—my reality, ripping its claws in.

"I should kill you," Dieter snarls, and I'm sure he means it to be menacing. His broken teeth flashing, the blade pressing in, his eyes wildly unfocused. I lift my chin, and lean in, it stings when the blade splits a hairline slice in my skin. I can't bring myself to meet his gaze.

"Do it," I say, barely above a whisper. We both know this is the ending I deserve; pinned to the floor, at the mercy of someone who's second chance I took away. Besides, I can't go back to the Compound, I can't go back to the dark rooms, and the tests, and the dome fights. If he doesn't finish me off, I will. I'll snap my own neck before they ever get me out the door.

"No, you can't," Sky gasps. Dieter curves the knife, setting the handlemost edge to my throat in preparation to slash a clean, deep line. I tilt my head back and exhale for the last time.

This is okay. I'm okay.

3 1 | One Last Time

"That's enough, Dieter." King's pillars sink into the earth. My eyes fly open. I catch myself before I crack my skull on the tile.

Sky barrels into me, rolling with me over and over until a wall stops us.

"Mate, what the hell was that?" He shoves off me and jumping to his feet. The look of utter betrayal he gives me hurts more than any physical blow could. And then he's collapsing, electricity scorching through his nerves and flooring him.

I should follow him, given the crashing going on across the room. Instead, I deflate. Numbness creeps over me, a fog of empty and deathly calm. I touch my neck gingerly, blood comes off on the tips of my fingers from the nick I gave myself. Hm. I sigh and let my hand drop onto my side. A dish shatters against the wall beside me, I don't flinch. I feel like I should feel something, but I don't. I can't. It's like floating but in reverse. Instead of me drifting outside my body, hanging on by a narrow thread to all the roiling emotions, the emotions are outside, and I'm held captive inside.

Yana is near, her hair falls in thick, loose curls over her face. Half her hairpins are scattered on the floor where she fell. Her legs wobble, her arms quiver, but she clutches an iron frying pan with both hands, gripped so tight her knuckles are bloodless.

Delilah fights in from the outskirts. Her loose clothes billow around her, the only part of her not charged with tense energy is her nerve-damaged pinky. She makes some leeway, but she's holding back. She keeps stopping to catch debris, to stop it from shattering or breaking holes in the walls.

And there, in the midst of it all, are King and Dieter, at each others' throats. The violence grows more volatile by the second. Pillars erupt from the floor, five in the blink of an eye, all gunning for Dieter. Magno-blasts crumble them and pummel King from whatever angle Dieter can get to. King's jaw is set, his nostrils flared, he dances in the cramped space. His feet kick and stomp and drag over the floor, each tap of his heels calling up new rocks from new angles. He has the skill, the experience, to beat Dieter any day.

Except, maybe, today. Dieter's rage is white-hot, he fights like a rabid bear, flinging himself at King, knife swinging, and when that gets batted across the room he settles for curling his hands into claws. He screams, spit flying, magno-blasts erupting at random and destroying everything they come in contact with. King is good, but the worried glint in his eyes is getting easier and easier to read. The table smashes on its side with a house-shaking bang and Dieter wastes no time scurrying over and ripping one of the legs off with help from his magnokinesis.

He turns on King, a war cry ripping from his throat. A massive wave explodes out from his core, sending everything and everyone flying. My head whips back and drives a hole into the wall, the headache is instantaneous. I blink away the black stars in time to see Dieter straddling King, table leg lofted above his head. King convulses, the shock restraints leaving him paralyzed and helpless against Dieter's attack. Suddenly I lurch back into myself.

King, the stake, Dieter.

I launch myself off the floor and crash into him at the same time the makeshift stake rams through King's sternum. We hit the wall and Dieter magno-blasts me across the room. Damn it! Blood pools thick and fast, pouring out of King. He claws at the table leg and wheezes a final, ragged gasp. The light leaves his eyes and his body stays rigid for a few seconds longer, like it doesn't realize he's gone.

I crack the tile on my fist. *Damn it.*

Dieter magno-blasts my head hard against the floor, blinding me for a few seconds more. I scramble to my feet, too dizzy to tell which direction is up. Staggering forward with my arms flailing for something to steady myself on, my vision clears in time for me to see Delilah nail Dieter in the ribs once, twice, raising a snarl from him. He grabs a fistful of her hair and cuffs her over the back of the head, magno-blast striking her skull point-blank. One more and she sags, two more and she drops like a sack of bricks.

No, damn it, *no.*

His cold blue eyes meet mine, pupils blown and framed by mottled skin. He turns and hauls Delilah out of the kitchen with him. I race after them, straight into the muzzle of a red-shirted guard's gun. The frigid metal presses into my chest for the barest of moments, sending a chill through my body. I grab the guard's wrist and twist, the gun clatters across the coffee table and lands with a thud on the floor. The guard has time to look sufficiently scared before I bash his nose into his brain and toss him aside.

Amiah yelps from outside. I burst through the empty hole of the front door. Dieter is at the end of the driveway, shoving Delilah's limp body into the back of a white cargo van. Amiah clutches her nose at the bottom of the stoop, blood drips on the sidewalk and runs down her arm. Steadying herself, she draws a sleek black handgun from a holster hidden under her jacket. With one hand pinching her nose and the other aiming the gun, she fires off three rounds at the van as it guns it out of the driveway and down the street.

She spits obscenities, dropping her hand to reveal blood-stained teeth and a gushing nose. She raises the handgun to fire again, but the van hits the main street, and the flow of other vehicles engulfs it.

"Start your car," I say, turning to run back into the house.

In the house, I glance at the Redcoat's body on my way past. His chest rises and falls shallowly, but the ugly bruise on his face says he won't be awake for a good long time. In the kitchen, I find Yana crumpled against the oven. She, too, is unconscious but breathing. I crouch beside her to check for any serious injuries. There's a nasty goose egg on the back of her head, but no blood spilling from her ears or nose.

"Mate." Sky limps into the room from the hallway, splinters and plaster decorate his greasy hair and torn clothes.

Stepping over King's body, I reach Sky and jam my fingers under the black band around his neck.

"Dude, dude, dude," he tenses under my touch. I grimace and with a quick jerk, snap the collar, then crouch to snap off the ankle restraints. When I stand, he traps me in a tight hug, the metal ex-fix biting into my scar.

"Don't you dare ever pull a stunt like that again," he demands, pulling away. "You scared the daylights out of me."

I grab his shoulders, give him a little shake to get his mind in the right place. I can't promise him anything, and now is not the time to discuss that. Our lives are on the line, the clock is ticking faster with each second we waste.

"Can you fight?" I ask.

"Of course."

I spot the block of kitchen knives toppled on the counter. "With a knife?"

"Yes."

"Good." I push the biggest knife from the block at him. "Let's go."

Outside, a car horn blares. Sky and I exchange glances, him with his knife gripped in his hand and determination gritted between his teeth, and me with nothing left to lose. I take a final moment to carry Yana to the living room and lay her on the couch with her mini newstab beside her. Away from King's body. Grabbing the Redcoat by the ankle on my way out, I drag him out onto the front lawn and throw him into the shrubs. I hope Amiah doesn't mind her greenery getting crushed.

I climb into the backseat of the car and shut the door. A wooden bat lays across Sky's lap, Amiah's handgun is stuck in the cupholder. The tires squeal as she punches it out of the driveway.

A since of finality hangs in the air, mingling with the rage evaporating off of me. I know this will be the last time I ever go back to the Compound.

"Where are we headed?" Amiah asks once we've hit the main flow of traffic. Sky is already turning green, pressing his forehead to the cool glass.

"East of the city," he answers, his shaky tone draws Amiah's attention. She spares one glance at him and grimaces. Reaching over, she pops open a compartment set in the front of the vehicle.

"There's a package of anti-nausea pills in there," she says. Sky fishes them out with a grateful grunt. He pops two little round pills out of their tin foil barrier, then passes the package back to me. "Okay, now, there are a million roads headed east out of this place, so I really need you to be specific."

"It's, um… roads… " A frustrated groan escapes Sky and he strikes the doorframe open-handed. He doesn't know the way to the Compound, neither of us do. I press my knuckles to my teeth, and for the first time since charging out the door, the spark of rage-fueled fire in my stomach begins to flicker.

Amiah stomps on the brakes and wrenches the car to the side of the road, sending us all crashing against our seatbelts. The car is barely stopped when she throws open the compartment between the front seats and fishes out a miniature newstab.

"This place was on the news a while back, the lab the Americans attacked, right?" she asks, pulling something up on the newstab screen.

"That's the one," I say, easing back into my proper seat. Her fingers fly over the screen, tapping here and there too fast for me to catch what she's doing. In thirty seconds she has a map up on the newstab screen and is grinning triumphantly to herself.

"Got it." She passes the newstab to Sky, flips a switch beside the steering wheel, and rockets back onto the road. "Okay, now save that image to memory, wipe the browser history, and disconnect the newstab from everything."

"Why?" Sky asks, already pressing buttons to get the image saved as the car lurches across several lanes of traffic.

"Because what I did for that map is illegal as hell and the police will stop us from getting to the Compound."

Sky taps with more speed. At the first red light we hit, Amiah snatches the newstab from him and pulls up the image of the map.

"Where did you learn to do this?"

"Old job," Amiah answers tersely. The light turns green, she drops the newstab in Sky's lap and hits the gas, she spins the steering wheel with alarming speed, and I throw my hands out to brace against the seats. I don't want to be tossed out of this forsaken contraption before we get to the Compound. "Map says we're sixty minutes away from the Compound. So we'll be there in twenty," she says, then burns through a red light.

With twenty minutes of racing hearts and close brushes with fatal accidents ahead of us, I lean back and try to keep all of my self inside my skin. It's difficult, especially in the silence, and the knowledge that we're headed straight for the Compound makes it a hundred thousand times worse.

"Hey," I tap Sky's shoulder. He turns in his seat to face me, eyebrows up. "How's your hand?"

The eyebrows go down, but he doesn't answer right away.

"It's fine," he says at last.

"No, how bad is it?"

He looks away and sets his knife in the cupholder next to Amiah's gun. Sighing, he runs his hand through his hair and gives a half-hearted shrug. "It's shattered, but it… it doesn't hurt much," he admits at last.

My fingers find the edge of the burn scar of their own accord. The action is becoming familiar, habitual almost.

"Were you serious when you told Dieter to kill you?"

"It doesn't matter." I bite my tongue and turn to look out the window at the light posts racing by. Sky leans back into his seat and falls uncharacteristically silent. We pull onto a road with dwindling traffic, Amiah speeding around every car in our path with frightening agility. Soon the light posts are replaced by trees, and the traffic has vanished. The road we're on winds like a snake through the forest, and more than once Amiah swerves on two wheels to avoid a car-killing pothole. We're so near I can taste it, like bile washing over my tongue. My stomach is resting up in my throat, dangerously close to spilling out.

Amiah leans into a tight turn. Unexpectedly, the road ends. The brakes screech in protest as Amiah goes from pressing the accelerator to the floor, to standing on the brake pedal. We skid across a gravel patch, stones flying, and stop a breath from smashing the front end of the car into the trunk of a pine tree. I think my seatbelt might be permanently embedded in my collarbone. In the front seat, Sky undoes his seatbelt with a shaking hand, muttering to himself.

"A concussion, whiplash, what's next? A broken nose? Sprained ankle?" He's too busy trying to pop his neck to spot the movement in the bushes.

"Get down!" I shout, diving for the floor. Mere moments later a spray of bullets shatters the front window, glass flies everywhere, the back seat explodes in torn fabric and burst foam. Amiah, slumped so low she's at eye-level with the bottom of the steering wheel, grabs her gun. When the gunfire stops, she levers herself up, takes aim, and fires over and over and over, until the chamber clicks empty. There's no return fire.

I sit up, ears ringing. Sky is crunched under the dashboard, brushing glass from his hair. Amiah keeps her handgun raised, her sleeve is torn at the shoulder revealing red skin and beads of blood underneath, but it looks like a graze. She's two shades paler, her hands tremble despite her death grip on the gun.

"Breathe," I say, because she looks like she's forgotten how to.

"I think—I think I just—killed someone," she says.

"Are you hurt?"

She gulps air in, holds it, and lets it out with a big whoosh. When she does, she lowers her empty gun. "No, I'm okay."

"Good, stay here. If we're not back in ten minutes, leave. Okay?" I take the bat from the passenger side and hand it to her. She takes it with one hand, staring at the handle as if it's a foreign object. "Hey, did you hear me? Ten minutes only, after that, get out of here. Bring the police back if you can but don't try to go in yourself."

"Yeah, okay yeah, half an hour, got it." Her grip on the bat tightens, and she loses the shell-shocked expression long enough to convince me she's alright. I climb out of the glass-littered back seat.

The gravel crunches under our feet, damp from the melted snow, on the horizon is a storm head creeping our way. A slight breeze rustles the tops of the trees, and the sun shines down with mild warmth. Not bad weather, for a doomsday. I shut the car door, trying to make as little noise as possible. Sky follows suit.

"Ready?" I ask. I'm not, standing so close to that place makes my skin crawl and my lungs contract.

"No," Sky answers, then laughs a short, tense chuckle.

"Great. Let's go then."

A wide swath of woods separates the parking lot from the field surrounding the Compound. We sneak through it, our steps crunching on dead leaves and fallen twigs the whole way. When we reach the edge of the tree line, a rumble rings out from the Compound. We drop like lead to the forest floor. Sweat drips down my temple as I skim the ruined Compound for signs of life.

The fence is burst open inwards on our side, the white van lays crumpled on its side on the basketball court. Sky breaks for it.

"Dead Redcoat," he says, back at my side in the blink of an eye. A dead 'coat, an open fence, and not a living guard in sight. Something's not right. Another rumble, my eyes snap to the source of the din.

"Look," I whisper, pointing to the silhouette of a person creeping out of the infirmary.

"I see him," Sky whispers back.

The silhouette moves slowly at first, checking over his shoulder at the infirmary. As he reaches the edge of the circle of destruction around the burned building, he breaks into a sprint. He doesn't slow until he disappears into the last standing cell block.

"Infirmary?" I ask.

"Infirmary." Sky agrees.

A burned-out fire is a sad and ugly thing. There's nothing left except fine clumps of ash and blackened charcoal, and the cloying stench of spent smoke lingers everywhere. A burned-out fire after a storm is worse.

We tiptoe over a heavy mess of reeking sludge, our footsteps squelch. Globs of the stuff have been flung against the sides of the remaining buildings and left to dry, and the black leaks out of the cooked building skeletons and onto the surrounding area, leaving sickly trails of greyish ooze. The only upside to this sticky nightmare is the lack of dust flying up to choke me. That, and I can see the paths other people have taken all throughout the remains of the Compound.

A spray of red against the otherwise monochrome ground catches my attention. It's blood, splattered in a wide circle and still shiny wet. There's a fat drop of it a few feet away, and another beyond that, an entire trail leading behind the infirmary. I follow the trail to the back of the infirm and all the way to the double doors of the laboratory. A light shove opens them.

Muck caked on the soles of my shoes sloughs off on the floor in wet grey puddles. An ominous streak is smeared across the righthand wall, not more than two steps in, a scream like that of a tortured animal erupts from the direction of the dueling dome. A body smashes into the corner of the wall where the corridor splits, another goes flying past at the same time and bangs into a wall out of sight. The one on the floor sports a dirty lab coat, blood stains the wall where he cracked his head, he groans but his eyes stay closed.

"Looks like Dieter is in a good mood," Sky whispers.

I creep forward, for the barest of seconds my eyes unfocus, the body on the floor becomes a meaningless lump, the blood on the wall stretches out into pale almost-oblivion. Then every edge, every speck, and line, and teeny tiny detail snaps into sharp focus. The door to the dome is wide open, the handle embedded in the wall.

"Come on in!" Dieter barks, strolling into view with his hands up. "What's next, sedatives? A long stick to me with?" he sings in a mocking high-pitched voice. He pauses when he spots me, hands frozen in the air. Then a slow smile lifts the corners of his lips and spreads until it looks like someone has peeled his lips back and push-pinned them to his cheeks. "Took you long enough."

I step over the threshold, my footsteps echo on the chipped cement floor. The dome unfolds before me, dirty from ages of viciousness and brutality. A section of the metal rods that make up the roof are caved in where Delilah landed on it the last time we were here, and beneath that lays a sprinkling of debris. In the center of it all is Dieter, standing over Delilah's body.

"She's hurt." Sky bolts from behind me. Dieter explodes. He throws his magno-blast at us only for it to rocket upwards and rattle debris lose from the dome. He glares up at it. The distraction leaves him open, giving Sky a break to skirt him and lift Delilah from the floor with his good hand. He stumbles to a stop just short of the door and drops her onto her feet, wincing.

She groans, leaning hard on Sky. Awake, barely. A growing red patch stains the side of her shirt and leaks between her fingers, her sweaty face is ashen and taut. Suddenly she thrusts her arm out, a gust of howling wind sends Dieter sailing smack into the farthest wall moments before another of his blasts crumbles the doorframe.

She lists to one side, Sky catches her in the nick of time and we share worried looks. I can see her fading even as she fights to stay upright.

"Get her out of here," I say, turning to the place where Dieter is peeling himself off the ground. I don't have to last long against him, just long enough for Sky and Delilah to get far away.

33 | Dirty Ash, Dirty Floor

"Are you here to stop me?" Dieter asks. His twisted grin has fallen away into a menacing snarl, his left eye twitches. "Hypocritical of you, hypocrite. I'll do to you what I did to that menace they made follow me."

Bakari, I want to say, his name was Bakari and you killed him for no reason.

He whips a pulse of magnetic energy at me. I wrench to the side, backpedaling right to the wall. The edge of the blast buzzes too close for comfort.

Watch his arms.

Close the distance.

My feet move of their own accord, my body more prepared for this fight than I am. The next blast hits the wall shy of my heels. I jump to the side again, picking up the pace. Always moving. Always watching his arms wheeling. I've been fighting him like he was a geokinetic, but I should have been treating him like an aerokinetic. I won't make that mistake again.

Closer, closer, closer. Dieter spins, throwing magno-blasts, missing by fractions of space every time. I draw the spiral tighter, the fractions get smaller. Magnetic energy skims my skin, electric and spectral in a way that would make my brain hurt if I weren't too busy trying to keep ahead of it. Dieter slows, I count the seconds between his blasts.

Count, breathe in, a blast.

Count, breathe out, a blast.

In, blast. Out, I close the final bit of space between us, sliding into that bubble of free seconds, fist drawn back.

Not perfect enough. The blast rips me off my feet, stars in my eyes and mouth when I roll to a stop on the cold floor. Dieter cackles. Two more pulses strike me in the head and gut, warm blood sprays from my nose and drips over my lips. My side throbs, those ribs won't ever heal at this rate.

"Hurts, doesn't it?" Dieter purrs, edging closer to examine his handiwork. Damn creepy kid. Rolling to my feet, I wipe the blood off my face and spit out the red iron building up on my tongue.

My blow catches him off-guard and now he's prying himself off the floor across the dome. He's sloppy, flinging at random in hopes of dinging me. I dive out of the path of a magno-blast and come up swinging, my fist connects with the side of his head. Bone crunches, Dieter screams, and my knuckles buzz from the impact. I grab him by the collar of his grungy shirt and pull back my arm to pummel him again.

"No no no no please please please no," he moans, eyes wide. Pink drool spills too fast from his trembling lips, two of his cracked teeth are on the floor. I punch him again, red mist paints his face and mine, one of his eye teeth sticks to my knuckle briefly before falling to join its brothers. His swelling eyes roll back in his head, and I prepare to strike again.

The magno-blast comes out of nowhere. Too weak to fling me away, it goes through me like a shudder, buzzing every molecule for an instant. My stomach flips and my head pounds, and then it hits my legs.

And suddenly, I'm the one screaming. Collapsing as the rods and pins holding my bones together shift. Metal grinding bone. Dieter flops in front of me, sobbing.

"Please don't hurt me, don't hurt me anymore, don't—" he begs, hammering another magno-blast into me. Nuclear pain shatters my legs into glass shreds. Like in the forest, only a hundred thousand times worse.

And I'm back, trapped under the impossibly heavy weight.

Trapped under Dieter.

He does it again, wrenching screams out of my chest like physical things. Something gives and I feel it burn a crater all the way out of my shin.

He's babbling, whimpering, he lifts his hands to strike again. I swipe at him. Miss.

His pushes down, except the blast erupts from his back. The lab ceiling bursts open, showering dust and debris. I shield my eyes from the worst of it. When I drop my arms, prepared to catch Dieter before he can strike again, I see him folded over. He clutches his arm, his shoulder hanging out of its socket.

He hiccups and the blast that bursts from him throws me across the room. I hit the wall hard and sag to the concrete, breathless. It takes precious seconds for my vision to clear up. In the meantime, I drag myself onto my hands and knees and nearly pass out when my brain and everything attached short-circuits.

Get up. The voice in my head demands it. Get up.

I can hear Dieter crying, the echoes bounce around the concrete basin making it difficult to pinpoint him. But he's not attacking. I blink away static and tears and notice I'm close to the door. Sky and Delilah should be long gone. If I can just get to my feet. If I can just make my limbs work. I look down at the blood pooling below me, dark arterial red. There's a tear in my pantleg and too much blood pouring out to see the damage underneath. Gritting my teeth and gripping the doorframe, I drag myself onto ruined legs.

The metal frame groans, it's the only thing keeping me upright. One foot in front of the other. The dome shudders under the wrath of another magno-blast. With a deafening pop, a section of the webbing comes loose and crashes to the floor. Debris and concrete dust create flurries in the air, blocking out the weak flickering light. And under all the chaos, a kid whimpers.

I look back. Dieter cowers in the center of the dome, one arm drooping uselessly at his side and the other held out from his body like something alien and dangerous. He stares wide-eyed at the destruction. Terrified. He flinches at a chunk of cinderblock hitting the floor, and the blast that explodes out of his chest puts a dent in the concrete. Bone snaps audibly. Crying out, he caves on himself, holding his ribs.

He can't stop it, I realize. I pushed him too far.

The empty corridor calls to me, I can practically feel how many steps through the familiar hall will take me to safety.

Forty-nine.

My own blood soaks my leg, my ribs ache, and every inch of my skin is a bruise beginning to form. But the fight is almost over and that's all that matters.

I let go of the doorframe and limp toward Dieter

"What are you doing? Stop, *stop*." He flings his hand at me. The blast bursts from his leg, toppling him. The vibration threatens to knock me over, too.

"Dieter," I say, grasping for the right words, "Dieter, I'm sorry. I'm not going to hurt you anymore."

"Yes you will!" he shrieks. His face is swelling and broken, and it's not even the first time I've done that to him. Guilt clenches its fist around my heart.

"Not this time," I promise. "What the Whitecoats did to you isn't fair. What *I* did to you wasn't fair."

Magno-blasts slip out of him while I inch closer. Destruction rains. I have to shout to be heard over the mayhem. The rumbles succeed in taking me to my knees in front of him.

"I know it hurts," I say.

He stares at me with eyes bloodshot and full of tears. Glances at the hand I offer him.

"Can you make it stop?" he asks.

"Yes."

He rests his hand in mine. A blast propels him forward, smashing him into me. I curl around him, absorbing as much of the blow as I can. When he tries to right himself, another blast whips him back down. My hand grinds a new dent in the concrete keeping us both up.

"Stay there, it'll be okay," I say, wrapping my other arm over him. He shudders, breathing labored, remnants of his teeth chattering. He tries to hold in the sobs wracking his body, but they and the magno-blasts that come with them are relentless.

"You're going to be fine, Dieter."

I hug him. A hand on the back of his neck. A quick squeeze.

The bone snaps, and it's over.

34 | Cracked Bones

The last magno-blast supernovas out of Dieter, decimating everything in its path. The first second slows and stretches on for years. I feel the buzz of every charged molecule and every brand new fissure about to be carved into the floor. And the skip of my heart getting hit too hard, too wrong. And the cooling blood from Dieter, and the warm blood sloughing out of my leg.

The dome bursts apart, and the ceiling above it. Years of abuse crushed and flung into the open air.

The first drops of rain splash on my head like a taunt. I fix my gaze on the steely rainclouds above, bloated with rain that threatens to come crashing down and soak us. I never liked the rain here, it's so much colder, so much harder than the rain back home.

My skull cracks the concrete and the world goes pitch, empty black for the last time.

Dígame un historia

"Come on, mate, breathe. Just breathe. It's over. We won, it's all over, please don't do this to me."

Numbness, except against the rain. It's pouring hard now, I'm drenched, the roar of it is deafening. Or maybe that's my ears ringing. There's pressure on my chest. Dull and heavy and *ow*—something snapped.

"Don't give up yet."

Another snap.

"Don't you dare quit." Sky presses again, grinding my broken bones, "*you* asshole."

More chest crushing, the numbness is ebbing and now I know for sure it's raining, and the droplets are tiny rocks banging down on me. The comforting barricade of numbness grows thinner, and on the other side is agony like I've never experienced in my life. I can taste it like sulfur on my tongue and I recoil, willing the numbness to hold steady. I don't want to go back. I'm free for the first time since the world ended and for once in my life, nothing hurts.

I want to go home

Tengo miedo.

I'm humming that tune again.

Everything in every direction is a damp grey shade, seamless and glassy. Like the surface of a puddle when the sun hides and the wind doesn't blow. I look down at my feet, there's a gash in my leg. I guess I could be standing but I could also be lying down, it's hard to tell when there are no shadows.

The hum gets louder, though I stay quiet. It grows to fill the grey, echoing off walls that aren't there, surging louder and louder until the beat of it thrums in my chest in place of a heartbeat. It folds over me a hundred times, a warm blanket.

"Do you remember the words?" In the impossibly tiny fraction of space between one moment and the next, Elle appears at my side. It feels like she's been there for a hundred years, squished into the span of a second. This is a timeless place. She reaches for my hand, I take hers and pull her into a hug. She's warm, her skin is soft, and the points of her bones are all smoothed over where they used to jut. She's healthy.

"Look at you," I breathe, a faint smile ghosting my lips. I brush her curly hair away from her rosy round cheeks, she wrinkles her nose in pretend annoyance. That look flickers when her eyes dart over me.

"*Miraté*," she whispers, her brow furrowing. "*¿Qué es esto?*"

"It doesn't matter," I shake my head. "Look, it doesn't hurt." I press the ragged edge of the wound on my arm to prove my point. Hot blood makes my skin slippery, and sloughs over my fingertips. Bad choice of examples. I grimace and move my hand up to press over the gash, my palm scrapes over the jagged edge of a bone. The realization that I'm mid-fight strikes like a truck.

Elle can't be in the dome.

I jolt to my feet. I fall head over heels. Search for my opponent in the grey. They could by anywhere, behind, above.

A small fist knots the remnants of the hem of my shirt and blood gushes in sheets from my stomach.

"You're dying."

"I don't feel it." I take her hand, pulling her close to me, where it will be easier to shield her. The lullaby is frantic in my ears. I search again for my opponent but there is only grey grey grey.

Elle pulls both legs into the air and sits.

"Sit with me," she asks.

"Not now," I say, turning in a circles. "We need to—run, we should run." I cough and blood splashes the back of my teeth. Elle tugs my arm.

"*Está bien*," she says, "nobody else is here. Sit with me."

Nothing but grey. Red on the grey.

That's right, the fight is over.

I sink down next to her. The lullaby hums on in the background, it's so familiar I feel it singing through my veins. If this is death, it's more peaceful than I could've asked for. It's better than what the Whitecoats will give me if they ever manage to scrape me off the dome floor.

I cough, more blood painting the walls of my throat. Blood gushes in sheets to the floor, drenching anything in its path. Elle leans against me, warm, her curls springing in every direction. I smooth them down and wrap my arm around her. Infinity passes, Elle taking up the hum of the lullaby somewhere between then and now.

"I'll tell you the words next time," she says, stepping back.

"Next time?" The directionless grey begins to tilt on an imaginary axis as if I'm falling in slow motion. Blood loss makes everything fuzzy, and it's starting to get difficult to breathe for an entirely different reason than the lake of blood sitting outside my body instead of inside it. Still, I try to blink away the dizziness. My little sister is right beside me, I can't collapse.

"You can't die yet. You have to fight." Fierceness permeates her words, she sounds determined enough for both of us. But my heart sinks at the mention of fighting. I'm too tired for that. I don't want to spend another day fighting, I don't want to break any more bones, I don't want to hurt anyone else.

"No," I say. The falling sensation doubles, stretching us apart. The space between us bubbles out, swelling with grey. I reach for her. She takes my hand, but blood makes my skin slick. "Elle, when I fight I hurt people. I don't want to do that anymore."

It echoes. I hurt people, I hurt people, I hurt.

"You never hurt me." The lullaby stops, and in the heaviness that follows, she throws her arms around me, pulling me into a hug so tight it's almost violent. Blood soaks us both, but she ignores it, clinging to me. I hug her back until grey static blinds me. Numbness blocks out all but the pressure of Elle's hug and the warmth seeping from her to me. A part of me wishes the lullaby was still playing. A different part of me wonders if it is and I just can't hear it anymore.

"I'll see you later. *Te amo*, Hendrix."

I wake up suffocating on something foul jammed down my throat. Ridged edges scrape at the raw corners of my lips and snake down my mouth. I gag, the tube jerks but won't come out. Two seconds awake and I'm already choking to death. Figures. I try to grab at whatever holds the tube in place, but my hands don't move. I can't move, can't breathe, can't think straight. What is this? *What is this? What's happening?*

"He's awake!"

Everything is dark, too heavy to be real. My eyes are stuck shut, and that's the part that terrifies me the most. I gag again, violently. Fighting to get my hand up, to get this thing out of me, to do anything.

"Yana!"

I recognize Delilah's voice, like a punch to the gut. She's not supposed to be here, we sent her home. We sent her to safety.

"What are you doing?"

"Sedating him."

My heartbeat thrums hummingbird-like against my ribcage, lungs convulsing. The edges of the tube cut grooves into the inside of my throat and the taste of iron floods my mouth.

"He just woke up."

"He need more time to heal before we can take tube out."

Warmth spreads up one of my arms, surprising me. It travels like wildfire, somewhere in the chaos I recognize the feeling of sedative coursing into my veins. Seconds later it hits my head, plunging me into an ocean of oblivious warmth. I feel no less suffocated, no less threatened, but a moment more and unconsciousness relieves me of thought.

Countless times I wake up the same way. Countless times they put me under again. Elle never returns, the grey never makes a re-appearance. There is only void black and bare snippets of the lullaby that ebbs and flows on no particular beat.

My throat burns, but this time the hard plastic edges don't scratch away my tongue. Air moves in and out of my lungs the way it should. And I can open my eyes.

The first thing I see is the blurry panels of a false ceiling. I stare at them for ages, until my eyes stop burning and the tiny holes look more like speckles than smears. I feel heavy, as if layers and layers of sand are piled on top of me. Everything hurts but in a dull, muted way, except for my right leg. That I can't feel much of at all. I tilt my head to get a better look at my surroundings and figure out where I am.

The room is small, glass sliding doors take up one wall and give a view into what looks like a miniature, empty lobby. A wooden door to the left of the glass wall is half-open, beyond it is a toilet and a sink, and further to the left, a stuffed red chair is crammed into the corner. I know by the glass wall that this isn't the Compound, the chair and bathroom confirm it.

"Morning, sunshine."

I turn my head towards the sound. Standing at the side of my bed is Delilah, a row of stitches curves down her left temple, scattered around the cut are burst blood vessels. She looks rested though, and clean.

"Here." She holds a cold spoon to my mouth. "Ice chips, Yana said to give you some if you woke up."

Never in my entire life has ice tasted so good. Cool trickles of water soothe the cotton balls that coat the inside of my throat. While I suck on the ice chips, Delilah perches on the edge of the bed. "You really had us going for a while there, the doctors didn't know if you'd make it past the first hour. But here you are."

"Don't sound so happy," I make a poor attempt at a joke, my voice is too hoarse to rise above a whisper. She smiles wanly and offers another spoonful of ice. My side aches something awful.

"You've woken up a couple times now, I'm waiting to see if it sticks."

"I think it will," I mumble around the ice chips.

"That's what you said last time, too," she says.

"Oh."

Minutes pass in silence, Delilah feeds a few more spoonfuls of ice into me and the burning in my throat settles down. I wince and scratch at the sore spot under my thin hospital gown. There's a stiff, swollen line zippering my abdomen. I run my fingers across it again, it feels like stitches, but I don't remember getting stabbed there.

"Your spleen burst, they had to take it out," Delilah says in response to my puzzled expression. My mind flickers back to the moment in the grey, with all the blood. I let my hand linger on the stitches.

It's dim in the room, the blinds are open but the soft glow of a streetlamp is the only light. There is one other chair in the room, tucked into the far corner beside the window. Sky is curled up on it, snoring. Unlike Delilah, he's a mess. His greasy hair sticks up all over his head. purple rings stain the skin around his eyes and his broken hand sticks out at an awkward angle over his knees.

"He looks bad," I say, I can't stop looking at the cage on his hand. Delilah shrugs, more to herself than me.

"He's been having nightmares. We die in them," she says, leaning her elbows on her knees. "Sleeping in here kind of helps though, so I try not to wake him up when he dozes."

"Only Sky would sleep better in the same room as the guy who broke his hand," I mutter. Delilah slides a critical gaze over me from the corner of her eye. I don't remember telling her that I was the one who crushed Sky's hand, but someone must have because she doesn't flinch or pull away. Maybe it's just not a surprise. We were built for violence, after all.

"I don't think he cares about that part," she says. I can't help the pang of guilt that goes through me. As if sensing it, Delilah pats my shoulder. "Just stay alive this time, would you?"

"I'll try."

"Good."

"And you?"

Delilah hesitates, and my heart stutters hard enough that the monitor beeping beside my bed stutters too. I can't hear it very well, it's on the same side as the ear that bullet grazed.

"Woah, hey, take it easy," she says, eyeing the jumping lines on the monitor. "I'm alright. A concussion, I think a bit of metal got me when the van crashed but I'm all patched up now."

"Good," I sigh. I try to prop myself up, only to discover that one of my arms is trapped. A thick cast envelopes my arm from my shoulder to my wrist.

"Shattered your humerus," she says.

"Is that all?" I ask, examining the rest of me. I should have checked myself over earlier, but nothing hurt enough to catch my attention. A broken arm and a missing spleen—whatever that is—doesn't seem too bad after everything that happened.

"Ha, you wish. You also have thirteen broken ribs, a bruised liver and kidney, a torn rotator cuff, and they say your spine is cracked but they don't know how bad it is yet."

"Wow, I don't feel any of that."

"With the painkillers you're on, it'd be more surprising if you did," she answers. "You tie for worst injuries from that fight."

"What poor kid tied with me?" I ask, my mind flashing to Dieter. Delilah snorts.

"He's a Whitecoat," she informs me, a sneer on her face. "An electrokinetic fried him in the middle of the riot and he got trampled."

Suddenly I have no sympathy for him.

"There was a riot?"

"There was a shockwave from the dome. It took down that building and popped a bunch of the cell doors. Most of us went after the Whitecoats, until the police got there. Amiah got arrested," she tacks the last part on casually, pausing to pop an ice chip in her mouth. "For something she did with her newstab? They let her go. They arrested a lot of us and let us go. You missed a lot of boring legal stuff."

"Oh damn," I feign disappointment.

Delilah rolls her eyes. Crunching down more ice she says, "you're lucky you got to sleep through most of it. You're lucky Sky found you, too, he kept you alive."

There's no tube in my throat but I feel choked anyways. Imagining Sky coming back for me, the idea that he might have had to hurt himself more, is too much.

"He shouldn't have done that," my voice is a bare whisper, struggling to get around the suffocating lump in my throat. Delilah slides that critical gaze over me again, expression unreadable. She opens her mouth to say something, but it's Sky's voice that fills the room next.

"Don't say that," We both jump, neither of us had noticed the lack of snoring from Sky's chair. He stands, watching me from behind red-rimmed eyes. In the next moment, he's throwing himself on me, hugging me as tightly as he can without disturbing all the medical junk attached to me. "I thought you were dead."

I lift my unbroken arm to hug him back. My movements are sluggish, too dulled for me to squeeze properly. I do my best, and he doesn't seem to mind when I thump him a little too hard.

When he finally settles, retreating to the end of the bed, there's a shakiness to him. "You can't say things like that anymore, Trick."

"Sorry," I say automatically.

"I can't keep watching my friends die," his voice cracks. Tears well in his eyes, dark spots bloom on his sleeve. Delilah does what I can't and smooths a comforting hand over his bent spine.

"I'm sorry," I say again, knowing the blood of those friends is on my hands. Even before the escape I might have killed them in the Dome. Hundreds of evils sit on me, I will never be clean of them. I can never live in this world. I press my thumb into the stitches at my side.

"I can't fight anymore." And the admission feels like death. Violence is all I am. Fighting is what the Whitecoats made me for, the only thing they made me for. Everything beneath my breastbone crushes into a tight ball, distantly I hear the monitor stuttering.

Delilah's calloused hand finds mine.

"You don't have to fight, " she says, "it's over, we're free."

It doesn't feel real. But Delilah is there, hand on mine, and Sky is there, at the end of the bed.

"We are proper free," he says.

And a teeny tiny fractured part of me begins to believe, for a split second, that we are free.

37 | My Name Is

Three weeks later

They don't give me nearly enough medication to stave off the combined pain of the injuries with the fibro. They say it will get better with time, they also say it would get better faster if I slowed down but I can't stand sitting still.

I sit on the edge of the bed in Amiah's guest bedroom, grimacing to myself as I wrestle with the straps of the back brace. It's a tight, unforgiving thing that keeps my lower back steady as I move around. I'm not supposed to take it off, but I needed space last night. Today we're holding a memorial for Elle, and all I could see until the sun came up was her face.

"Need some help?" Yana appears in the door, she doesn't even try to hide her exasperation. This is the third time I've taken the brace off. The third time she knows of anyways.

"Yes, please," I say, pretending not to see her narrowed eyes. These braces aren't designed for accessibility, one-arming it is like gluing water to a tree. Yana walks over and kneels to adjust the brace.

"You shouldn't be taking this off," she scolds, cinching the straps.

"I know."

"It could damage your back."

"I know," I repeat, watching her fasten the final Velcro seal. "It's hard to do breathing exercises when I'm wearing it."

Yana frowns but doesn't argue. The breathing exercises are from therapy. I started last week, one-on-one with a doctor twice, and a group talk once. Some of the therapy helps, some of it doesn't, and maybe that's as far as it will ever go. I'll keep trying though.

I grab the curved handle of the silver cane beside the bed. It takes a little help from Yana and a big push off the bed, but I manage to get to my feet. I pause, balancing on one foot to fasten my borrowed button-up shirt, then, with my cane acting as a third foot, I head for the door. Unlike the back brace, the cane is a permanent installment. The numbness in my right leg never went away, and it never will, courtesy of the crack in my spine. Technically I'm advised against walking until my back heals more, but I hated the wheelchair with a passion. It all hurts the same anyways.

"You look nice." I say as Yana and I round the corner into the hallway.

For today, her usual gaggle of hairpins is missing, leaving her curls loose to frame her delicate face. Her dress is long and indigo to match the paint on her nails.

"Thank you," she says, reaching up to straighten the collar of my shirt and ruffle my hair. She does that a lot lately, "you do too."

"Thanks for coming today."

"Of course."

Delilah, Amiah, Sky, and his parents are all waiting outside, gathered around the doorstep. Arin and Justine Jones are lovely people if I've ever met any. They flew in mere days after the first global news report came out with a list of surviving Experiments and a call for relatives to rejoin their missing family members. I doubt Justine has let go of her son since they first hugged at the airport, and I don't think Sky minds in the least. Arin dips his chin at me as I step out the door and I return the gesture. He's a man of few words, unlike his son.

"Ready to go?" Delilah asks, skimming me as she speaks. The scar on her temple is thin and pink, no longer in need of stitches, and the wound on her side is healing well, too. She follows the doctors' orders much better than I do.

"As I'll ever be," I answer.

We all clamber into the van Amiah rented and buckle in for the trek to the bitsy church where the pastor giving the memorial resides. Elle's ashes are in a sealed urn, wrapped in a scarf in the middle front seat. The idea of locking her body in a box and hiding it underground seemed wrong. One day I'll take her home.

The people in the van lapse into silence, listening to the music that filters through the ancient radio. I, for one, think about the future. I'm looking for a job, but not many people are keen on hiring a disabled liability. I'll find something, though, and in the meantime Amiah has agreed to let me stay at her place under the condition that I no longer, in her words, mope around.

Skyelar is headed back to England with his parents, he promises to visit often, and I plan to hold him to it since it's a day's run for him to get here. And Delilah got herself a job at a nearby library. It's a peaceful job and she's not the first soldier to pass through. The other library staff are very understanding, from what I hear.

We pull into a tiny parking lot as the final refrains of a soft song play out. I ease my way onto solid ground, thankful for the anti-nausea meds that come with my painkillers. The soft green buds of spring are beginning to erupt into bright summer foliage, the last remnants of snow are running off into the ditches and the trees that line the parking lot drink in the warm sun. High above, the oceanic sky is dotted with triangles of white birds, migrating home. Once steady, I lean over and take Elle's urn from its place. I unwrap it delicately, place the scarf on the seat of the van, and settle the urn in the crook of my cast so I can carry it in.

Delilah appears at my side, holding a necklace in her hands. "We went by the jewelers this morning to pick it up." She reaches up to fasten it around my neck. It's a heavy oval locket on a simple beaded chain. Inside, safely behind a seamless glass seal, are the tips of Elle's horns and a thimbleful of her ashes. A final, preserved piece of not only her, but our home that will be safe no matter what happens.

"Thank you," I say as she tucks it under my shirt. The cool metal locket rests on my skin, right above my heart. Sky slings his arm over my shoulders, throwing his other hand out to stabilize Elle.

"Looks cramped in there," I say, nodding at the squat white building at the end of the parking lot.

"Yeah," he agrees, "it's one big room inside though."

"Doesn't sound too bad."

We all turn towards the church.

My name is Hendrix Sanchez-Fernandez. I am nineteen years old. Today is the day that I rebuild my world.

the end

ACKNOWLEDGEMENTS

A great big thank you to all my incredibly patient and helpful beta readers; Katrina Matt, A.S. Carmody, Brooke Timothy, Jaimes Weber, and Gerry Saunders. Laura Stapleton for her help editing. Ingrid Perez, for correcting my attempts at Spanish in the nicest way possible. Snow, who wrote the lullaby that gets stuck in my head to this day.

Thank you to Dane Low for creating the cover, and to Rodney Smith for editing my new name onto it.

To countless Wattpaders and Kidpubbers, who lended their encouragement and help on everything from descriptor choices to Russian translations.

And of course, my mom and dad for being all-around good parents, and in particular for only complaining a little about my house troll lifestyle.

Finally, thank you to Sasha, who will always get first reader privileges. Love you.